PR/
THE FRESH-E

"Engaging...a cozy distinguished by its appealing characters and mouthwatering recipes."

—Publishers Weekly

"This is a great cozy to get you into the holiday spirit—because even though there's a murderer on the loose, there's lots of holiday cheer (and some yummy-sounding recipes at the end of this book)."

—AnnArbor.com

"[A] fun and captivating read...full of holiday cheer, mystery, murder, delicious treats, endearing characters, and evil villains...a cute and grippingly good read."

—Examiner.com

"Washburn has a refreshing way with words and knows how to tell an exciting story."

—Midwest Book Review

"This mystery is nicely crafted, with a believable ending. The camaraderie of the Fresh-Baked Mystery series' cast of retired schoolteachers who share a home is endearing. Phyllis is an intelligent and keen sleuth who can bake a mean funnel cake. Delicious recipes are included!"

—RT Book Reviews

"The whodunit is fun and the recipes [are] mouthwatering."

—The Best Reviews

## Other Fresh-Baked Mysteries

*A Peach of a Murder*

*Murder by the Slice*

*The Christmas Cookie Killer*

*Killer Crab Cakes*

*The Pumpkin Muffin Murder*

*The Gingerbread Bump-off*

*Wedding Cake Killer*

*The Fatal Funnel Cake*

*Trick or Deadly Treat*

*The Candy Cane Cupcake Killer*

*Black and Blueberry Die*

*The Great Chili Kill-Off*

*Baker's Deadly Dozen*

*Death Bakes a Pecan Pie*

# Never Trifle With Murder

*A Fresh Baked Mystery*

# Livia J. Washburn

Fire Star Press

Dedicated to my amazing husband, James, and my beautiful daughters, Joanna and Shayna, for always being willing to read a passage or sample a new recipe.

# Chapter 1

Phyllis Newsom watched as her friend Sam Fletcher intently studied the dominoes arrayed in front of him. He frowned in thought, put the tip of his index finger on one of them, then moved it to another. After a couple of seconds, he picked up that domino and placed it with the other two that had already been played in the center of the table.

The man to Sam's left slid one of his dominoes out to join the others. Sam's partner, seated across the table from him, sighed and turned all six of his dominoes face down, then began shoving them to the center. Sam and the other two players did likewise. The sound of the dominoes hitting the table and then clicking together was almost musical.

"That was the *first* play in that hand," Phyllis said. "And it's over?"

"Well, we were set," Sam said.

His partner, former hardware store owner Ansel Hovey,

shook his head and said, "I shouldn't'a bid on sixes. I knew better." He gave Sam a mock glare. "I figured you'd have somethin' better than what you threw out there."

The man to Sam's left, who had played the decisive domino, grinned and said, "Now, don't give Sam a hard time, Ansel. You can only play the dominoes you're dealt."

"Thanks, Patrick," Sam said. He turned his head to look up at Phyllis, who stood behind his left shoulder. "You see, once Patrick took that trick, there was no way we could make what Ansel bid. There wasn't enough count left."

Carolyn Wilbarger, who stood behind Sam to the right, said, "You don't have to mansplain the game of Forty-Two to us. We're all from Texas, you know."

"And I've been playing Forty-Two for as far back as I can remember," Phyllis added. "I understand the concept of what you're saying, Sam. My brain's just never been able to work fast enough to see how the whole rest of the hand is going to play out based on the first one or two tricks."

"Your brain works plenty fast," Sam told her. "If it didn't, you wouldn't have been able to solve all those murders."

The player called Patrick turned to smile up at Phyllis. "That's right, you're the lady who's famous for catching killers. I've heard a lot about you."

"Most of it greatly exaggerated, I'm sure," Phyllis said.

Sam said, "You and Patrick ought to get together sometime and compare notes. He used to be a homicide detective before he retired, you know."

Phyllis shook her head. "No, I didn't know that. Where did you work, Mr. Flanagan?"

"Several places. New York, St. Louis, and finally retired from the Dallas PD." Flanagan was a stocky man wearing a polo shirt and khakis. He still had a full head of brown hair streaked with gray, and a brush-like mustache that was a mixture of those shades, as well. He didn't really look like a cop to Phyllis, but she had been around enough police officers and sheriff's deputies to know that they came in all different varieties, including her son Mike, who worked for the Parker County Sheriff's Department.

The fourth man at the table in the Weatherford Senior Center, Carl Benford, leaned forward and said, "Well, if nobody else is gonna shake those bones, I will." He rested his hands on the cluster of face-down dominoes in the center of the table and started shuffling them.

"Thank goodness," Carolyn said. "There's the man we're here to see, Phyllis. Now we don't have to stand around and watch these fossils play Forty-Two."

Sam chuckled and said, "Don't rush off. We might play straight dominoes when we finish this game. Or even Chickenfoot. Could get downright excitin'."

Carolyn said, "Hmmph," and linked arms with Phyllis. She steered both of them toward the far side of the big main room.

Three people had just entered the senior center. The one in the lead looked a little out of place here. Not because of his age; his hair was silver and his deeply tanned face showed the weathering of years. He was old enough to be considered a senior citizen. He was the only man wearing a suit, though, in a roomful of casually dressed people.

And an expensive, three-piece suit complete with vest, at that. A stickpin glittered in his silk tie. Elegance, success, and sophistication seemed to radiate from him.

He glanced over his shoulder at the two much younger people following him and said, "I'll find out where we're supposed to set up." His voice was deep, powerful, and self-assured.

His companions were a young man and woman, probably in their mid-twenties. The woman was very pretty, with blond hair pulled back in a long ponytail and a trim shape in jeans and short-sleeved knit top. The young man with her had dark hair, thick and a little floppy, and was well-built without looking athletic.

Two women who had been talking on the other side of the room hurried forward to meet the three newcomers. One of the pair was Eve Turner, a retired teacher who shared a big, two-story house on one of Weatherford's tree-shaded side streets with Phyllis, Carolyn, and Sam, all of whom had had long careers as educators. The house belonged to Phyllis, and after her husband passed away, she had come up with the idea of renting out rooms to other retired teachers, instead of rattling around in the big old place by herself.

By this point, the foursome weren't just housemates. They were family.

The woman with Eve was Darla Kirby, the director of the senior center. She held out her hand to the distinguished gentleman in the expensive suit and said, "You must be Mr. Dorrington."

He took her hand, then clasped it with his other hand as well. His smile was warm as he said, "Indeed I am. And you, without a doubt, are Ms. Kirby. I recognize your charming voice from our phone conversations."

Phyllis could tell that Darla wanted to giggle and flutter at the flattery, but she kept it under control as she said, "Yes, I, uh, I'm the director of the center here."

Eve didn't bother keeping her natural response to a handsome older gentleman under control. She swooped in and took Dorrington's hand as soon as Darla let go of it, and she used the man's own move on him by wrapping both hands around his.

"And I'm Eve Turner," she introduced herself in a honeyed voice.

"Ms. Turner," Dorrington said. Not to be outdone, he added his left hand to the mix and wrapped it around both of Eve's.

"Oh, for heaven's sake," Carolyn muttered to Phyllis as they crossed the room. "Why doesn't she just challenge him to wrestle?"

"Don't give her any ideas," Phyllis responded quietly.

Dorrington extricated his hands from Eve's and gestured vaguely toward his two younger companions. "My assistant, Becky Thackery."

He didn't introduce the young man.

Dorrington rubbed his hands together with a slight, papery whisper and went on, "Now, where should we set up?"

"The kitchen is right here," Darla said, pointing toward a door next to a large window with a pull-down shutter closing it off from the main room. "I hope it's big enough to hold the class. If not, we can open that up and some of the ladies can watch from out here. I know you like to have your students get right in there and do the work themselves, though."

"Hands-on experience," Dorrington agreed. "By far the best way to learn anything."

"That's what I've always believed," Eve said. She looked over as Phyllis and Carolyn came up and put her flirting aside for the moment as she went on, "Oh, you have to meet these two. Phyllis Newsom and Carolyn Wilbarger. Between them, they've won most of the cooking and baking competitions around here for the past few years."

"Ladies," Dorrington greeted them. He stopped short of giving them a courtly bow, but Phyllis thought he looked like the idea crossed his mind. "It's an honor to be in your presence, let alone to have you attend some of my classes. You *are* going to attend, aren't you?"

"That's why we're here," Carolyn said. "And we're just amateurs, not some fancy chef like you."

"It's been my experience that some of the best cooks in the world have never worked their magic outside their own kitchens. I'm sure you'll do wonderfully, and I hope you enjoy and can make use of what little expertise I have to pass on."

That was false modesty if she'd ever heard it, thought Phyllis. Alfred Dorrington was an expert in the kitchen, and he darned well knew it. He owned a ritzy restaurant in Dallas, and even though he had retired from its day-to-day operation, he still had a reputation as one of the top chefs in Texas.

He was from England, originally, but had lived in the States for the past thirty years, as Phyllis had learned from talking to Darla Kirby, but that was all she really knew about the man other than the fact that he traveled around the North Texas area giving classes in British cooking and, in an intriguing twist, a cross between Texas and British cooking at places such as senior and community centers. He did that because he enjoyed it, according to Darla, not because he needed the money.

"We're looking forward to seeing what we can learn from you," Phyllis told him.

"What's on the agenda for today's class?" Carolyn asked.

"If I wanted to be coy about it, I could say that you'll find out soon enough," Dorrington replied. Then he leaned forward with a twinkle in his eyes and lowered his voice to a conspiratorial tone. "But I don't mind letting you on it, my dear. Today we'll be learning how to make the world's best scones and a traditional Bubble and Squeak that's to die for!"

He turned, motioned toward the door, and told the two young people with him, "Come along, children."

They disappeared into the kitchen. Eve watched them go, sighed, and said, "I just love a man with a British accent."

"You love a man with any accent, as long as he's breathing," Carolyn said. Then she looked at Phyllis and went on, "And I really wish he hadn't said that about a Bubble and Squeak that's to die for. He doesn't know who he's dealing with here!"

# Chapter 2

The two young people spent the next ten minutes bringing things from a vehicle parked outside and carrying them into the center's kitchen. Phyllis heard pots and pans clinking together as the young man placed a large, zippered fabric bag on the counter. The young woman brought in cardboard boxes that were probably full of ingredients for that day's lesson. Through the open door, Phyllis saw them starting to unload the containers while Alfred Dorrington emerged from the kitchen and resumed chatting with Phyllis, Carolyn, Eve, and Darla Kirby.

When Carolyn could get a word in through Eve's coquettish remarks, she asked, "Did you have any formal training as a chef, Mr. Dorrington?"

"You mean, did I attend any of the famous cooking schools such as Saint Emilion or Le Cordon Bleu London?" Dorrington smiled and shook his head. "Alas, no. I got my start as a scullery lad at a fish and chips shop. But when I got a chance, I proved to have a knack for more than washing dishes and sweeping out the place." He laughed. "Of course, there's only so much you can do with fish and chips! But I experimented with various combinations of seasonings, and they proved popular, to the point that the owner began to resent me and fired me. Word had gotten around, though, and it didn't take long for me to catch on as the cook at a small pub. Again, there's only so much you can do with simple fare such as that, but it opened up a whole new world of intriguing possibilities for me. Eventually I started my own place on little more than the proverbial wing and a prayer and parleyed my success with it into opening a larger, more elegant establishment."

The story had a practiced air to it that made Phyllis think that Dorrington had probably told it numerous times before, probably at every one of these classes he gave. She knew from her years of experience as a history teacher that keeping your students engaged and entertained made it easier for them to grasp what you were trying to teach.

"I suppose it didn't take much to be more elegant than a fish and chips shop or a pub," Carolyn said.

Instead of taking offense at that, as he might have, Dorrington laughed and said, "A blunt but very accurate assessment, Carolyn. With luck and hard work, I was able to turn my little endeavor into a successful restaurant."

Carolyn shook her head. "No, I'm afraid I don't know anything about restaurants in London. I've never been to England, or anywhere else in Europe."

"Well...not to sound disloyal to queen and country, mind you... I've come to greatly appreciate living in America, as well. I consider myself an American now and have for quite some time. If fact, I've been in Texas so long I've adapted some spices popular in this great state to my staple foods at my restaurant, so that it's becoming more Tex-Brit foods, shall we say." Dorrington smiled at his own cleverness.

"Well, I hope we get to try some of those," Carolyn said. Phyllis could tell that Dorrington's easy affability was beginning to have an effect on her friend, despite Carolyn's naturally skeptical personality. She was hard to win over, but once she was on your side, she would stick by you, no matter what.

Dorrington smiled and said, "Of course, but today we're starting with very traditional British foods."

The shutter in the big window between the kitchen and the center's main room rolled up, rattling a little as it did so. Dorrington's assistant, Becky Thackery, looked through the opening and said, "We're almost ready in here, Alfred."

"Excellent." Dorrington rubbed his hands together again and smiled at the group of four women gathered around him. "I need to go and make my own preparations, ladies. The class will begin shortly."

"We can't wait," Eve said.

"Are you going to take the class, Eve?" Dorrington asked.

"No, I'll just be an interested observer." Eve waved a hand. "I've never been that skilled…in the kitchen."

"Well, it takes talents of all kinds in this world, doesn't it?" Dorrington returned with his already familiar twinkle. He went into the kitchen and left them standing there.

When he was gone, Carolyn asked Eve, "Are you ever going to grow up and stop being such a shameless cliché?"

"Goodness, I hope not. What fun would that be?"

A few minutes later, Dorrington came to the window. He had removed his suit coat but still wore his vest, snowy white shirt, and tie. He had donned an apron with what looked like some sort of British coat of arms emblazoned on the front. Phyllis didn't know if it was an *actual* coat of arms or just a design made to look like that, but she had to admit, it seemed very appropriate on the apron worn by Alfred Dorrington.

He nodded to Darla Kirby, who turned and raised her voice above the usual hubbub. "Will everyone who signed up for the British cooking class come to the kitchen now, please?"

A dozen women, including Phyllis, Carolyn, and Eve, started toward the door. Before the three of them got there, however, a couple of the others moved to block their path.

"You're not going in there, Turner," one of those two said with a scowl.

Eve looked surprised, but she answered quickly, "Yes, I am."

The other woman who had stopped them shook her head firmly.

"We saw the sign-up sheet for the class," she declared, "and your name wasn't on it."

"And we just heard you tell Mr. Dorrington that you're just observing, not actually taking the class," the other one said. "That means you can *observe* from out here, through the window."

"But I'd rather be up close where I can see—" Eve began.

"You mean where you can bat your eyelashes at that man and act like some...some high school cheerleader drooling over the star quarterback!"

"Hold on, now," Carolyn said. "You shouldn't talk to Eve like that."

"Why not? I've heard you say worse than that to her when she starts chasing after men like some TV show caricature."

"But I'm her friend!"

"What difference does that make?"

Eve said coolly, "It makes a difference, I assure you. Now, please, let's all go in there and behave like civilized adults, why don't we?"

That sounded like a good idea to Phyllis, but she didn't know if the two women who had planted themselves so resolutely in front of them would agree to it.

Phyllis was acquainted with them from other activities here at the center, but she hadn't been able to recall their names right away. She'd been trying to retrieve that information from her brain while they were talking to Eve and Carolyn, and now she succeeded.

The lanky, graying brunette was Sheila Trent. The heavyset blonde was Ingrid Gustafson. Phyllis wouldn't have guessed that they were particularly close friends with each other, but evidently they had teamed up on this attempt to keep Eve out of the kitchen.

Phyllis had mixed emotions about that. On the one hand, she could see the point that Sheila and Ingrid were making. If space was limited in the kitchen, then it wasn't right for Eve to take up some of it simply because she was smitten with Alfred Dorrington. On the other hand, Eve was her friend, and Phyllis didn't like seeing her being treated in such an obnoxious manner, even if the objection might be justified.

And Eve was right: Carolyn could make comments that wouldn't be welcome from others.

Darla Kirby came up and asked, "What's the hold-up here? I think Mr. Dorrington is just about ready to begin."

Ingrid pointed at Eve and said, "You need to keep her out of there. She didn't sign up for the class. She doesn't belong."

"Well, we've never really worried too much about things like that unless there are some specific restrictions—"

"The sign-up sheet said space was limited," Sheila broke in. "That means people can't come crowding in just because they've got hot pants for the teacher."

Eve's eyes widened in outrage. So did Carolyn's, at that

crude attack on her friend. Phyllis was starting to get angry, too.

Before any of them could say or do anything else, Alfred Dorrington's deep, cultured voice asked, "Is there a problem out here, ladies?" He had come out of the kitchen to join them.

Darla turned to him and replied quickly, "No, no problem—"

"We don't think she ought to be in the kitchen," Ingrid declared, pointing at Eve in an accusatory manner. "She's trying to bull her way in when she didn't even sign up for the class."

"I would have," Eve said, "if I'd known who was going to be teaching it."

Through clenched teeth, Sheila said, "His picture was on the flyer that Darla tacked up. You just never paid any attention to it because it was about cooking, and you couldn't care less about that."

"I'm surprised she didn't notice anyway," added Ingrid. "Turner's like a bloodhound. She catches the scent of every attractive man within a mile."

So it wasn't just a matter of how much space there was in the center's kitchen, Phyllis thought, or whether it was fair to let in someone who hadn't signed up for the class. Ingrid was attracted to Alfred Dorrington, too, and judging by the glances that Sheila sent his way, she was, as well. And they didn't want Eve in there flirting shamelessly with Dorrington and trying to monopolize his time…as Eve tended to do on occasion.

"Now, now, there's no need for a kerfuffle," Dorrington said as he held up both hands and patted the air in a conciliatory gesture. "Eve, dear, it really is important that the students have the opportunity to get right in there close and see what I'm doing, and since you said yourself that culinary skills aren't your strong suit…"

Eve sighed and said, "Oh, all right." She glared at Sheila and Ingrid as self-congratulatory smirks appeared on their faces.

"But since you're so charming," Dorrington went on, "I thought perhaps you might like to share a scone and a cup of tea with me after the class is concluded."

That suggestion brightened Eve's mood immediately and brought the scowls back to Sheila and Ingrid.

"Of course," she told Dorrington. "I'd be very happy to."

"Excellent! Then, if you will, ladies…"

He held out his hand to usher them into the kitchen in a grand manner, as if they were about to enter a ballroom in Buckingham Palace.

# Chapter 3

"That was mighty good," Sam declared as he pushed the small paper plate a short distance away from him on the table. "I hope I didn't ruin my supper."

The dominoes had been pushed to the side and the games gladly postponed when Phyllis and Carolyn came over and asked the four men if they wanted to be guinea pigs for the dishes they'd prepared in class. The answer had been yes, of course, and the men had sampled the scones and Bubble and Squeak with great gusto.

Patrick Flanagan said, "I really liked that, what did you call that potato thing, Bluster and Squawk?"

"Bubble and Squeak," Carolyn said. She and Phyllis had pulled a couple of chairs up to the table and sat down to enjoy the food themselves.

Flanagan laughed. "Oh, yes, that's right. I suppose when I think about Englishmen, blustering and squawking come to mind."

"You don't like Englishmen?" Carolyn asked.

"I like 'em just fine. Haven't really been around that many of them, to tell you the truth. Some of them just strike me as being a little full of themselves, that's all."

Flanagan leaned his head toward the table on the other side of the room where Eve sat with Alfred Dorrington, laughing and talking as they had scones—on paper plates—and tea—in foam cups. It wasn't exactly fine china.

"Although that fella, from what I've seen of him, seems to be pretty friendly and down to earth," Flanagan went on. "Other than the fact that he dresses pretty fancy for around here."

"Well, he does own a restaurant in Highland Park. His customers there would expect him to be well-dressed."

Flanagan nodded and said, "Yeah, it's a pretty snooty neighborhood. Bound to rub off on you."

Sam asked Phyllis, "Did you enjoy the class?"

"Yes, I did," she said. "It's always nice to learn something new. I don't like it when I hear somebody say that they're too old to learn anything. The way I see it, you're never too old until you *stop* learning things."

"Words to live by," Sam said.

Ansel Hovey licked the plastic fork he'd been using, making sure he got the last little bit of food off it, then said, "How many more of these classes are there, anyway?"

"Two more," Phyllis told him. "On Wednesday and Friday."

"Same time?"

"Yes, I believe so."

Hovey grinned at the other men. "Reckon I'll see you again for those, boys."

Carl Benford returned the grin and said, "I'll be here." He cocked his head a little to the side. "You know, I wasn't sure

I'd care much for British cooking. My wife used to watch that TV show about it, and if you ask me, a lot of the things they fixed on there didn't sound good to me at all. But these biscuits—"

"Scones," Carolyn corrected him.

"Scooones," Benford said, drawing out the word in an exaggerated British accent. "Anyway, they ain't bad."

Becky Thackery and the young man, whose name Phyllis still hadn't heard, had been cleaning up in the kitchen, following Dorrington's orders to leave everything as spotless as it had been starting out. Phyllis had heard kitchen noises coming from in there as they worked, but it had gotten quiet now. The door was partially open, but the shutter over the big window had been pulled down.

She happened to be looking that direction as Darla Kirby walked over to the door and stepped into the kitchen. She came right back out with a speed that surprised Phyllis. She said something through the open doorway, then turned and walked away with an uncomfortable frown on her face.

Her curiosity aroused, Phyllis stood up and moved over to intercept Darla as the woman headed toward the door of the small office that she used as the center's director. Quietly, Phyllis asked, "Is something wrong, Darla?"

Darla stopped short and looked confused for a second as she said, "What?"

"I saw you go into the kitchen just now, and you came back out in a hurry, like something might be wrong."

"Oh." Darla nodded in understanding. She might still be uncomfortable, but she had gotten her mental balance after whatever had just happened. "No, nothing's wrong. I was just…surprised, that's all. And I don't know *why* I was. I'm not sure I should have been. There was nothing wrong with it, after all."

"Now you've lost me," Phyllis said.

"Well, I stepped in there to ask Ms. Thackery if she needed any help. I mean, she and her friend might not have known where we keep everything in the kitchen."

"Her friend?" Phyllis repeated.

"I hope they're friends." Darla lowered her voice and her face turned a slight, almost indistinguishable shade of pink. "When I went in there, they were *kissing*."

"Neither of them was wearing a wedding ring," Phyllis said. She wasn't aware until this moment that she had even noticed such a thing…but she had gotten in the habit of being as observant as she could. It had come in handy on a number of occasions and trapped more killers than she liked to think about.

She went on, "But I suppose it's certainly possible that they could be boyfriend and girlfriend. I know those terms are old-fashioned, but I think young people still use them." She paused and smiled. "And honestly, in this day and age, if all you caught them doing was kissing, you were probably lucky."

"Oh, I know what you mean. And it's not just the kids. You wouldn't believe some of the things I've seen here at the center. Why, one time I saw Ansel Hovey and Claire Duncan—" Darla stopped herself and held up a hand. "No, no, I'm sorry. I shouldn't be gossiping like this. I mean, I have a responsibility as the center's director to be discreet."

"Don't worry, I won't say anything," Phyllis assured her. "And for what it's worth, I already knew about Ansel and Claire."

Darla laughed. "Now, *that* doesn't surprise me in the least.

Anyway, what those two young people do is none of my business, so I'm going to leave it at that. Did you enjoy the class?"

"Very much so," Phyllis said.

"Good. I'm glad we arranged it, then."

Darla turned toward the door again, but Phyllis asked her, "*Did* Ms. Thackery and her friend need any help? In the kitchen, I mean."

"Not as far as I could see," Darla said, then laughed. "And she assured me that they had things well under control."

"Well, there you go," Phyllis said, and started to head back to the table where her friends were still sitting.

Before she got there, she saw Becky Thackery emerge from the kitchen carrying one of the boxes she had brought in earlier. On a whim, Phyllis changed course and reached the center's front door in time to hold it open for the young woman, who had her arms full.

"Thank you," Becky said with a polite smile. The young man wasn't far behind her, with the big tote bag in one hand and a box tucked under the other arm. Phyllis held the door open for him, too, and then followed them outside into the parking lot. It seemed like a natural thing to do.

"Thank *you*, Ms. Thackery," Phyllis said as she came alongside the young woman. "It was a very enjoyable class."

"Oh, well, that's Mr. Dorrington's doing…"

"Yes, but you helped." Phyllis gave the young man a smile, too. "Both of you did."

He nodded to her, but it was barely more than a polite acknowledgment of her comment.

"I'm Phyllis Newsom, by the way," she added.

"Yes, I remember your name being mentioned in class. And you know mine." Becky inclined her head toward the young man, since, with her arms full, she couldn't point or indicate him any other way. "This is my friend Cliff Reynolds."

"Hello, Mr. Reynolds."

"Hi," he said, not actually surly but without any hint of friendliness.

"Cliff insisted on helping me out today," Becky went on. "He's not normally part of the class."

"Dorrington makes you lug too much stuff around," Cliff said. "He could carry some stuff himself, you know."

"Yes, but he's the boss." Phyllis could tell that Becky was trying to keep her voice light, but she had a hunch this job was the source of some friction between the two young people. "And I *am* paid to be his assistant."

"Yeah, but that's all."

They had reached a large, dark blue SUV. Cliff went around to the back with the things he was carrying and set the tote bag on the ground. He dug in his pocket with that hand and brought out a keyless remote fob. The SUV beeped as the doors unlocked. Becky said to Phyllis, "Since you're here, would you mind getting that side door on the passenger side?"

"Of course not." Phyllis opened the door, and Becky leaned in to place the box she held on the floorboard. Cliff was putting the other things into the cargo area in the back. Phyllis noticed that one of the rear seats had been removed to provide more storage room.

Cliff headed back into the senior center to fetch more of the things they had brought with them. Becky lowered her voice and said to Phyllis, "Don't mind Cliff. He's just got his nose a little out of joint today."

Phyllis smiled and said, "I didn't know young people used phrases like 'nose out of joint' anymore."

Becky returned the smile. "Well, I'm around Mr. Dorrington an awful lot, and he's so distinguished and British and, well, mature, that I suppose I've picked up some of his expressions. One time Cliff brought in some groceries and started to put them up, and I told him just to leave them alone, that I'd get that lot sorted."

"I'll remember that line and use it on my friend Sam sometime."

Becky laughed and said, "Be my guest." They started back toward the door. "And thank you for coming today. Will you be back on Wednesday for the next class?"

"Oh, I'll be here," Phyllis said.

# Chapter 4

Ronnie was waiting when Phyllis, Sam, Carolyn, and Eve got back to the house later that afternoon.

Veronica Ericson was Sam's granddaughter. Nearly two years earlier, after a long series of arguments with her parents—Sam's daughter Vanessa and her husband Phil—Ronnie had run away from their home in Pennsylvania and showed up unannounced here in Weatherford, planning to move in with her grandfather. Sam hadn't been sure that was a good idea, but Phyllis hadn't raised any objection, and to keep peace in the family, Sam had agreed to let Ronnie stay temporarily.

Time had passed, though, and then Ronnie had been in her senior year of high school and wanted to stay so she could graduate with the new friends she'd made here. After a couple of visits home and some long discussions with her parents, everybody had decided that would be all right. But then Ronnie would return home and attend college in Pennsylvania in the fall.

Phyllis was going to miss her when she left. Ronnie had never been a bad girl, just a teenager with a normal rebellious streak that manifested itself in blue hair and a bit of an attitude at times. The somewhat slower pace of life here in Texas—slower compared to her home, anyway, although Phyllis thought that Weatherford had gotten way too big and busy—had mellowed Ronnie. The blue tint in her hair had faded away, and now it was her natural blond again. Her grades had improved. In fact, she would be graduating in a few days ranked twelfth in her class, a considerable jump from where she'd started. And despite the difference in their ages, she actually seemed to enjoy spending time with her grandfather and his housemates.

Phyllis saw Ronnie sitting in the glider on the front porch with Buck, Sam's Dalmation, lying at her feet. The girl had her phone in her hand, naturally, but she looked up and waved with the other hand when Phyllis turned her Lincoln into the driveway. Phyllis left the garage door open, so that when the four of them got out of the car, they could go along the walk and up the three steps to the porch to join Ronnie.

"Hi," she greeted them. "We got our cap-and-gowns today!"

Sam grinned. "You'll have to model the get-up for us."

"You'll see them at the graduation ceremony."

Phyllis said, "Yes, and we'll take a lot of pictures before then, too."

Ronnie shrugged. "I guess that's all right. Hey, how'd the cooking class go? You show that British guy Texas cooks are better?"

"I wouldn't go so far as to say that. We've baked scones before, but I can honestly say that today is the first time Carolyn and I have attempted to make Bubble and Squeak!"

Ronnie laughed and shook her head. "That name always cracks me up. At least they didn't have you making Spotted Dick!"

"I think that's another class," Sam drawled.

"Hush and take this on inside," Phyllis said as she handed him the foil-wrapped plate that held the leftover scones from the class. Between them and the men at the domino table, they had polished off the Bubble and Squeak.

Sam chuckled and took the scones in. Carolyn and Eve followed him. Phyllis sat down at the other end of the glider from Ronnie and reached over to scratch Buck's ears. He panted happily.

"I suppose you're excited about graduating," she said.

Ronnie tucked her phone in her back pocket. "Yeah, sure. I guess so. I mean…it's kind of a big deal." A more serious tone came into her voice as she went on, "But it's sad, too. It's the end of so many things."

"But it's also the beginning of so many other things," Phyllis pointed out.

"Yeah, that's what all the valedictorian speeches say, isn't it? And it's true. But it's so final! It's like…you walk across the stage, and they hand you a diploma, and then you take a step…and there's no going back. It's over. Everything that's gone before…it's gone and you can't reclaim it. Yesterday might as well be a million years ago. They're both equally far out of your reach."

"That's why you look to the future instead of the past," Phyllis said. "It's fine to remember your accomplishments and take pride in them…to recall with joy all the good times you've experienced…but most of your thoughts need to be turned toward what's still to come."

Ronnie sighed. "I know you're right. Sometimes it just feels like all the memories…all the regrets…they just try to pull you down. They weigh so much you *can't* turn away from them."

She was solemn, so serious, and Phyllis didn't want to point out that she was talking about the weight of eighteen years, not more than seven *decades*.

Anyway, such a comparison wasn't even fair. No matter how old you were, there was always someone older, someone who had walked a longer, harder road. No one could escape the occasional wallow in the trough of nostalgia, melancholy, and regret, but Phyllis tried not to allow herself to get down in that muck too often.

It was much better to think about her friends and family, and now, she considered Ronnie part of that family, too.

She moved closer to the girl and put her arm around her shoulders. "It'll be all right," she said. "Times like this are the reason they invented the word *bittersweet*."

"Yeah, I think you're right. It's just a shame we can't reach back and touch the past now and then, just for a minute."

"It's a pretty thing to think about," Phyllis said."

That evening, after loading the dishwasher, Phyllis went into the living room and found Sam sitting in his recliner, his feet up and an old Western paperback in his hands. He owned an e-reader and read many books that way, but he had a good collection of old paperbacks and retained a special fondness for them. As he had once said to Phyllis, "These old eyes of mine may like the big font in ebooks, but they sure don't smell as nice as an old Gold Medal or Ace Double."

Carolyn was sitting on the sofa on the other side of the room with a book, as well. In her case, it was a cookbook full of British recipes. Phyllis smiled and said, "I don't recall Mr. Dorrington giving us any homework."

"He said we'd be doing Yorkshire pudding and shepherd's pie next time," Carolyn replied. "I don't see any harm in being prepared."

"None at all," Phyllis agreed. "Where's Eve?"

"Upstairs. Writing."

"Another novel?"

Carolyn shrugged. "I have no idea. You know she never likes to talk about what she's working on."

A few years earlier, Eve had written and sold a novel loosely based on the four of them, including Phyllis's role in solving a number of murders. The book had sold reasonably well, according to Eve; Phyllis had never seen her friend's royalty statements and didn't want to.

But it had drawn the interest of Hollywood, leading to a film crew descending on Weatherford to make a movie based on the book. That hadn't ended well, and while the property wasn't exactly dead, it was stuck in development hell, as Eve phrased it.

Phyllis sat on the sofa with Carolyn and said, "I had a little talk with Ronnie after we got back this afternoon."

Sam lowered his paperback and slipped a finger into it to mark his place. "I noticed the two of you sittin' out there on the porch for a while after the rest of us came in," he said. "Anything wrong?"

"Not really. I just thought she looked a little down, and as it turned out, she was."

Sam shook his head. "She seemed fine to me."

"That's why it's a good thing the rest of us are around," Carolyn said. "Someone like you isn't as likely to notice such things."

"You mean a man...or an *old* man?"

"Both."

Phyllis said, "It's fine, Sam, don't worry. She's not unhappy. She was just feeling a little sad because high school's about to be over."

Sam nodded slowly and said, "Yeah, I understand. We used to see that all the time in the kids when we were teachin'. It gets to be the last week or so of school, with graduation loomin' up right in front of 'em, and the finality of the whole deal starts to sink in."

"That's exactly what Ronnie was talking about. Things coming to an end, and never being able to go back to them except in memories."

"That's what life is," Carolyn said. "One day, and then the next. Until there aren't any more."

Sam said, "Now *I'm* startin' to feel a mite down in the mouth."

"No need for that," Phyllis assured him. "We're all fairly healthy for our ages, and there's no reason to think we don't have plenty of good years left—"

"That sounds like we're appliances," Carolyn said. "Or cars."

"Yeah, you can still get parts for us," Sam said, "but it gets harder, and sooner or later you get to the point where you have to ask yourself, is it worth it to fix up this old thing one more time, or should you just get a new one?"

Phyllis was about to sigh with exasperation at both of them, but then she saw the smile lurking around the corners of Sam's mouth and knew he was just joking. She glanced over at Carolyn and saw that her friend had returned her attention to the British cookbook, or at least was pretending to.

"Anyway, Ronnie's all right," Phyllis said. "We had a nice

talk. She'll miss her friends, but she's looking forward to college this fall, too, even though she's a little nervous about it."

Carolyn said, "That *is* one thing I don't like about being old. We try to keep active, of course, and like you said, Phyllis, we try to learn new things, but at our age, there aren't any real adventures to look forward to, are there?"

"I wouldn't say that," Sam responded. "Look at all the ruckuses we've been mixed up in, these past few years. I don't reckon when we retired that any of us saw *that* comin'."

Phyllis laughed and said, "Well, that's true. And some of those ruckuses, as you call them, I would have just as soon done without!"

Sam stroked his chin and looked like he was thinking.

"You never know," he mused. "Could be somethin' else excitin' comin' up, right around the corner."

Phyllis wondered what he meant by that.

# Chapter 5

The rest of that evening passed uneventfully, except for Ronnie coming downstairs wearing her cap and gown, as she'd promised. It was very impressive, and Phyllis told her she looked very mature and intelligent. Ronnie laughed at that, but Phyllis could tell that she was pleased.

The next day went by pleasantly as well, and then right after lunch on Wednesday afternoon, the four housemates headed for the senior center again for the second British cooking class with Alfred Dorrington.

As Phyllis pulled into the center's parking lot, she saw that Dorrington's SUV was already there. Dorrington and his helpers must have arrived not long before, because she saw Cliff Reynolds taking the big tote bag out of the back. He started toward the center with it. Phyllis didn't see Dorrington or Becky Thackery and assumed they were already inside.

Patrick Flanagan, Ansel Hovey, and Carl Benford were waiting at the domino table for Sam. The dominoes were already in the middle of the table, face down.

"There you are, Sam," Flanagan greeted. "Good to see you again."

"You didn't reckon I'd miss it, did you?" Sam said to the retired cop. He noticed that the empty chair at the table was directly across from Flanagan. "Are we playin' partners this time?"

"Is that all right with you?" Hovey asked. "We thought we'd shake things up a little. Patrick hasn't been one of us for that awful long. Carl and I figured he ought to take his turn carryin' you." His amiable grin took any sting out of the words.

Flanagan chuckled. "Ah, they'll be singing a different tune when we're done mopping the floor with them, won't they, Sam?"

"Yeah, and I'll enjoy listenin' to it," Sam said with a smile as he sat down.

Flanagan turned his head, smiled up at Carolyn, and said, "And how are you today, Miz Wilbarger? It's good to see you again, too."

Carolyn frowned slightly. Phyllis could tell she was surprised by Flanagan's question and comment. But then Carolyn said, "I'm fine, thank you. And you?"

"Oh, just dandy," Flanagan told her. "Looking forward to an enjoyable afternoon."

"Yes, me, too." Carolyn cleared her throat and moved on toward the kitchen.

Phyllis patted Sam on the shoulder and said, "Enjoy your game."

"I intend to. Have fun cookin'." Then, as Phyllis and Eve followed Carolyn, he went on, "All right, boys, what're we playin' today?"

Carolyn still seemed a little confused. She wasn't moving

very fast, and she glanced over her shoulder at the domino table a couple of times. Phyllis and Eve moved up alongside her, flanking her.

Eve leaned in and said quietly, "That man was flirting with you, Carolyn. You know that, don't you?"

"Mr. Flanagan? Don't be absurd."

"Take my word for it. I know flirting when I see it. I should, I've done enough of it over the years."

"Well, I'm not going to argue about *that*," Carolyn muttered. "But in this case, you're wrong. There's absolutely no reason that man would be flirting with me."

"Of course there is. We're the three best-looking women here. Phyllis and Sam are a couple, obviously, and I'm out of poor Mr. Flanagan's league, so that leaves you."

"Thanks." The word had ice around its edges. "You *are* insane, you know that?"

Eve didn't answer, because at that moment Sheila Trent and Ingrid Gustafson intercepted them. The two women planted their feet, crossed their arms, and glared.

Phyllis, Carolyn, and Eve had no choice but to come to a stop, unless they wanted to run over the other two. Sheila and Ingrid had chosen a spot between tables to form their blockade. It was an effective location.

"That's far enough," Sheila said.

"We want to get something clear," Ingrid added.

"Oh, for heaven's sake," Eve said. "We went through this last time. I agreed to stay out of the kitchen, and I kept my word, didn't I?"

"And then you proceeded to steal all the rest of the time that Alfred was here," Sheila said. "Nobody else really got to talk to him except for a second or two."

"I believe that was his idea, not mine. *He* invited *me* to share tea and scones with him." Eve smiled, but the expression held no warmth or friendliness. "And based on that, I believe if anyone here has a right to call him Alfred, it would be me, not you, dear."

Sheila's eyes narrowed. She looked like she wanted to lunge at Eve. Phyllis hoped the woman wouldn't lose her temper. At their age, none of them needed a brawl. That would be a rash of broken hips just waiting to happen.

Ingrid stepped forward and a little to the side, so that she was between Sheila and Eve. She said, "We're just putting you on notice, Turner. If Mr. Dorrington's gonna be sharing Yorkshire pudding with anybody after class today, it's going to be me and Sheila."

"We'll see what Alfred has to say about that," Eve said.

What Dorrington had to say at that moment, as soon as the window between the center's main room and the kitchen had rattled up, was, "All right, ladies, those of you in the class please come into the kitchen."

For a second, it appeared that Sheila and Ingrid were going to continue blocking the path, but then they moved aside with obvious reluctance and turned toward the kitchen door. Phyllis and Carolyn followed. Eve stayed where she was, scowling at the retreating backs of her two self-appointed nemeses.

The class was every bit as enjoyable as the first one, as Alfred Dorrington punctuated his instructions and demonstrations with stories about things that had happened in his London restaurant, most of them involving royalty and/or celebrities. Some of the tales were just racy enough to draw laughter from the class participants and the small audience watching through the big, open window.

Becky Thackery assisted Dorrington with brisk efficiency, but Cliff Reynolds remained in a corner of the kitchen, one hip propped against a counter while he crossed his arms and watched with a somewhat impatient half-frown. Phyllis noticed that and remembered how the young man hadn't been pleased with how Dorrington treated his girlfriend. Becky didn't appear upset about the situation, though. She laughed and smiled and seemed to be having a fine time working with Dorrington.

The shepherd pies went in the oven first and then the class members began working on their Yorkshire puddings, following Dorrington's directions. After the class, those who had signed up for it would receive copies of the recipes by email. That was another job actually handled by Becky Thackery, Phyllis suspected.

When the Yorkshire pudding went in the second oven, there was a short break so the class members could visit the restroom or just move around. Sam was waiting outside the kitchen door when Phyllis emerged.

"What happened to the domino game?" she asked him.

"Oh, we're takin' a break, too," he said. "You know how it is. Bones and muscles as old as ours can't just sit there for too long a time. Got to get up and shake a leg now and then." He grinned. "Besides, Ansel and Carl are tryin' to figure out a way to get Patrick and me to switch partners again. We've whipped 'em twice at Forty-Two, once at straight dominoes, and we're ahead again in the game right now."

"So the two of you are working well together."

"You could say that. Of course, it's helped that we've been gettin' good dominoes. You can only play what you're dealt."

"A statement that applies to life, as well."

"Yeah, I reckon. If you want to get philosophical about it." Sam shook his head. "That's a mite weighty for me." He paused, then went on, "I hope you're plannin' to bring samples of those goodies you're fixin' over to the table when you're done, like you did last time. The boys'll sure be disappointed if you don't."

Phyllis smiled and said, "Oh, I imagine that can be arranged."

"And when you do," Sam continued, "maybe you could kind of see to it...without bein' obvious about it, you know...that Carolyn sits next to ol' Flanagan."

Phyllis cocked her head to the side. "Really? Eve told Carolyn that Mr. Flanagan was flirting with her, but Carolyn didn't believe it. I wasn't completely convinced myself, either. You think he likes her?"

"I believe the thought has crossed his mind," Sam said with a solemn nod. "He hasn't come right out and said anything, but he's asked me a few questions about her...Just idle conversation, you know...And I saw the way he looked at her a time or two. I think there's some interest stirrin'." His shoulders rose and fell. "Whether or not it'll ever amount to anything, who knows?"

"Well, I'll see what I can do," Phyllis promised. "Without meddling, of course."

"Of course," Sam agreed, although he was smiling when he said it. He added, "You can sit by me."

"That's what I had in mind." A bit of curiosity sparked in her mind. "What prompted you to say that?"

"Well..." Sam suddenly looked and sounded a little hesitant. "Patrick was askin' me some questions about *you*, too. I don't think he meant anything by it, you understand. It's more

like he feels like the two of you are, I don't know, kindred spirits. Him bein' a retired detective and all, and so are you. Well,
you're not retired from *bein'* a detective, but you *are* retired
and you *are* a detective…"

"I know what you mean, Sam," Phyllis said, rescuing him.
"I don't think Mr. Flanagan has any romantic interest in me,
either. Eve mentioned that very thing earlier."

"She did? What did she say?"

"That you and I are obviously a couple," Phyllis said as she
rested a hand against his upper arm. "I didn't argue with her."

Sam smiled and said, "No reason to."

# Chapter 6

The shepherd's pie and Yorkshire pudding were both successful. Phyllis divided the ones she had made onto three small paper plates and carried them over to the domino table. She gave one to Carl Benford, set a plate in front of Sam, and took the other herself at the empty chair Sam had waiting for her.

Phyllis had made an effort to get there first so that Carolyn would have to share her dishes with Patrick Flanagan and Ansel Hovey. That was what she did when she walked up to the table a minute or so after Phyllis did.

After thanking her, Flanagan patted the empty chair beside him and said, "Sit right down here and join us, Miz Wilbarger."

"All right," she said. As she took the chair, she added, "I suppose it would be all right if you were to call me Carolyn. We're regulars here at the center, so I assume we'll be seeing a lot of you and we'll all be friends."

Flanagan smiled and pointed across the table at Sam. "As

long as that towering fellow remains my partner in these games. We're proving well nigh invincible so far, aren't we, Sam?"

"That's the way it looks to me," Sam agreed.

Carolyn asked, "How long have you lived in Weatherford, Mr. Flanagan? I know I've seen you around for a while, but it doesn't seem like it's been all that long."

He held up a finger and waved it back and forth. "Now, if I'm to call you Carolyn, then you have to call me Patrick. As for how long I've been in these parts, I moved over here from Dallas a couple of months ago." His eyes rolled dramatically. "Talk about a difference between night and day! The traffic over there is terrible. It's so peaceful here."

"Those of us who've been here for a while will tell you, the traffic *here* is a lot worse than it used to be. It wasn't long ago that Weatherford was just a little country town."

"Not long at all," Sam said. "Just forty years ago."

"No, it couldn't be—" Carolyn began. Then she stopped, frowned, and shook her head. "Forty years ago was...Oh, never mind! It seems like not that long ago to me. Anyway, I'm sure it really is a lot different from Dallas."

"Do you miss it?" Phyllis asked Flanagan.

"The dirt, the bad air, the crime, *and* the traffic?" He shook his head. "No, I don't miss it. Some people, when they've lived in big cities all their lives, think that life in the country or in a small town is too slow and boring. There's nothing to do, they say. Well, I've done things already. More things than I like to think about, actually. And as far as I'm concerned, at this point in my existence on this earth, I'm just fine with sitting back and taking life easy."

"I couldn't agree more," Carolyn said.

"Of course," Flanagan went on, "having some fine food to

eat makes it even better." He pointed with the plastic fork he'd picked up from the plate with small portions of shepherd's pie and Yorkshire pudding on it. "And I think I'll dig in right now."

The others sitting around the table followed his example. Compliments on the cooking flowed from the men to Phyllis and Carolyn, neither of whom were afflicted with false modesty. They accepted the praise and were grateful for it.

Although Sam did point out that the Yorkshire Pudding wasn't exactly what he'd been expecting from the name.

"This is more like a biscuit," he said as he poked at the dish with his plastic fork. "Why would they call somethin' a pudding when it's clearly *not* a pudding?" Then he answered his own question by saying, "Oh, well, they're British."

Patrick Flanagan chuckled and said, "And to them a biscuit is a cookie, my friend."

Carolyn said under her breath, "Oh, no."

"What is it?" Phyllis asked her. "Something wrong?"

Carolyn nodded toward the kitchen, where Alfred Dorrington had just emerged into the main room. He had taken off his coat-of-arms apron and donned his suit jacket again. He was talking to two women, and even though their backs were to her, Phyllis recognized Sheila Trent and Ingrid Gustafson.

She also saw Eve, sitting by herself at a table not far away with an expectant expression on her face. Phyllis realized that was probably what had prompted the worried reaction from Carolyn.

Sure enough, looking somewhat distracted and impatient, Dorrington spoke to Sheila and Ingrid, but only for a moment before he deftly sidestepped them and started toward the table where Eve was sitting. The two women turned to watch him, and their faces reddened with anger as Dorrington took a seat at the table and reached across it to clasp one of Eve's hands in both of his.

"Do you think we should go over there to help her?" Phyllis asked Carolyn.

"Help who?" Sam put in, having overheard the question.

"Eve. There, ah, may be an argument."

"With those two ladies glarin' at her and Dorrington like warmed-over death? I'm not sure argument is the right word. It looks to me like they might be fixin' to go to hair-pullin' and eye-gougin'."

"Never underestimate the female of the species," Flanagan said. "That's one thing I learned as a copper. Any time you answered a domestic disturbance call, the woman was liable to turn out to be more of a danger than the man."

Phyllis started to push her chair back. "Maybe we should—"

She didn't finish the sentence, because at that moment the senior center's front door opened, and most of the eyes in the room swung toward the woman who entered the room, her slim shape silhouetted against the afternoon sunlight outside.

She came in a couple of steps and then stopped. She wore a stylish, obviously expensive beige outfit that went well with her coloring and dark blond hair. She took off the sunglasses she had worn into the building and slipped them into the bag that hung from her left shoulder. Several rings glittered on her long, slender fingers. Her outfit, which included high heels, set her apart from the other women in the room. She wasn't young, but she carried herself well.

Alfred Dorrington stood up and said to the newcomer, "Sophia, darling—"

At that moment, Becky Thackery stepped out of the kitchen carrying two small plates with Yorkshire pudding on them.

She began, "Alfred, here are the puddings you wanted—"

She stopped short, too, at the sight of the tall, slender, elegant woman who had just come into the senior center.

The woman smiled and resumed her walk toward the table where Eve sat and beside which Dorrington stood. She didn't move exactly like a model on a catwalk, Phyllis thought, but there was an air of grace and sinuousness about her that said she was used to people watching her...and took such attention as her due.

"Hello, Alfred," she said as she came up to him. She glanced at Eve, but her eyes didn't hold any real curiosity, just hostility. Phyllis was able to tell that from across the room. The woman went on, "I see that, as is customary, you're not lacking for female companionship."

"This is one of my students," Dorrington said, his voice as cool as the expression on the newcomer's face. "Actually, allow me to rephrase that. Eve *isn't* one of my students, but some of her friends are, and she's very pleasant company."

"Thank you, Alfred," Eve said.

The woman he had called Sophia turned her chilly smile on Eve. "Don't assume that he actually means anything by what he just said, dear. Alfred may have all the charm in the world, but it's quite easy to tell when he's lying: his lips are moving."

Eve stood up and said, "I don't know who you are, but I'm not sure you belong here."

"Why don't you tell her who I am, Alfred?" Sophia said. She waved her hand, a gesture that took in the entire room. "In fact, why don't you tell all these lovely people that I'm your wife?"

At one of the tables nearby, Sheila Trent exclaimed, "Wife?"

Ingrid Gustafson added, "He didn't say anything about being married?"

"And why would I?" asked Dorrington. "My marital status is hardly germane to how to make shepherd's pie or Yorkshire pudding."

"Speaking of Yorkshire pudding," Sophia said, "why don't you tell your little doxy to take those back into the kitchen? She looks rather uncomfortable standing there holding them."

Becky lifted her chin and glared defiantly at Sophia. "You can't talk about me like that."

"My dear, I'll say anything I please to the little home-wrecker who's trying to steal my husband," Sophia snapped back at her.

"That's a lie! I'm not trying to do anything of the sort."

Sophia shook her head. "Don't bother denying it. Alfred is absolutely incapable of keeping his hands off any attractive young woman around whom he spends any amount of time. You think I haven't seen that sordid little scenario play out again and again over the years?" She let out a brittle laugh. "Trust me, there's nothing special about you. You're just one of a long line of little chippies he keeps on his string. Something young and fresh to keep him amused when he's not busy pursuing ancient tramps like this one!"

She flung a hand dismissively toward Eve.

"That's about enough," Eve said as she started out from behind the table.

At the same time, an angry cry of "I knew it!" came from the kitchen door. Cliff Reynolds stalked out, headed toward Becky, and went on, "I knew there was something going on between you and Dorrington!"

Over at the domino table, Patrick Flanagan muttered, "This isn't shaping up well."

Phyllis agreed with that. Everyone had fallen silent to watch the confrontation going on in front of the big window between the main room and the kitchen. Becky Thackery had gone pale as her gaze cut back and forth between Dorrington, Sophia, and Reynolds. Suddenly she turned and set the samples of Yorkshire pudding on a nearby table and then moved to get in front of Reynolds, who appeared to be heading for Dorrington.

"Cliff, stop," she said with a degree of urgency in her voice. "Mrs. Dorrington doesn't know what she's talking about."

"Is that right?" Sophia asked in a malevolent purr. "What if I said I have proof—"

"You'd be lying," Dorrington interrupted her. "You can't prove something that doesn't exist."

Sophia nodded toward Reynolds and said, "Then perhaps I should show this boy the pictures I have."

"I don't need any pictures," Reynolds said as he stepped around Becky and shrugged off the hand she put on his arm. "I already know good and well what's going on!"

With that, a long step brought him within arm's reach of Alfred Dorrington. He swung a punch at the older man's head.

# Chapter 7

Sam and the other three men at the table were on their feet immediately. Alfred Dorrington was probably three times Cliff Reynolds' age, and he might need help fending off the angry young man's attack.

However, that didn't appear to be the case. The punch never landed. Without even seeming to move quickly, Dorrington leaned to the side. Reynolds' fist flew harmlessly past his head.

The young man's momentum had brought him close already. Dorrington stepped even closer and jammed his open right hand into Reynolds' midsection. The stiffened fingers dug deep into Reynold's body, just below his breastbone. Reynolds bent forward sharply. Phyllis could see his face, so she was able to observe how his eyes suddenly got big with pain and surprise. His mouth opened in a gasp.

Then he staggered back, both arms crossed over the injured area. His mouth opened and closed like a fish as he struggled to catch his breath.

"Cliff!" Becky cried. She hurried to his side and caught

hold of his arm, steadying him as he swayed and seemed to be on the verge of falling down.

"I'm sorry I had to do that, son," Dorrington told him. "You gave me no choice."

Sophia said, "No, he's not sorry at all. He takes great pleasure in hurting people. It's just that normally it's not physical pain he inflicts. He'd rather torture someone mentally and emotionally."

Darla Kirby must have heard the commotion from her office. She came up with a worried look on her face and said, "Please, we don't want any trouble here."

"Then you shouldn't have hired a liar and a serial philanderer," Sophia said. She sniffed, looked at Dorrington, and went on, "I've said what I came to say. I'm on to you, Alfred, and if you want to get this sorted, it's going to take some serious groveling on your part. Even that may not be enough."

"I have no intention of groveling, serious or otherwise, I assure you," Dorrington said. He shook his head. "Sophia, darling, you have everything wrong, as usual. Now, please, don't cause any further disruption among these poor, innocent people."

Sophia glanced at Eve and said, "I doubt if *that one* has been innocent for a very long time."

Carolyn stepped forward, suddenly a formidable presence in defense of her friend. "That's enough," she said. "I really think you should leave."

Sophia regarded her coldly but said, "That's precisely what I intend to do."

She turned and walked toward the door with the same sort of unhurried, cat-like grace she had displayed when she came in.

Eve looked like she wanted to go after the woman, but

Phyllis put a hand on her arm and gave a slight shake of her head.

Sam came up to Dorrington and asked, "Are you all right, Mr. Dorrington?"

The Englishman smiled and straightened the lapels of his suit jacket, settling the garment.

"Of course," he said. "Completely unharmed. Never better, in fact."

"I don't think that young fella can say the same," Ansel Hovey said as he nodded toward Cliff Reynolds. Becky had led him over to one of the tables and was helping him sit down. His face was pale, and his eyes still seemed a little larger than normal.

He muttered angrily, though, as he said something to Becky and all but pushed her away from him. A look of despair came over her face.

Dorrington started toward them, but Becky noticed, caught his eye, and shook her head. Dorrington hesitated, then shrugged and nodded. Phyllis thought maybe he wanted to apologize, but she agreed with Becky: now was not the time. Emotions were still running too high.

Instead, Dorrington turned to Eve and said, "I'm appalled that you had to endure that little display of pique, my dear."

"Is that woman really your wife?" Eve asked.

"I'm afraid so."

"She's very pretty," Eve said grudgingly. "For her age, that is."

"Unfortunately, physical beauty is no substitute for a sweet, gracious nature...something that you have in spades, Eve, darling."

Eve's eyes narrowed. "You're what we used to call a silver-tongued devil, aren't you? Flattery just comes naturally to you, especially where women are concerned."

Dorrington spread his hands as if in helplessness. "Guilty as charged, I'm afraid."

"And married, to boot." Eve shook her head. "Alfred Dorrington, you're a scoundrel. A charming one, but still a scoundrel." She looked past him at the table where Becky Thackery had sat down next to Cliff Reynolds. He still looked surly and half-sick, but he didn't jerk away as she rested her hand on his arm and leaned in to talk quietly to him. "Are you taking advantage of that poor girl?"

"That was a heinous lie on Sophia's part," he declared. "Ms. Thackery is a friend, and an exceptional assistant, as anyone in the class can tell you. That's all there is between us."

"Well..." Eve considered and then slowly nodded her head. "I think I believe you about that. And as for the other..." She smiled. "I don't suppose I can blame you. I *am* wonderful company."

"Wonderful, indeed!"

Phyllis and the others had been standing nearby, listening to this conversation. Now Darla Kirby stepped forward again and asked, "Are you going to continue with the final class, Mr. Dorrington?"

"Of course! There was never any doubt in my mind about that. Nothing that happened here today will change my plans. We'll put this misunderstanding behind us and continue as scheduled. The next class will be focused solely on desserts. A sticky toffee pudding and a delicious trifle." Dorrington paused. "Assuming, of course, that you *want* me to continue...?"

Darla nodded. "I certainly hope you do. It might cause hard feelings if we had to cancel the final class. Not to mention some people would want their money back."

"We can't have that. Have no fear, I'll proceed as planned on Friday."

"Will your, ah, assistant be able to help you?"

Dorrington glanced toward Becky. "That will be entirely up to Ms. Thackery, but I most definitely hope she'll continue in her current capacity. I've become accustomed to having her assistance. But if she feels too uncomfortable because of to-day's unfortunate incidents, I'll just have to soldier on as best I can."

With that settled, Darla looked relieved. She said, "If you need any help loading your things, I'm sure some of the men would be glad to pitch in."

"Sure," Sam said. "Let us give you a hand."

"Much appreciated, but I can handle it nicely. And I think I had best get started."

"But we never had our Yorkshire pudding," Eve said.

Dorrington looked a little surprised. "Under the circum-stances, I assumed you'd prefer not to associate with me any-more, Eve."

"Oh, I'm a little peeved at you for not mentioning that you're married," she said, "but we were just having some pleasant conversation, weren't we? It didn't amount to any more than that."

"Unfortunately, it didn't," Dorrington admitted. "But it *was* very pleasant."

"Yes," said Eve. "While it lasted."

Everyone returned to where they had been sitting earlier. Phyllis noticed that Patrick Flanagan had hung back a little when the other men went to help Dorrington. She supposed that was because of what he had said about his experiences with domestic disturbances when he was a police officer. She knew from listening to her son Mike talk that officers always dreaded those calls.

Cliff Reynolds stood up and went back into the kitchen, still looking shaken. Becky Thackery followed him, still talking quietly but intensely to him. Phyllis couldn't hear any of what the young woman was saying, but she wondered if Becky was trying to convince her boyfriend there was no truth to the accusations Sophia Dorrington had made.

Dorrington went over to the table where Becky had left the samples of Yorkshire pudding. He picked them up and carried them back to the table where Eve had resumed her seat. She still looked a little wary, but as they began talking and eating the pudding, she relaxed. Phyllis knew Eve well enough to be able to tell that from across the room.

As she and Carolyn settled back into the chairs at the domino table, Flanagan asked, "Is there always this much excitement whenever you're around, Miz Newsom?"

"Oh, you just don't know," Carolyn said before Phyllis could answer. "Trouble seems to follow her like a magnet."

"I'm not sure that's fair," Sam said. "We've done plenty of things where nothin' bad happened."

Phyllis nodded and said, "That's true enough. But I think all of us have seen more than our fair share of...unexpected developments."

Ansel Hovey grinned. "Murder's what she means."

"Yes, I've read about some of the cases you've been involved in," Flanagan said. "From the sound of it, you've done some mighty fine detective work."

"It's just a matter of keeping my eyes open and being willing to consider things from different angles until they fit together," she said.

"Kind of like puttin' together a jigsaw puzzle," Sam added.

"Only the stakes are higher," Flanagan said with a slow nod. "Life and death, sometimes."

"I never asked for any of that," Phyllis said.

"Those of us in our line of work seldom do," Flanagan said, and Phyllis recalled what Sam had said earlier about the retired detective regarding them as kindred spirits. But chances were, in his years of carrying a badge, he had probably seen a lot uglier things than she'd had to deal with.

She hoped she would never have to sort out anything like that again.

# Chapter 8

After the men had finished their shepherd's pie and Yorkshire pudding, they resumed their domino game. Each team had a rectangular piece of wood cut out of a one-by-four, with fifty small holes drilled in it in five rows of ten. Each hole represented five points, with the first team to two hundred and fifty being the winner. The wood had been stained and varnished, and each team also had a little wooden peg to move from hole to hole as they scored.

Phyllis knew that Sam had made those score-keeping boards in his workshop in her garage, and he was proud of the craftsmanship that had gone into them. Of course, it was just as easy to keep score using a pen or pencil and a piece of scrap paper, but some people took their dominoes more seriously than that.

She could have stayed and watched the game, but when she saw Cliff Reynolds come out of the kitchen alone, carrying the tote bag full of equipment, she stood up and headed in that direction. Carolyn came along as well.

"What are we doing?" Carolyn asked.

"I want to make sure Miss Thackery's all right," Phyllis said. "She was having to hold it together to keep her young man under control, but she had to be upset by what happened, too."

They found Becky in the kitchen, packing away supplies in a cardboard box. Her eyes were a little red. Phyllis knew she had been crying. She appeared to be keeping a tight rein on her emotions at the moment, however.

"Oh, hi," she said as Phyllis and Carolyn came into the kitchen. The shutter on the big window was rolled down. "Can I help you?"

"We wanted to make sure you were all right," Phyllis told her, keeping her voice friendly and level.

"I'm fine," Becky said. "It's nothing to worry about. Cliff... Well, Cliff can be a little volatile."

Carolyn said, "Jealous seems to be the word for it."

Becky stopped what she was doing, sighed, and shook her head. "He's not like that all the time. He just gets ideas in his head, and it's hard to convince him that he's wrong. Having Mrs. Dorrington show up and start throwing around crazy accusations like that certainly didn't help matters."

"Has she done things like that before?" Phyllis asked.

"Sophia? Not while I was around. Alfred... Mr. Dorrington...has mentioned in the past that she has a jealous streak, too. A lot like Cliff, I suppose. But he said it was nothing to worry about."

Carolyn said, "I think I'd worry if I were you. That woman looked...vicious, I guess is the word. And very cold-blooded, too."

"She'd never do anything," Becky replied with a shake of her head. "Mr. Dorrington says she's very conscious of her place in society. She wouldn't want to risk a scandal by getting in a fight with some woman she suspected of being her husband's mistress."

"They're actually married, not separated or divorced?" Phyllis said.

"That's right. They still live together." Becky looked embarrassed as she added, "I don't think they have much of a real marriage anymore. But I'm gossiping now, and I shouldn't be doing that. I just work for Mr. Dorrington. Whatever goes on between him and his wife is none of my business."

"That's a very sensible attitude to take," Carolyn told her. "How did you wind up working for him, anyway?"

"I worked for him at the restaurant in Dallas. He asked me if I'd like to be his personal assistant and help him with the classes he gives. I thought it would be a good opportunity to learn more. You know, to observe him cooking up close, one on one, almost."

"You want to be a chef?" Phyllis asked, smiling.

"That's my goal, someday. I don't want to own a restaurant, though, like so many chefs do." Becky shook her head. "I can't imagine having to keep up with all the details of running a business. I just want to cook."

Carolyn nodded and said, "It's a very admirable profession, I think. Everybody has to eat, and it might as well be good food."

"Exactly." Becky turned back to the box on the counter. "I need to finish packing everything up. Mr. Dorrington probably will be ready to go before much longer."

Phyllis noticed that Cliff hadn't returned. She said, "Is Mr. Reynolds going to drive back to Dallas with you?"

"Yes. He's probably sitting out there in the SUV, brooding,

but he promised me he wouldn't lose his temper anymore."

"You convinced him there was nothing to what Mrs. Dorrington said?"

"Well...he claimed he believed me." Becky sighed. "I'm not sure he really does. You see, several times he's walked in while Mr. Dorrington was showing me something...about cooking, you know...and our heads would be pretty close together over the pot or pan or mixing bowl or whatever. That's what got him suspicious in the first place. But nothing ever happened, and I told him that over and over. Like I said..." She shrugged. "Once he gets an idea in his head..."

"Maybe it would be a good idea if he didn't come with you in the future," Carolyn suggested.

"I thought about that, but then it seemed to me like he might be even more convinced I was trying to hide something. I'm not sure there *is* a good solution, short of him just believing what I tell him."

"That would be best," Phyllis agreed. "So he's coming back with you Friday?"

"Right now, I just don't know." Becky smiled sadly. "And I don't know what to hope for, either. Now, if you'll excuse me..."

"Of course. We'll let you get back to work. We just wanted to make sure you were all right."

"I will be," Becky said confidently. "I'm sure we'll work everything out, one way or another."

She picked up the box and carried it out of the kitchen.

Carolyn watched her go and said, "That poor girl. Do you believe her?"

"She sounded sincere," Phyllis said. "But it's really hard to be sure of anything."

"One thing *I'm* sure of...that's probably going to be a long, chilly ride back to Dallas with the three of them in that SUV."

Phyllis couldn't disagree with that."

They went back out into the center's main room and saw that Eve and Alfred Dorrington were both on their feet. The plates that had held samples of Yorkshire pudding sat empty on the table. Dorrington took Eve's hand and said, "I hope I'll see you back here on Friday, my dear."

"Oh, I'll be here," Eve assured him. "If there are any more fireworks, I wouldn't want to miss them."

Dorrington winced. "No fireworks, I promise. I'm going to have a long talk with Sophia and try to put her fevered mind to rest. She really has to stop making scenes like that."

Phyllis and Carolyn had moved up to the table while Eve and Dorrington were talking. Phyllis said, "Mrs. Dorrington has made accusations like that against you before?"

"Unfortunately, my darling Sophia has a very possessive, competitive personality. Jealousy comes naturally to her, I'm afraid."

"I hate to see a nice young woman like Miss Thackery get caught in the middle of such ugliness."

"As do I, Mrs. Newsom, I assure you. Poor Becky is totally blameless in this matter." Dorrington shrugged. "Fate has seen fit to pair us both with suspicious, impulsive partners."

Eve said, "Is it going to be safe for you to travel all the way back to Dallas with that Reynolds boy?"

Dorrington smiled. "Cliff Reynolds may be young and agile, but he's no threat to me. I know how to handle his type."

"Yes, you demonstrated as much," Phyllis said. "Where did you learn to fight like that?"

Dorrington chuckled and said, "The restaurant business is surprisingly cutthroat, especially in London. I was involved in a number of rough-and-tumbles when I was younger, and I've tried to keep myself in shape over the years. In fighting trim, you might say."

"And you've done a fine job of it," Eve said.

"I appreciate that, my dear," Dorrington said. "Now, I really must be going." He smiled around at them. "I'll see you all Friday."

When he had walked across the room and gone out the front door, Carolyn frowned at Eve and said, "After everything that happened, you still had to flirt with him, there at the end? Tell him what good shape he was in?"

"Force of habit, I suppose," Eve replied. "Although there wasn't anything untrue about what I said. He really must be in good shape, to have handled a much younger man attacking him like that. I don't think he was frightened, even for a second."

"He didn't appear to be," Phyllis agreed. "Did he say anything to you about his relationship with Becky Thackery?"

"Only that she used to work at his restaurant, and she's been his assistant for a while." Eve frowned. "Don't tell me you believe any of that wild-eyed woman's accusations, Phyllis."

Carolyn said, "Sophia Dorrington didn't strike me as being all that wild-eyed. In fact, she seemed very calm and collected. Cold-blooded, even."

"Cold-blooded...like a snake."

"Carolyn and I talked to Becky," Phyllis said. "She told us the same thing about working in the restaurant first. She said her boyfriend saw her and Dorrington working together in close proximity while they were cooking and misinterpreted what was going on."

"That sounds perfectly plausible to me."

"Yes, it does. But then, Sophia Dorrington mentioned something about having pictures…photographs, I assume she meant…but she didn't go into any detail about what might be in them…"

"She was bluffing," Eve said. "There couldn't be pictures of something that never happened."

"No, I suppose not." Phyllis looked over toward the table where the domino game was going on. Sam was leaning forward, his long arms extended over the table as he shuffled the dominoes for the next hand. "I believe I'll go watch the boys play for a while."

She didn't want to think any more about the tangled relationships that had been on display here today. That was strictly the business of Alfred Dorrington, his wife, and the two young people.

"There's another table and another set of dominoes," Carolyn said. "And there are three of us. I'll bet we could find a fourth and get a game of our own going."

"Now that's a good idea," Phyllis said. The solidness of the dominoes and the spots imprinted on them seemed very appealing to her right now.

# Chapter 9

Final exams were over at the high school. Grades were in, class order was determined, and all that was left was graduation practice on Thursday and the graduation ceremony itself on Friday night. For many years while Phyllis was teaching, graduation had been held at the high school football stadium, but several instances of bad weather—thunderstorms were nearly always possible in Texas during the spring—had prompted the district to start holding the ceremony indoors. The only place in the area large enough was an indoor arena over in Fort Worth. Buses would take the students there for the practice on Thursday. That was the only thing the seniors had to do that day, since classes were effectively over.

That morning, Phyllis could tell how excited Ronnie was about what she'd be doing that day. Over coffee, bacon, and pancakes, she said, "I'm glad to see you're not worried about graduating anymore."

Ronnie laughed. "Oh, I wouldn't say that," she replied. "It's still a big deal, and it doesn't help that I haven't decided what I want to do with my life or even what I want to major in next fall when I go to college! But it's going to happen anyway, whether I worry about it or not."

Sam was sitting at the other end of the table. He took a sip of coffee and set the cup down, then said, "That's a pretty good way of lookin' at it. And you've still got plenty of time to decide what you're gonna do. That's part of what college is for, givin' you a chance to figure things out."

"Yeah, but you knew all along that you wanted to be a teacher, didn't you?"

Sam grinned. "Not hardly. I was gonna play pro ball. But Oscar Robertson and Jerry West came outta college the same year I did, so all the NBA teams decided they could get along just fine without me. I already knew I liked coachin', though. My coach in college said I was almost like a coach on the floor when I was out there. I'd minored in education, anyway…most Phys Ed majors did, either that or business…so it was easy to slide right into teachin'. Once I did, it didn't take me long to realize that was what I was born to do."

"See, that's it," Ronnie said. "I don't think that I was *born* to do anything."

"You were. You just haven't run across it yet."

"Maybe." She shrugged. "Like I said, it's going to happen no matter what I do, so I might as well just go along for the ride and enjoy it."

When Ronnie had left the kitchen a few minutes later, Phyllis lingered over her coffee and said to Sam, "I didn't know you wanted to play professional basketball. If we've ever talked about that, I'm afraid I've forgotten it." She smiled. "It's sort of nice to realize there are still things I don't know about you."

"Oh, it was never much of a dream," Sam said. "I was tall

enough to play center on a little country high school team, and they made me a forward in college, but at my size, I'd have had to play guard in the pros, and I never had the ball-handlin' or shootin' skill for that. Might've been nice to get a tryout, just so I could say that I'd done it and maybe played against some of the really good players, even if it was just in practice. But that never happened, and I'll tell you the truth… I've never lost a blasted second of sleep over it, either."

"You've lived a fulfilling life anyway."

"Yes, ma'am, I sure have. I got to be a positive influence on a bunch of kids over the years, or at least I hope I was—"

"You were," Phyllis said. "I have absolutely no doubt of that."

"I was married for a lot of years to a good woman," Sam went on. "Raised a good kid. Got to see my granddaughter grow up some. And, these last few years, I've made the best friends I've ever had in my life."

"I'm glad I could be one of them." Phyllis smiled. "At least I hope I am."

"You're more than that, and you know it."

They looked at each other over the table for a long moment of silence, then Sam cleared his throat and looked around at the counter. "There's still a couple of pieces of bacon…"

"You can have them," Phyllis said. "You don't even have to ask."

When Ronnie got back that afternoon, she seemed pleased with the way the graduation practice had gone. She went out with her friends that evening…the last time they would do so as high school seniors, she pointed out.

Phyllis, Sam, Carolyn, and Eve watched a movie after supper, then Carolyn and Eve went upstairs, leaving Phyllis and Sam in the living room. Phyllis checked her email on the computer in the corner while Sam picked up the paperback on the table next to his recliner, but after a few minutes, he said, "What's that picture on the monitor? Looks good."

Phyllis had finished with the email and moved on to a food website. She smiled back over her shoulder at Sam and said, "That's a Tex-Brit trifle, which is an English dish but Texas style. That's what we'll be making tomorrow. It's a Texas Margarita trifle with cake, cheesecake pudding, strawberry Jell-O with tequila, and fresh strawberries and blueberries, and a whipped cream topping."

"Sounds good, too," Sam said. "Maybe a little overwhelmin' with all those ingredients."

"Yes, I'm sure it'll be a little rich and it has tequila and triple sec rather than rum or brandy. Not to mention it's a bit tricky, with those different layers."

"Sort of like a seven-layer burrito."

Phyllis laughed. "Well, not really."

"Or three-bean salad. No, wait, you just mix up the different kinds of beans in that, don't you? It doesn't have layers."

"Well, I suppose it would be like a seven-layer Mexican dip."

"That's what I was thinking of! I knew something had seven layers."

That drew another laugh from Phyllis.

Ronnie didn't have anything to do on Friday except the graduation ceremony that evening, so Phyllis let her sleep in.

She and Carolyn went to the grocery store to make sure there was enough food on hand for the weekend, then, after lunch, the four friends got in Phyllis's car to head for the senior center.

"I certainly hope Mr. Dorrington got all of his, ah, personal drama settled," Carolyn commented from the back seat of Phyllis's Lincoln. "It was too tense the other day." She looked at Eve. "And you might do well to stay away from him. You never know what that wife of his might do. She struck me as a little crazy."

Some people might have thought Carolyn was being too blunt to say such a thing, but she and Eve had been friends for decades and Eve didn't seem to take any offense.

"I don't have any intention of sharing anything with Alfred Dorrington except some polite conversation...and maybe a sample of whatever you're baking today."

"Sticky toffee pudding and a trifle," Phyllis said, supplying the information from behind the wheel.

Carolyn said to Eve, "You're over your crush on him, then?"

Eve waved a hand dismissively. "Oh, I never had a crush on him, not really."

"You could have fooled me, the way you were playing up to him."

"Like I said, habit. I haven't gotten to know the man well enough to have any sort of genuine feeling for him. Oh, he's very handsome and charming, no doubt about that."

"So you *had* to flirt with him. You didn't have any choice in the matter."

"Of course. Be honest now, dear." Eve smiled. "You would have been disappointed in me if I *hadn't* flirted with him, wouldn't you?"

Sam looked around with a smile and said, "She's got a point there."

"Anyway, he had no genuine interest in me, either," Eve went on. "I knew that right away. You see, it's a matter of habit with *him*, too. Whenever he encounters an attractive woman, something inside him makes him turn on the charm. He can't help it any more than I can."

"Maybe so," Carolyn allowed. "And Sam's right. If you *hadn't* gone after him, I might have started wondering what was wrong with you."

A few minutes later, they reached the senior center, which was on the west side of town not far from the public library. As Phyllis pulled into the parking lot, she checked to see if Dorrington's big SUV was already there. She didn't spot it anywhere in the parking lot, but it was still early, she reminded herself. The previous two classes, Dorrington and his two companions had arrived well after Phyllis and her friends did. The domino games had been well underway.

"I'm in the mood for a little Forty-Two again today," Sam said as they walked inside. "Hope the other fellas are all right with that."

The first person Phyllis saw was Darla Kirby, and she realized immediately that the middle-aged center director looked worried. She and Carolyn and Eve walked over to Darla while Sam headed for the domino table. Patrick Flanagan, Ansel Hovey, and Carl Benford were already sitting there, talking and laughing.

"Something wrong, Darla?" Phyllis asked.

"I got an email last night from Mr. Dorrington saying that he might not be able to make it today after all," Darla said. "I know that's going to cause disappointment and hurt feelings if it happens."

"Did he say why he might not be here?"

"No, he just apologized and blamed unforeseen circumstances." Darla sighed. "But I'll bet it has something to do with his wife showing up and making a scene day before yesterday."

"It's bound to," Carolyn said. "He probably doesn't want to risk it happening again."

"I don't know," Eve said. "Alfred Dorrington doesn't strike me as the sort of man who'd be frightened off easily—"

A chime came from the cell phone in Darla's pocket. She pulled it out, thumbed the home button, and said, "Oh, thank goodness. It's a text from Mr. Dorrington. He says he's on the way and will be here shortly…and that this will be the best class yet."

# Chapter 10

The trio of Flanagan, Hovey, and Benford were happy to engage in another Forty-Two battle royal, and soon they were leaning forward, intently studying the dominoes they had drawn, and announcing, "Bid thirty." "Thirty-one." "Thirty-*two*." "We'll just set you, then. Go ahead."

The spots began to fly. Dominoes slapped down with chuckles from one side and groans from the other. Phyllis smiled as she watched Sam enjoy himself, caught up in the game.

Darla Kirby distracted her by sighing and saying, "I almost don't know what to hope for today."

"I do," Carolyn said. "No more trouble."

"Well, of course," Darla agreed. "But I was really having some mixed emotions when I didn't know whether Mr. Dorrington was going to show up. It would have been bad if he didn't, of course...but on the other hand, that would have meant there wouldn't be any more arguments."

"Maybe there won't be. Maybe that Reynolds boy won't

come with them today. After what happened last time, I wouldn't want to come along, if I was him. I'd be too embarrassed to."

Eve said, "Unless he's afraid to leave his girlfriend alone with Alfred."

Carolyn shrugged. "There's that to consider."

It wouldn't be long before they had their answer, Phyllis thought, and sure enough, less than half an hour had gone by when the front door opened and Cliff Reynolds came into the senior center, carrying the tote bag full of gear just as he had on the two previous occasions.

Alfred Dorrington was close behind him, holding the door open for Becky Thackery, who came in laden with two cardboard boxes, stacked one on top of the other. At least they didn't appear to be too heavy. She wasn't straining much to carry them.

"Hello, ladies," Dorrington greeted the little group as he came into the center. "Are you ready for the final class?"

"We are," Carolyn said. "We—"

"Mr. Dorrington," a new voice interrupted her. Phyllis looked around to see Sheila Trent and Ingrid Gustafson standing there with determined expressions on their faces. Sheila was the one who had spoken.

"Yes, my dear?" Dorrington responded with his usual easy smile.

"We want to thank you for coming over here and giving these lessons this week," Sheila went on. "And we want to apologize for any unpleasantness we might have contributed to."

Ingrid glared at Eve for a second, then forced a smile onto her face and added, "We probably overreacted a little, now and then."

"Nonsense," Dorrington said heartily. "Passion is a necessary ingredient in all great cooking. If we don't *care*, anything we make will be bland and tasteless."

"Well, we want to bury the hatchet," Ingrid said. She thrust out a hand toward Eve. "Truce, Turner?"

"Of course," Eve said. She took Ingrid's hand and smiled. "It's not like there was any sort of real competition, anyway."

Anger sparked in Ingrid's eyes again, and for a second Phyllis thought the blonde was going to squeeze Eve's hand too hard, but Eve never flinched and Ingrid got control of herself.

Sheila shook hands with Eve, as well, then turned back to Dorrington and said, "I hope you'll sample my trifle when I'm done with it."

"I look forward to it," Dorrington assured her. "Now, if all you ladies will excuse me, there are preparations to make."

He headed for the kitchen and disappeared through the door. The shutter on the big window stayed down. No angry voices came from inside the kitchen, and Cliff Reynolds left the center and came back in a couple of times, bringing in more boxes. Today's class would involve a lot of different ingredients.

Finally, the shutter went up, and Alfred Dorrington looked out and nodded to Darla, who had been watching and waiting for that signal. With a mixture of relief and trepidation on her face, she turned to face the room and called, "All right, those who are taking the cooking class can go on in the kitchen. If you'd like to watch but aren't taking part, you can gather here around the window."

Phyllis and Eve started toward the kitchen door. From the corner of her eye, Phyllis saw Sam and the other three men stand up from the domino table and head in the same direction. That surprised her, and she paused.

"What is it?" Carolyn asked. "Is something wrong?"

"I don't know. It looks like Sam and his friends are coming over here."

"What in the world for? Sam's not interested in cooking, unless it's that chili of his."

"I know," Phyllis said. She waited until the men came up and then asked Sam, "What are you doing?"

He grinned. "We thought we'd watch the cookin' class. Maybe pick up a few pointers. All four of us are single men, you know."

Phyllis just gave him a dubious look.

"Well, fact of the matter is, we just finished a game and wanted to stretch our legs for a few minutes before we started another one."

"I have circulation problems," Flanagan put in. "I need to get up and move around fairly often, or my legs start bothering me."

"Oh. Well, that makes sense, I suppose." Phyllis nodded to Flanagan. "And I'm sorry to hear about your issues."

He waved a hand. "It's nothing to worry about. Just another of the great perks of getting old."

Carolyn said, "We'd better get in there, or we'll be stuck at the back and won't be able to see."

Eve added, "Yes, Sheila and Ingrid are liable to hog all the space up front, even if they did promise to play nice from now on." She shook her head. "I don't believe that for a second. They're up to something."

Phyllis thought the two women had been sincere, for the most part, and that Eve was being a little paranoid, but she didn't say that. She just went to the door with Carolyn and moved into the kitchen, joining the half-circle of students gathered around the island counter where an apron-wearing Alfred Dorrington was standing with a number of mixing bowls and utensils in front of him. Becky Thackery stood at the end of the island, wearing an apron like Dorrington's.

Cliff Reynolds was leaning against the counter in the corner, apart from the others. He wasn't glaring, but Phyllis got the impression he was making an effort to keep his face expressionless so as not to reveal whatever he was actually feeling.

Eve, Sam, and the other three domino players were among the group gathered just on the other side of the window between rooms.

"All right, everyone," Dorrington said. "We'll begin with the gelatin that'll need to chill for the trifle, then we'll move on to the sticky toffee pudding.

"While the sticky toffee pudding is strictly a traditional British dessert that has a dark, dense sponge cake made with chopped dates topped with a sweet toffee sauce, to give it a Texas twist, we serve it with Texas' Blue Bell Homemade Vanilla ice cream. Now the trifle is a little different. We're going to make the gelatin into a Margarita delight."

Phyllis didn't see any sign of anything untoward or unprofessional as Becky assisted Dorrington in his efforts. She was right there whenever he needed something, but there was no unnecessary contact between them and Dorrington didn't waste any words whenever he asked her for something or gave her instructions. Clearly, he was making an effort not to provide anyone with an excuse to think there was anything improper between them.

That was probably difficult for him, Phyllis mused, accustomed as he was to smiling and flirting with most women and calling them "my dear" or "darling".

The class made the gelatin for the trifle and put the trifle containers in the refrigerator to chill, and then they started making the sticky toffee pudding. As the class went on, Dorrington seemed to relax, although he was still careful about how he spoke to Becky. Smiles appeared more often on his face, and the somewhat stiff manner he had displayed starting out eased. Clearly, he was caught up in the enjoyment of what he was doing. He was a man who loved to cook.

They finished with the sticky toffee pudding, leaving the warm toffee off the pudding until it was time to serve. It was time to move back to the Texas Margarita Trifle.

"Hand me that bowl there, darling," Dorrington said to Becky as he put out his hand. She seemed to have anticipated what he was going to say and was already turning to reach across the island and pick up the bowl he wanted.

As both of them moved at the same time, their outstretched arms crossed. It was an innocent accident, but their arms tangled, and as Dorrington continued his turn, they linked and Becky had to pivot toward him. That left them standing only inches apart, face to face, and the unintentional intimacy seemed to paralyze both of them. The casual smile disappeared from Dorrington's face, replaced by a look of intense solemnity. From where Phyllis was, she could see how their gazes locked, just as their arms had.

And if she could see that, so could everyone else in the kitchen, and those watching from the other side of the window, as well. A little hush hung over the scene.

That hush was broken by a shrill, angry voice crying, "I knew it! I knew it!"

"Wait!" That startled exclamation came from Darla Kirby. "You can't—Oh!"

The group of students inside the kitchen parted involuntarily. Sophia Dorrington came through them, bulling aside even the very solidly built Ingrid Gustafson. Instead of an elegant dress, today she wore tight, stylish jeans and a knit top, more suited for action.

And action was clearly what she had in mind, as she threw herself at Becky Thackery, hands outstretched and fingers hooked to claw as she cried, "You little slut! I'll teach you to leave my husband alone!"

Sophia's sudden, aggressive entrance took everyone by surprise, freezing them momentarily, even Alfred Dorrington, who had reacted so swiftly the last time violence broke out. Sophia rushed past him and barreled into Becky, knocking her back a step, away from Dorrington. He reached for Sophia and shouted, "Stop it! Stop that, you crazy woman!"

He wasn't watching Cliff Reynolds, and that was a mistake. The young man leaped forward, and this time the punch he threw at Dorrington landed squarely on the older man's jaw and knocked him back. Dorrington sprawled on the kitchen floor as Cliff crowded in, obviously intent on doing more damage.

# Chapter 11

Before Reynolds could reach Dorrington, Sam and the other three men from the domino game charged through the same opening that Sophia had made. Patrick Flanagan wrapped his arms around Reynolds and pulled him away, saying, "Hold it, son! Settle down!"

At the same time, Sam got hold of Sophia's shoulders and held her back from Becky Thackery. "You don't want to do that, Miz Dorrington," he told her as he tried to wrestle her away from the young woman.

"She deserves it! She deserves whatever she gets!"

The disturbance had everybody talking loudly and asking questions. Commotion and hubbub filled the big kitchen.

Flanagan suddenly went, "Ooof!" Phyllis, who was trying to take in everything at once, glanced that way and saw the stocky retired cop stumbling backward, holding his stomach where Cliff Reynolds had just rammed an elbow into it.

But by grabbing Reynolds like he had, Flanagan had delayed the young man's attack long enough for Dorrington to climb back to his feet. Dorrington's graying hair wasn't so sleek and neat anymore, and a bruise was starting to form on his jaw already. He staggered and had to put a hand on the island to keep from falling down again as Reynolds broke free from Flanagan.

Ansel Hovey tried to get between them. "Stop it, you young fool—" Hovey got out before Reynolds punched him in the stomach. He turned green and bent over, but he was still in Reynolds' way. The young man had to shove him aside.

That gave Flanagan time to recover. He grabbed Reynolds from behind and pushed him forward. They careened into the island.

Sam looked distinctly uncomfortable as he wrapped his long arms around Sophia Dorrington from behind and lifted her completely off the floor. Her legs kicked wildly as he swung her around, away from Becky. She screamed, "Let me go!" and added some choice blue language.

"Gangway, ladies!" Sam said as he started toward the door, intent on carrying Sophia out of the kitchen.

Flanagan bent Cliff Reynolds forward over the island. Bowls and pans clattered as the two men struggled and knocked them here and there. Flanagan got hold of the young man's right arm and bent it up behind his back in a hammer-lock.

"I don't want to hurt you, young fella, but you'd better settle down and do it quick, lad!"

Cliff's dark hair had fallen down in front of his face. He panted, "All…all right. Just…let go of me." He groaned. "You're breaking my arm!"

"I will if I have to."

"Let him go," Dorrington told Flanagan. He swiped his own disarrayed hair back. "I can handle him now. He took me by surprise, that's all."

"Are you sure about that, mister?"

"I'm sure," Dorrington said.

"All right." Flanagan released Cliff Reynolds and stepped back. He looked ready to spring into action again if he needed to, though.

Sam had reached the door with Sophia and wrestled her through it into the center's main room. Phyllis was torn between following them and staying here in the kitchen to keep an eye on Cliff Reynolds. It was obvious that despite what everyone involved had said, *nothing* had been settled when it came to the jealous suspicions flying around Alfred Dorrington and Becky Thackery.

She decided to follow Sam. As she reached the door and went into the main room, she saw him let go of Sophia and give her a little push that propelled her farther away from the kitchen. She caught her balance and turned, her eyes snapping with fury.

She wasn't the only one who was mad, though. Darla Kirby hurried out of the kitchen and came toward Sophia, shaking a finger as she approached.

"How dare you come in here and act like that?" she demanded. "You could have hurt someone!"

Sophia regarded her coldly and said, "That was my intention. But only Alfred and his little tramp would have been hurt." She sniffed. "I would have scratched up that girl so she wouldn't be so pretty anymore! And Alfred... Well, let's just say he deserves a good swift kick in the most appropriate place."

"Not in my senior center, he doesn't," Darla said. "I'm going to call the police."

Sophia pushed back her dark blond hair and sneered. "Do

whatever you want. I don't care."

"You deserve to be arrested," Darla went on. "So does that young man. I can't believe he knocked Mr. Dorrington down like that!"

"Good thing Patrick was here," Sam said. "I don't know if any of the rest of us could've handled that fella, as mad as he was."

Darla pointed at Sophia and said, "Don't you move. I'm calling the police."

Alfred Dorrington came out of the kitchen and said, "I really wish you wouldn't, my dear Mrs. Kirby."

Darla frowned in surprise. "You don't want those two arrested, after what they did?"

"They allowed their emotions to run away with them, that's all," Dorrington said. "Haven't we all been guilty of that at certain times in our lives?"

"Maybe," Darla muttered, "but I never tried to slug anybody like that boy did to you."

Dorrington smiled faintly, lifted a hand to his chin, and made a show of working his jaw back and forth.

"No real harm done," he said. "I'll have a bruise—"

"You already have one," Eve told him. She had come over to join them. "But it makes you look dashing."

That turned Dorrington's smile into a grin, then a grimace from the resulting twinge of pain. "Please, dear," he said to Eve, "don't make me laugh right now."

Becky Thackery came out of the kitchen. She held tightly to Cliff Reynolds' arm as he walked beside her.

"I'm not going to apologize," he said. "You can just forget that!"

"I haven't asked for an apology," Dorrington responded coolly. "Anyway, if you owe such a thing to anyone, it's Miss

Thackery. She's the one you've wronged." He shrugged. "A little physical altercation is nothing."

"It would have been something, all right," Reynolds snapped, "if that old guy hadn't grabbed me."

Most of the others had streamed out of the kitchen, following the two young people. Phyllis saw Carolyn, Sheila Trent, and Ingrid Gustafson.

Sheila said, "We tried to straighten everything up in there, Mr. Dorrington. Things got a little scattered around."

"Thank you, dear lady," he told her.

"Where's Patrick?" Sam asked, looking around with a frown.

"Here he comes with Ansel," Phyllis said.

Flanagan emerged from the kitchen with Ansel Hovey. He had hold of Hovey's arm as the other man leaned on him for support.

"That punch to the breadbasket has Ansel feeling a bit poorly," Flanagan explained. "I think he should sit down."

"Of course," Phyllis said. "Bring him over here." They went to the domino table, where Phyllis had a chair pulled out and ready as Flanagan helped Hovey sit down in it.

"What about the police?" Darla asked. "Are you sure you don't want me to call them? What about you, Ansel? He attacked you, too."

Still looking a little green, Ansel shook his head. "Naw, I'm all right," he said. "I don't want the boy to get in trouble."

"You're more inclined to mercy than I am, my friend," Flanagan said. "I like to see people get what's coming to them."

Darla turned to Dorrington. "And you don't want to press charges?"

"No, I don't. I just want the lad to get it through his head that he's wrong about Miss Thackery."

Becky said, "Thank you, Mr. Dorrington. I...I don't want Cliff to get in trouble, either."

Darla pointed to Sophia, who still wore a sneer. "What about her?"

Becky shook her head. "Can't we just let it all go?"

Darla drew in a deep breath, then let it out in a sigh. "All right. I suppose we can do that." She glared at Sophia, then turned the same expression on Cliff Reynolds. "I don't like what you did here today, though, either of you. In fact, if either of you ever set foot in here again after you leave, I'll consider it trespassing, and I *will* call the cops."

"Why in the world would I ever come back to a dingy place full of smelly old people?" Sophia asked.

Dorrington said, "My dear, you should remember that you're older than some of these people."

She just glowered down her nose at him.

"And I'm not coming back, either," Cliff Reynolds said. "I'm through with this. Through with everything."

Becky put her hand on his arm and said, "Oh, Cliff—"

He jerked away from her. "That includes you, too. We're finished, Becky. I could never trust you again."

"But Cliff, nothing happened!"

"Sure," he said, but it was obvious from his tone of voice that he didn't mean it. He picked up a chair, carried it over to a corner, and thumped it down. As he sat in it and crossed his arms, he said, "I'll just sit right here, out of the way. You just go ahead and do whatever you want. It's none of my business anymore."

Becky looked like she wanted to cry or argue with him, or both, but she drew in a deep, shaky breath and said, "I guess we'd better start packing up."

"Nonsense," Dorrington said. "We'd just gotten started on the trifle."

"You mean you're going to continue the lesson?" Darla asked.

"No one has ever been able to say that Alfred Dorrington backed out on a commitment, and they never will." With his charming smile back on his face, despite the bruise, he gestured toward the kitchen and went on, "Please, ladies, allow me to continue. Before the afternoon is over, you'll be sampling a delicious delicacy the likes of which you've never tasted before!"

# Chapter 12

It took a while for everyone to put the ruckus behind them and concentrate on the class again. Sophia Dorrington, who placed a chair next to Cliff Reynolds and sat down beside him, was a constant reminder of the altercation as she sat talking quietly with the young man. Phyllis had no idea what they were hatching, but she figured it couldn't be anything good. She was surprised that Sophia hadn't just left.

Eventually, however, those in the class turned their attention back to what Alfred Dorrington was saying as he demonstrated how to make the Tex-Brit dessert known as a Texas Margarita trifle made with strawberries and blueberries. The students spread out around the kitchen and began making their own trifles.

Once the layers were put together and the trifle needed to set, Dorrington looked around the room and said, "Ladies, I want to express my gratitude to each and every one of you. I love teaching, passing along all the little tricks and tips and techniques I've accumulated during my many years in the kitchen, so that I help you all become better cooks. It's been a real honor and a pleasure to conduct this class with you."

"Are you serious?" Carolyn asked with her customary bluntness—or maybe even with a little more bluntness than usual, Phyllis thought. "After everything that's happened, you still say it's been a pleasure?"

"Of course," Dorrington answered without hesitation. "Those momentary distractions are just that...distractions...and nothing more. True joy is in creation, and there's nothing more joyful than creating something delicious to eat. A feast for our bodies...*and* our senses. Such things are what lifts us above the animals, who consume food only for sustenance. Why, enjoying a good trifle is one of the most sensuous, passionate experiences anyone can ever have!"

He flung out a hand in a dramatic gesture to emphasize his words.

"That's what I've always said," Eve put in from the other side of the window. The comment drew a ripple of laughter and smiles even from Sheila Trent and Ingrid Gustafson. Eve might act like a shameless stereotype at times, but she did it with such enthusiasm you couldn't help but like her.

"At any rate," Dorrington went on, "I've enjoyed the class, and I hope that all of you have gotten something worthwhile out of it." He turned to smile at Becky and went on, "I also want to thank my assistant Ms. Thackery, who is going to be a very talented chef in her own right."

Becky blushed and said, "Thank you, Mr. Dorrington. I only hope I can live up to your example."

"You'll not only live up to it, I suspect you'll surpass it, my...my friend."

Phyllis could tell that he'd started to say "my dear" but had stopped himself and changed the term he had been about to use.

"No cook could ever ask for a better helper in the kitchen," Dorrington went on. "Now…" He clasped his hands together in front of him. "I think those trifles should be about ready for us to give them a try!"

Dorrington set the trifle he and Becky had made on the island and using a large serving spoon scooped down to the bottom of the serving dish to get a decent serving, making sure to include all of the layers and a strawberry from the top. He put it on a plate and slid it toward Becky.

"Here you are," he said. "I think you should have the honor of trying it first, since you contributed just as much to its making as I did."

"Oh, that's not necessary," she protested.

"I insist!" He handed her a plastic spoon. "It's not fine cutlery, but go ahead."

She smiled, still hesitating, but then said, "Oh, all right," and used the spoon to scoop a bite with a strawberry filled with Margarita gelatin, pudding, whipped cream, and a bit of cake. She lifted it to her lips.

Phyllis glanced around, aware that everyone in the kitchen was waiting for Becky to take the first bite. There was something almost symbolic about it. The window was crowded with others watching and waiting, as well, including the four men from the domino table, who must have taken another break from their game.

Phyllis didn't see Sophia Dorrington or Cliff Reynolds, though. They were still sitting in a corner of the main room, if they hadn't gone outside.

Becky looked embarrassed to be the center of such attention, but she must have known that the fascination wouldn't break until she had taken a bite. She drew in a deep breath, then opened her mouth and put in the spoonful of trifle. She seemed to savor the taste for a few seconds and then swallowed.

"Delicious," she pronounced, prompting a little wave of approving applause from the students. "It tastes really—"

She stopped short. A small frown creased her forehead. An intent look came over her entire face.

Dorrington asked, "Is something wrong, darling?" In his concern, he had allowed the endearment to slip out this time.

"No, it's just..." Becky's eyes were getting bigger. "I can't seem to get my...There's no air..."

The plate and the spoon slipped out of her fingers. The trifle *splatted* onto the island's countertop. Becky sagged forward, caught hold of the island's edge for a second, then her eyes rolled up in their sockets and she fell. Dorrington tried to grab her before she went down but missed.

"Becky!" he cried.

The sheer anguish in his voice must have been heard all through the center. As the students in the kitchen shrank back and the people looking through the big window leaned forward, Cliff Reynolds burst into the room and shouted, "Becky! Becky, what's wrong?"

Sophia Dorrington wasn't far behind him, saying, "Alfred? Are you all right?"

Reynolds skidded to a stop at the sight of Becky's crumpled form next to the island. He stared at her, his eyes so big they seemed about to fly right out of his head. After a second, his gaze switched to Dorrington, and he yelled, "You! What did you do to her?"

Becky's sudden collapse appeared to have shaken Dorrington even more than Reynolds' earlier attack. For the first time since Phyllis had met him, he looked old. Old and scared.

"I…I didn't do anything," he said. "She just fell down—"

"I can see that!" Reynolds rushed forward and fell to his knees beside her. He grabbed her shoulders and tried to lift her as he said, "Becky! Becky, wake up!"

Her head fell back limply on her shoulders as he lifted her. Her eyes were still open, but Phyllis could tell they weren't seeing anything.

"Here now!" Patrick Flanagan said urgently from the window between the rooms. "Stop that! Let go of her, lad. You might just do more damage."

Sam had left the window. He hurried into the kitchen now and raised his arms, spreading them and motioning for the students to move back.

"Patrick's right," he said in his loud, powerful teacher's voice. "Let 'em get some air. Y'all step back and give 'em some room."

He turned and glanced at Phyllis, and as their eyes met, they shared the same grim realization.

Giving Becky Thackery some room wasn't going to do any good. Both of them had seen enough bodies to know that she was gone.

Cliff Reynolds must have realized the same thing. He didn't let go of her. Rather, he pulled her up higher, wrapped his arms around her and cradled her limp form against his, and began to sob.

Sophia Dorrington looked shaken but not particularly mournful as she asked her husband, "What happened?"

"I…I don't know," Dorrington replied. "She just suddenly seemed like something was bothering her, and then she collapsed…" He stretched out a hand toward the trifle Becky had dropped on the island's countertop. "Right after she took a bite of that—"

"Don't touch it, Mr. Dorrington," Phyllis said, her voice as sharp as if she were reprimanding a misbehaving student back in her teaching days. "There may be something wrong with it, and you don't want to risk touching it."

"Wrong with it?" Dorrington repeated. "That's impossible! I made it myself. I know everything that went into it."

"Even so, it would be best if you didn't touch it, or the part you put on your own plate." Phyllis raised her voice. "Everyone else, set your own trifles aside. Don't taste them or even touch them."

The students in the kitchen hastily complied, setting their plates on the long counter that ran along the room's rear wall.

Carolyn looked at Phyllis and said, "I know what you're thinking. The same thought occurred to me as soon as that poor girl collapsed."

Cliff Reynolds, his face wet with tears and contorted by grief, looked up and demanded, "Why isn't somebody calling an ambulance? Somebody call 9-1-1, blast it!"

"I reckon he's right," Sam said as he slipped his phone from his shirt pocket. But he gave a little shake of his head as he said it, and Phyllis knew what he meant. The authorities had to be notified, but it wasn't going to do any good now.

Becky Thackery was beyond anybody's help. Struck down with no warning, in the prime of her life, it was too late for her.

But there were other matters to be resolved, and Phyllis's brain was already churning with them.

Patrick Flanagan lifted his arms to call for attention and said to the people in the kitchen, "All of you should go back out into the main room. Nobody leave the center, though." He looked at his domino-playing friends. "Ansel, Carl, go stand by the door and don't let anybody in or out except emergency personnel."

"What are you talking about?" Sophia Dorrington demanded. "You have no right to stop me or anyone else from doing whatever we want."

"Maybe not technically, ma'am, but I assure you, you're going to want to do what I've just suggested. Otherwise, it's liable to look pretty bad once the police get here."

"The police?"

"Yes, ma'am." Flanagan looked around and put into words what Phyllis had been thinking for several minutes. "This senior center is a crime scene. That poor girl was murdered."

# Chapter 13

"Murdered!" Alfred Dorrington said. "That's insane."

Phyllis said, "I'm afraid she showed signs of being poisoned, Mr. Dorrington. Even if she wasn't, the police will want to investigate to rule out the possibility. That always has to be considered when an apparently healthy person dies suddenly—"

"Stop it!" Cliff Reynolds cried from his sitting position on the floor, where he still held Becky. "Stop talking about her like she's dead! She's not dead! She can't be! I...I love her..."

His voice trailed off into another choked sob.

Sam moved over to him and rested a hand on his shoulder. "Come on, son," he said gently. "I called 9-1-1. The EMTs and police will be here any minute. We really ought to go back out into the other room—"

"No! I won't leave her!"

"You'll have to, eventually. Here, let me help you..."

Sam bent closer to ease Becky out of Reynolds' grip. For a second, Phyllis thought the young man was going to explode at him in rage and grief and shock, but then Reynolds, with Sam's help, lowered Becky carefully to the floor.

"Can't we at least...put something under her head?" he asked in a choked voice. "Maybe...maybe cover her face, anyway?"

Phyllis picked up a towel from the rear counter and folded it to make a small pad. She handed it to Sam and said, "Here, put this under her head." She opened a drawer under the counter and took out a folded dish towel. "And you can cover her with this."

Sam lifted Becky's head and slipped the folded towel underneath it, then unfolded the dish towel and draped it carefully over her face. Then he straightened to his feet and held out a hand to Reynolds.

"Come on, son."

Reynolds hesitated, then clasped Sam's hand. Sam helped him to his feet and slipped an arm around the young man's shoulders to steer him toward the door.

"We'll go in the other room and sit down," Sam said. Reynolds looked back over his shoulder once as Sam led him out of the kitchen, but he didn't try to return to Becky.

Patrick Flanagan said, "All the rest of you should go in the other room, too." He crossed his arms over his chest. "I can keep an eye on the crime scene."

Sophia began, "What gives you the right to—"

"I'm a retired police officer, ma'am. I'm familiar with the procedures."

Alfred Dorrington said, "Yes, yes, very well." He sounded very weary and distracted. He put a hand on Sophia's arm and continued, "Come along, dear."

She pulled away from him and responded icily, "Just because some tragedy happened, that doesn't mean I've for-given you, Alfred. I'm afraid that may not be possible any-more."

"I still insist that you're wrong, my dear. I never—" He stopped and shook his head. "We can have that discussion later. For now, let's just deal with this unfortunate incident."

Phyllis thought it was a lot more than an unfortunate inci-dent, but she didn't want to read too much into Dorrington's rather callous turn of phrase. Everyone reacted differently in times of stress.

She and Carolyn were the last ones out of the kitchen. "I had a bad feeling about this," Carolyn murmured as they left the room. "I just knew something bad was going to happen."

"I was hoping it wouldn't," Phyllis said honestly.

But she would be lying if she tried to claim that she hadn't worried about the same thing."

Ansel Hovey and Carl Benford were standing guard at the center's front door as Patrick Flanagan had suggested. The two older men stood there conversing quietly and watching through the glass door for the arrival of the emergency per-sonnel.

Sam sat Cliff Reynolds down at one of the tables and pulled out the chair beside him. They didn't say anything as they sat there. Reynolds just stared forward with an empty gaze. No one approached him.

Dorrington and Sophia sat at opposite ends of a rectangu-lar table, not speaking to each other. Sophia still wore a cold, angry expression, while Dorrington just looked stunned.

Phyllis, Carolyn, and Eve sat together at another table. Eve asked quietly, "Do you have any idea what happened, Phyllis?"

"None at all, other than the fact that it appeared that poor girl might have been poisoned." Phyllis smiled faintly but without a trace of genuine amusement in the expression. "I haven't solved the case, if that what's you're asking."

"Well, of course you haven't," Eve said. "The murder just happened."

"If it actually *was* murder," Carolyn put in. "I mean, I think we're all pretty convinced that it was, but we don't *know* that yet."

"We certainly don't," Phyllis agreed. "I suppose it's possible some sort of natural affliction might have killed Miss Thackery."

Eve said, "People sometimes have things wrong with them and don't have any idea about it until they suddenly drop dead. Remember when that professional tennis player died on TV?"

"And that fellow who only ate healthy food from the wild," Carolyn said.

Phyllis nodded, recalling both instances of sudden, unexpected death. She said, "We can't rule it out...but that's not what it looked like to me."

Carolyn and Eve both agreed with her.

Darla Kirby came over to the table and sank down in an empty chair with a sigh. She frowned at Phyllis.

"I'm not blaming you, Mrs. Newsom," she began.

"And you shouldn't," Carolyn interrupted. "You know good and well that whatever this was, it wasn't Phyllis's fault."

"Still, you can't argue with the fact that these things seem to follow you around," Darla went on. "With all that anger and those emotional outbursts going on, I looked at you and thought to myself, you know, this is just the sort of situation where somebody's going to wind up dead. And then, sure enough…"

"Believe me, I don't like that tendency any more than you do," Phyllis told her. "I just wanted to learn how to make some nice British dishes."

At the front door, Ansel Hovey exclaimed, "Here they come!"

Phyllis heard a siren's growl taper off and end. A few moments later, Hovey held the door open as a couple of emergency medical technicians hurried in carrying bags of equipment and apparatus.

Patrick Flanagan beckoned to them from the kitchen door and said, "Back here, lads. I'll show you."

No sooner had they gone into the kitchen than two uniformed officers from the Weatherford Police Department came in the front door, too. Phyllis didn't know either of them, and she hadn't recognized the EMTs, either. She had met quite a few law enforcement officers through her son Mike, but the department was much too big for her to know everyone in it.

After all the murder investigations she had been mixed up in, though, she knew Chief Ralph Whitmire. She suspected she might be seeing him before this day was over.

One of the officers told the other to keep an eye on the door while he went into the kitchen. Ansel Hovey said, "Carl and me have been watchin' the door. Nobody's gone in or out."

"What about back doors?" the cop asked. "Are there other exits here?"

"Well, sure," Hovey said. He frowned. "Nobody said anything about guardin' them."

"But we've been watching all the folks, too," Carl Benford

said. "Nobody's left. Leastways, I don't think so."

The officer grunted. "We'll figure that out later. Right now I just need to find out exactly what we're dealing with here."

He walked across the room and disappeared through the kitchen door.

Less than a minute later, he reappeared. One of the EMTs was with him. The officer talked into the microphone clipped onto his shoulder, then said, "We're going to start getting names and addresses from everyone, folks. Just cooperate, and we'll be done here and let you go home as soon as we can."

The tone of finality in his voice made it clear that no one would be going home any time soon, though.

The officer went out to his vehicle and came back with a tablet that he used to enter names and addresses as he started around the room, gathering information. Patrick Flanagan drifted over to the table where Phyllis, Carolyn, and Eve were sitting and stood there beside it, shaking his head.

"Not like the old days when we wrote everything down in a notebook," he commented. "Of course, not much *is* like the old days anymore, is it?"

"That's fortunate in some ways," Carolyn said, "but in many it's not."

"Aye, that's the truth." He smiled at Carolyn. "I'm sorry you're having to go through this inconvenience."

Eve said, "Oh, that's all right. We're used to it."

"Indeed," Flanagan said, nodding. "I've read about the way murder seems to follow you ladies around. You're regular murder magnets, aren't you?"

Before any of them could respond to that comment, the center's front door opened again and a tall, attractive woman in her thirties entered. Her long dark hair was pulled into a ponytail that hung down her back. She wore jeans and a dark blue, short-sleeved top. A holstered sidearm and a badge were clipped to her belt.

Flanagan's eyebrows rose as he looked at her and murmured, "And who might this be?"

"Detective Isabel Largo," Phyllis said. "If she's here, it means there's a strong possibility the first officers on the scene think this might be murder."

"I see. Well, I don't think there's any doubt most of us were leaning that way right from the start, weren't we? That poor lass certainly acted like she was poisoned."

Isabel Largo had started across the room toward the kitchen when she stopped short and looked at Phyllis. After a couple of heartbeats, she changed course and came over to the table.

"Mrs. Newsom," she said. "Nobody told me you were going to be here."

"I was here when it happened," Phyllis said. She nodded toward Carolyn and Eve. "We all were. We were taking a cooking class—"

Largo held up a hand to stop her. "I'll talk to you later," she said. "Don't go anywhere."

"I wasn't planning to," Phyllis assured her.

Flanagan watched her go and said, "Did I detect a hint of professional jealousy there?"

"Detective Largo is a fine officer," Phyllis said. "I've never had any trouble from her or Chief Whitmire."

"Other than when they've arrested all three of us for murder, at one time or another," Carolyn pointed out.

Flanagan grinned and said, "You *have* had an adventurous retirement, haven't you, Mrs. Newsom?"

"Tell me about it," Phyllis said.

# Chapter 14

The hushed atmosphere in the center's main room continued as the minutes dragged past. There were low murmurs of conversation around the tables where people sat, but nobody wanted to speak up very loudly.

Sam and Cliff Reynolds didn't say anything at all. The young man just stared straight ahead as if his thoughts were a million miles away.

Dorrington and Sophia were equally silent. They had nothing to say to each other or anybody else.

Darla Kirby had stood up and wandered off to drift around the room, speaking in low tones to some of the older regulars at the center who looked frightened and upset. Phyllis knew she was trying to calm their nerves and assure them that whatever had happened, it had nothing to do with them and was an inconvenience, that's all.

Carolyn said, "You must have worked some murder cases when you were a police officer, Mr. Flanagan."

"Patrick," he reminded her.

"Patrick," Carolyn agreed with a nod.

"Aye," he said in answer to her question, "I've seen more death than I like to think about. Of course, you have to remember that most homicides are very simple. A spouse kills a spouse in a drunken rage over something. Criminals fall out over money. Someone who's been wronged takes their revenge. After a while, you get to where you can just look at the facts of a case and then point a finger at whoever you think is the killer, and nine times out of ten you'd be right."

Eve said, "That never seems to be the sort of thing that *we* run into. It's always more complicated than that."

"A rush to judgment is what you're talking about," Carolyn said. "Jumping to conclusions. It's thinking like that by the police that landed all of us behind bars at one time or another." She blew out a disgusted breath. "I mean, honestly, can you imagine any of us committing murder, no matter what the circumstantial evidence might have looked like?"

"Indeed I can't," Flanagan replied, shaking his head. "But then, I'm acquainted with all three of you ladies. If I was still a cop...like your Detective Largo, for example...I'd have to follow where the evidence led me."

"She's hardly *our* Detective Largo. I think she resents Phyllis because of all the cases she's solved when the police didn't."

Phyllis said, "I think she's just happy those killers were caught, no matter who figured out the cases."

"Yes, well, you're more inclined to give people the benefit of the doubt than I am."

Before the discussion could continue, the officer on guard at the front door opened it, and several men and women wearing coveralls and latex gloves came in and headed for the kitchen, where Largo stood in the doorway and beckoned to them. Each of the newcomers carried an equipment case.

As they disappeared into the kitchen, Flanagan said, "That would be the crime scene techs, I take it?"

"That's right," Phyllis told him. "I recognized several of them."

Isabel Largo came back out of the kitchen and walked over to the table where Sam sat with Cliff Reynolds. She said, "Mr. Reynolds?"

He ignored her and didn't look up, just continued staring. She said his name again, sharper this time, and he finally raised his grief-dulled gaze to her.

"What do you want?"

"I need to talk with you for a few minutes."

What Largo meant was that she was going to question him, Phyllis thought.

The detective went on, "I'd like to use the center director's office. Is that all right with you, Mrs. Kirby?"

"Of course," Darla replied. "I'm sorry, it may be a little messy in there…"

"Don't worry about that," Largo told her with a thin, perfunctory smile.

Reynolds started to stand up, but then he stopped abruptly and sank back down in his chair. Crossing his arms over his chest, he frowned and said, "I've changed my mind. I'm not talking to you. Not without a lawyer."

"And why would you decide that?" Largo asked, not missing a beat and implying at the same time that Reynolds' refusal to be questioned was suspicious somehow.

"I'm too upset," he muttered. "I…I don't need to be talking to anybody right now. Not without a lawyer."

Largo looked at him intently for a moment and then shrugged. "You're within your rights to do that." She turned and walked over to the table where Dorrington and Sophia sat. "You're Alfred Dorrington?"

"That's right," he said. No *my dear* or *darling* this time, Phyllis noted. Clearly, he was too shaken by what had happened to fall back on his old habits.

"Are you willing to talk to me, Mr. Dorrington?"

Slowly, he shook his head. "I'll give you my attorney's name and phone number, if you insist."

"Not just yet." Largo sounded calm and collected, but Phyllis could tell that she was getting frustrated. To Sophia, she said, "Mrs. Dorrington?"

"No comment," Sophia snapped.

"I'm not a newspaper reporter, Mrs. Dorrington. Are you refusing to answer my questions?"

Sophia sniffed, stared straight ahead, and didn't say anything.

"You know I'm going to find out what happened, whether you talk to me or not, don't you?"

Neither Dorrington nor Sophia even looked at her.

Largo let out a humorless little laugh. She swung around, and her gaze landed on Phyllis.

"Mrs. Newsom—"

"You can't arrest her," Carolyn blurted out. "It wasn't her trifle that killed that poor girl. None of us had anything to do with it this time. We just happened to be here."

"Of course you were," Largo said as she came over to the table where Phyllis and the others sat. "I'd appreciate it if you could give me an idea of what happened, though, Mrs. Newsom. I know how observant you are."

"You should," Carolyn said under her breath. Largo appeared to ignore the comment, but Phyllis was pretty sure she heard it.

Phyllis got to her feet and said, "Yes, I'll talk to you, but I can't tell you anything that two dozen other people can't tell you, too."

"Maybe not, but right now, I want to talk to you. If you don't mind coming with me...?"

Phyllis went with her to Darla Kirby's office. Largo closed the door behind them and gestured toward the chair in front of Darla's paper-littered desk.

As she sat down in the swivel chair behind the desk, the detective said, "Mrs. Wilbarger is right. From what I've gathered so far from talking to the first officers on the scene, none of you are even remotely suspects. You barely knew the victim, isn't that right?"

"We never saw her except during the cooking classes this week. A few hours on Monday, Wednesday, and today."

"Did you ever talk to her, one on one?"

"A little," Phyllis said. "Not much at all, and nothing that amounted to anything."

"But was that enough for you to believe that someone might have had a reason to kill her?"

Phyllis regarded the younger woman for a few seconds, then said, "You already referred to Miss Thackery as the victim, and now you're asking me if I think anyone had a motive to kill her. That makes it pretty clear you believe her death was murder."

"I believe any time an apparently healthy 23-year-old drops dead with no warning, the case has to be considered a possible homicide." Largo sighed. "I don't want to play games with you, Mrs. Newsom. That poor girl was poisoned, and we both know it. The autopsy will confirm it. It's just a matter of time. Now, is it possible the poisoning was an accident?" She shrugged and went on, "Accidents happen, of course. But that has to be proven, one way or the other. Why don't you just tell me what you saw in the kitchen?"

Phyllis couldn't think of any reason to refuse the request. As she had mentioned already, there were at least two dozen witnesses. Some of them might differ in the details—eyewitnesses never told exactly the same story—but the general outline of what had happened in the kitchen was obvious.

For the next few minutes, Phyllis sketched in the scene for Largo as best she remembered. The detective stopped her a few times to ask questions about everyone involved and the relationships between them.

"So this trouble between the Dorringtons, Ms. Thackery, and her boyfriend has been building up all week?" Largo asked. "And no telling for how long before that?"

"All I can tell you is what I saw and heard," Phyllis said. "Anything that happened before this week, you'll have to get them to tell you...if you can get them to talk."

Largo grunted. "Yeah, it looks pretty suspicious when everybody starts to lawyer up as soon as the police come in the door. But I guess that's what the world's like now. Movies and TV have taught people not to trust us."

"Well, as you said, they're within their rights."

Largo made a face but nodded.

"Is there anything else?" Phyllis asked.

"No, you gave me a pretty clear picture of what happened, and I trust your account. But I'm going to question some more of the witnesses anyway, just to verify what you've told me."

"Of course." Phyllis paused, then said, "I suppose what you're really doing is waiting for the crime scene techs to finish their initial examination of the scene."

"I'm not at liberty to discuss that with you."

"No, I didn't think you would be."

Phyllis stood up and left the room. Largo followed her out and said to Darla, "Mrs. Kirby, would you mind joining me in your office?"

Darla looked a little surprised by the request, but she said, "Oh. Okay, sure."

Once the office door was closed again, Carolyn asked, "Is she going to interrogate everyone who's here?"

"Probably not," Phyllis said. "I think that more than anything else, she's waiting on the crime scene unit to finish up in there."

Eve said, "It looks suspicious, doesn't it, that both Dorringtons and the Reynolds boy refused to answer questions?"

"You're not suggesting that they're all guilty, are you?" Carolyn asked. "That they worked together to kill that poor girl?"

"I don't think those three would be capable of cooperating on *anything*, let alone murder," Eve said.

"You'd be surprised," Flanagan said. "With a powerful enough motive, anything's possible."

Sam stood up from the table where he'd been sitting with Cliff Reynolds and came over to join them.

"I don't think that young fella's gonna go crazy or try to run away," he said as he sat down. "He seems to have gotten control of himself again after that shock. Anyway, there are cops around to take over if anything happens."

"Do you think he actually lost control of himself?" Carolyn asked. "Or was he just acting? Trying to make us think he was surprised by what happened, so as to cover up his own involvement?"

"Did he say anything to you to make you think he might have had something to do with that poor girl's death?" Eve added.

Sam shook his head. "He didn't say much of anything to me, period. I heard him say the girl's name under his breath a few times, and he muttered something to himself now and then, but I wasn't gonna ask him to repeat any of it. I didn't want to get him all stirred up again."

More time dragged by. Detective Largo questioned half a dozen more witnesses, but Phyllis still believed she was just marking time. There was no real question about *what* had happened...only *how* and *why*.

And who was responsible.

After a while, Sam checked the time on his phone and said with a frown, "Dang it, I hope Detective Largo's not plannin' on keepin' us here all evening. Ronnie's graduation is only a few hours away."

"Oh, my goodness," Carolyn exclaimed. "I had forgotten all about graduation."

Phyllis hadn't. She had thought about it a number of times, and if something didn't happen soon, she planned to appeal to Isabel Largo. The detective had no reason not to let them go home. She had contact information for all of them, and she'd admitted that they weren't suspects.

Before things could get that far, one of the crime scene techs emerged from the kitchen and went to the door of Darla Kirby's office. He knocked and went in.

Everyone in the room saw that. Carolyn leaned forward and said, "They found something."

"Or he's just making a preliminary report," Phyllis said with a note of caution in her voice.

She hoped, though, that the investigation had turned up some evidence that would bring this case to a speedy conclusion and allow them to attend Ronnie's graduation without any more trouble or delay.

Silence fell on the room again as Detective Largo came out of the office. All eyes were on her as she walked directly to the table where Alfred and Sophia Dorrington sat.

"Mr. Dorrington," she said, "if you still want to have your attorney present while you're being questioned, you had better go ahead and call him."

"Is that right, Detective?" Dorrington asked in a voice tight with strain.

"Yes, sir. Because you're coming with me."

# Chapter 15

Dorrington glared up at her and demanded, "What are you talking about?"

"I just told you. You're coming with me."

"You're arresting me?" Dorrington sounded astonished that such a thing could happen.

"I'm asking that you come with me to the police station for questioning."

Sophia Dorrington said, "You're insane."

"I'm not talking to you, ma'am," Largo said, making a visible effort to keep her temper under control. "Will you come with me voluntarily, Mr. Dorrington?"

Coldly, he said, "My attorney's office is in Dallas. I told you, I won't answer any questions without him present."

"And we'll wait for him. But we'll do it at headquarters."

"Then it sounds very much to me as if I am under arrest."

"You're being detained for questioning." Largo nodded to one of the uniformed officers who had followed her to the table, then said to Dorrington, "Will you please stand up and put your hands behind your back, sir?"

For a second, he looked like he was going to continue arguing, but then sighed and said, "If I agree to come with you, can we dispense with the restraints and the perp walk?"

Phyllis thought was going to refuse and tell him it was too late for that, but then she said, "I don't see why not."

"Very well." He put his hands on his knees and pushed himself to his feet. With the air of utter weariness that surrounded him, he looked every bit of his age now.

"You'll regret this," Sophia blustered. She might be angry at her husband; she might even hate him. But she didn't like seeing him being taken into custody.

With everyone in the room watching raptly, even Cliff Reynolds, two officers escorted Alfred Dorrington out of the senior center.

Once they were gone, Detective Largo turned to the others gathered in the senior center and said, "The rest of you are free to go, as long as you've given your contact information to one of the officers. For the time being, though, please don't leave the area without notifying me."

"Is the center closed?" Darla asked.

"For now, Mrs. Kirby. Until we make a determination of what happened here, we have to consider it a crime scene. But we'll allow it to reopen as soon as we can." Largo looked around. "I'm sorry for any inconvenience this causes."

She turned and left the building. Sam blew out a breath and said, "Well, thank goodness we've still got plenty of time to make it to graduation."

"Yes, there's that to be thankful for," Phyllis said as she got to her feet.

Carolyn said, "Earlier, I'd been thinking that we might have those trifles and the sticky toffee puddings we made for a snack when we get back tonight, but I suppose they're all evidence now."

"We'll make some more over the weekend," Phyllis said.

Patrick Flanagan said to Sam, "See you back here for more dominoes when all this is over and we're allowed to come back?"

"Sure."

"And I hope you'll be coming back, as well, even though there won't be any cooking classes," Flanagan said to Carolyn.

"We're here fairly often," she told him. "There are usually some sort of interesting activities going on. There'll be other classes."

"Then I can look forward to seeing you again?"

"Yes. Uh…yes." Carolyn looked a little uncomfortable.

Flanagan smiled and headed for the door, where people were filing out of the center. Eve watched him go and said to Carolyn, "You need to work on your banter, dear."

"Oh, leave me alone," Carolyn snapped. "And you're all wrong. Patrick Flanagan is just a polite gentleman and has no interest in me."

"Maybe," Eve said. "Maybe not."

Carolyn just rolled her eyes and shook her head.

They all started to drift toward the door. Phyllis noticed that Sophia Dorrington and Cliff Reynolds were still sitting at different tables, each of them alone. There was something stark about the two of them. Both looked lost and adrift, as if whatever moored them had been taken away. Phyllis told her friends to go on, then went over to the table where Reynolds sat.

"I'm sorry for your loss, Mr. Reynolds," she said. She didn't think anybody else had expressed any sympathy to him since Becky's death.

"I...I just can't believe it," he said without looking up at her. "I mean, yeah, sure, I was mad at her, but I never...I never wanted...never expected..."

"Of course you didn't," Phyllis said. "Everyone could tell how shocked you were."

Reynolds' forehead creased in a frown under the mop of hair that fell over it. "I wish I'd gotten my hands on his throat," he muttered. "I'd have killed him."

"You mean Mr. Dorrington?"

"It's all his fault. He's the one who...who got Becky mixed up with him in the first place. I saw what he was trying to do right away, how he played up to her and tried to charm her, the old goat. I tried to warn her. I even found out that he'd been involved with other young women who worked for him..." Reynolds' voice trailed off as he shook his head. "None of it did any good. She didn't care what he'd done in the past, and she didn't believe me when I told her he was after her. She just wanted to learn from him, she said." A bitter laugh came from the young man. "She learned from him, all right. And now look where it's gotten her."

There was no response Phyllis could make to that. But she thought that Reynolds sounded quite vindictive. Enough so to kill? He had been around all afternoon, without anyone paying much attention to him. He could have slipped something into the dishes they were making, either into the ingredients everyone used or into the trifle that Dorrington and Becky worked on specifically. He could have meant to poison them both, only Dorrington had ruined that plan by having Becky take the first bite...

Phyllis put those thoughts out of her head. Detective Largo must have had some reason to believe Alfred Dorrington was guilty, or else she wouldn't have taken him in for questioning.

It was entirely possible that by now, Dorrington had broken down and confessed. Phyllis didn't need to be spending her time constructing other possible theories.

But like a lot of other things, such speculation had become a habit.

Right now, she had other things to worry about, so she said quietly, "I'm sorry for your loss, Mr. Reynolds," and moved over to the table where Sophia Dorrington sat.

Before Phyllis could say anything, Sophia frowned up at her and asked, "Who are you? What do you want?"

"My name is Phyllis Newsom, Mrs. Dorrington. I just want to say that I'm sorry for all the trouble you've been through."

Sophia waved an exquisitely manicured hand. "This trouble is entirely my husband's fault, so there's no need for you to apologize, Mrs. Newsom. If Alfred wasn't such a randy old fool, none of this would have happened." She sighed. "He manages to convince himself that those young girls like him for himself, not because of his money or because they're angling for a better job. Male vanity leads to more ridiculous behavior than anything else in the world."

"Even so, I'm sure you must be upset about him being arrested."

"It's nothing," Sophia scoffed. "It won't take the authorities long to realize that Alfred Dorrington is utterly harmless and has been for a very long time."

Phyllis recalled how easily Dorrington had handled Cliff Reynolds the first time the young man attacked him. Having seen that, she wouldn't say that Dorrington was harmless. But she supposed that Sophia knew him better than anyone else.

"He has a good lawyer?"

"Of course." Sophia paused. "Although I suppose Alfred's

barrister is more accustomed to handling business matters, rather than mounting a criminal defense."

"If he needs to talk to anyone else, I know a good defense attorney here in town, Jimmy D'Angelo."

Sophia arched an elegantly curved eyebrow and said, "Really, dear, you're shilling for an ambulance chaser?"

Phyllis stiffened. "Just trying to help."

"Thank you," Sophia said in a chilly voice, "but there's no need."

She would take the woman at her word on that, Phyllis decided. She turned to leave and didn't look back as she walked out of the senior center."

"I don't like being in big crowds like this," Carolyn said quietly as they filed into the arena on the west side of Fort Worth a few hours later. "I never did."

"I don't care for it, either," Phyllis said. "But it's worth it to see Ronnie and all the other kids graduating. I don't know any of them very well except her, but Sam and I taught some of them when we were subbing at the high school a couple of years ago." She smiled. "Anyway, it's always good to see young people moving on with their lives."

"Of course it is. I just wish there was some way to do it in a less crowded venue."

Sam said, "There are too many people in the world, that's for sure. Crowds everywhere you go these days. But I don't reckon complainin' about it does any good." He shook his head. "Anyway, there are two people I thought might be here who aren't."

Phyllis knew he was talking about Vanessa and Phil, Ronnie's parents. They had talked about flying down from Pennsylvania for the graduation ceremony, but a couple of days earlier, on an Internet call with Ronnie, they had told her they couldn't make it. She'd passed it off as nothing, but Phyllis had a feeling it actually did bother her.

And clearly, Sam was disappointed, as well. But it was out of their control, and all they could do was enjoy seeing Ronnie walk the stage with her classmates, get her diploma, and move on to the rest of her life.

A few years ago, Becky Thackery would have been doing the same thing, Phyllis suddenly thought. The rest of *her* life had been cut short, whether by accident or design. If someone had murdered her, Phyllis hoped justice would catch up to the killer, even though she hadn't known Becky well. Murder was an outrage against the natural order.

Unfortunately, Fate had a way of laughing at the natural order...

She forced those dark thoughts away and turned her attention back to the crowd of people making their way into the arena. At this time of year, the sun was still well up in the sky at this hour, and the air was quite warm and filled with talk and laughter from the crowd. Plenty of bad things still went on in the world, of course, but right now, this evening, in this place, a feeling of lightheartedness and anticipation ruled, and Phyllis gave herself over to it.

The next two hours were given over to pomp and circumstance, as befitting the name of the march played by the high school band. Speeches were made by the district superintendent, the high school principal, the senior class president, the valedictorian, and the salutatorian. The band played more songs. One by one, hundreds of students walked across the stage to receive handshakes and their diplomas, with teachers from the school taking turns calling out their names. They walked through a gauntlet of teachers, shaking more hands. Finally, they moved the tassel on their caps from one side to the other, signifying that the ceremony was over and they were high school graduates at last. Caps flew high in the air, tossed from eager hands.

In other words, it was just like dozens of other high school graduations Phyllis had attended. In many ways, it was like her own graduation, almost six decades earlier. For one night, several thousand people had come together to commemorate a significant achievement.

And then it was tumultuous, joyous confusion, as friends and families sought out the graduates they had come here to celebrate.

It took a while for Phyllis, Sam, Carolyn, and Eve to find Ronnie in the vast, packed lobby. The noise in the place was almost deafening. But they spotted her waving her hand at them and worked their way through the crowd to her. They each hugged her, and then Sam stood with his arm proudly around her shoulders.

"I'll bet when I first came down here, you never thought you'd see this day," Ronnie raised her voice to say.

"Aw, shoot, I never doubted it," Sam told her. "I was a little surprised to see you, I won't deny that, but I sure am glad we got to spend the past couple o' years together."

"So am I," she said.

"We're all glad you stayed with us," Phyllis said.

"You've really brightened things up around the house," Eve added.

"And kept us on our toes," Carolyn said.

Tears sparkled in Ronnie's eyes. "I'm going to miss all of

you so much—" she began.

Then someone else called, "Ronnie! Ronnie!" over the hub-bub, and Phyllis turned to see a blond woman coming toward them through the crowd, followed by a tall, fair-haired man. She had seen enough pictures of them to recognize Vanessa and Phil Ericson, Sam's daughter and son-in-law.

"Mom!" Ronnie cried happily. "Dad! You made it after all!"

"Of course we did, dear," Vanessa said as Ronnie rushed into her arms. Phil folded his arms around both of them. "We were here to see you graduate."

"Took some doing at work," Phil rumbled, "but we decided we weren't going to miss this."

"I'm so glad," Ronnie said, almost sobbing now.

Sam stood there, a faint smile on his face. Phyllis moved next to him, linked her arm with his, and asked quietly, "Did you know they were coming?"

"Nope. Last I'd heard, they weren't. But I'm glad they were able to, after all. Look how happy that kid is."

"And that's what really matters to you, isn't it?"

"Well...she's my granddaughter. I want her to be happy. And her folks bein' here tonight... I reckon that's the last piece that was needed in puttin' her family back together again. She'll be able to go right on from here and live a good life."

"But you won't see her nearly as much," Phyllis pointed out.

Sam's shoulders rose and fell. "That's the way of the world. Kids grow up, and so do grandkids. It happens to all of us."

Phyllis nodded, thinking of her son Mike, his wife Sarah, and their son, her grandson, Bobby. Bobby was still a good number of years away from *his* high school graduation, but that day would get here, she mused. She hoped that she would still be around to see it when it did.

"That's the way it's designed to work," Sam went on, "and it's a good thing when it does, even though that means some of us get left alone."

"Not alone," Phyllis said, tightening the loop of her arm around his. "Never alone."

# Chapter 16

The morning after a much-anticipated event always left Phyllis feeling a little hollow. Not let down, actually; she had enjoyed going back to the house with everyone after the graduation. Everyone except Ronnie, that is. She had gone to attend the all-night party held at the high school.

Vanessa had worried about that, but Sam had assured her that Ronnie wasn't going to get into any trouble. The wild streak Ronnie had displayed a few years earlier hadn't been tamed, exactly, but rather she had grown out of it naturally when she hadn't had her parents around to push against.

They had stayed up late talking, and Phyllis enjoyed getting to know Vanessa and Phil better, too. If things had worked out differently, those trifles would have made good snacks for the after-graduation gathering, as Carolyn had suggested. But since that wasn't possible, they had made do with cookies — there were almost always homemade cookies at Phyllis's house — and ice cream.

Vanessa and Phil had a room at one of the local motels, so

they hadn't spent the night, but they planned to stay for a couple of days to visit more with Ronnie before returning home. While they were talking the night before, Sam had asked bluntly, "Are you takin' her back with you?"

"She wants to stay here with you for a while longer, Dad, at least for the first part of the summer," Vanessa had replied. "And we don't want to take that away from her."

"We can't tell you how much we appreciate everything you've done for her, Sam," Phil had added. Looking around the room at Phyllis, Carolyn, and Eve, he went on, "All of you. You've made a tremendous difference in her life, and we'll always be grateful to you."

"Ronnie has made quite a difference in our lives, too," Phyllis said. "Having her here has been wonderful."

Carolyn and Eve had echoed that sentiment. Smiling, Sam had said, "I reckon we're all about to get a little misty-eyed here, so we might ought to change the subject. Tell me about how that business of yours is doin', Phil."

So it had been a good evening all around, and now, in the early morning hours of the next day, Phyllis sat alone in the kitchen, nursing a cup of coffee while she waited for the lemon blueberry scones she had put into the oven to bake a short time earlier.

She heard the front door open and knew that only one person was likely to be coming in at this hour. She smiled a greeting as Ronnie walked into the kitchen and sank into one of the chairs at the table.

"Ohhhh," she groaned as she leaned forward and rested her head on her arms. "I think I'll sleep for a week."

"What are you talking about?" Phyllis asked. "You're young. You should be able to stay up all night without it making you tired."

"Yeah, maybe, but try telling that to my eyes. They won't stay open!"

"Would you like some coffee?"

Ronnie lifted her head and shook it from side to side. "I don't want anything that might keep me awake." She sniffed the air, then added, "But is that blueberry muffins I smell?"

"No, it's a blueberry lemon scone. The recipe is from the class we took. They should be ready soon. Do you think you can stay awake long enough to eat one?"

Ronnie laughed and said, "Maybe two. But if I doze off before they come out of the oven, be sure and wake me up." She leaned both elbows on the table and rested her chin in her cupped hands. "Any news on the murder?"

"How do you know about that?" Phyllis asked with a surprised frown. With all the excitement of getting ready for graduation, and then the ceremony itself, they hadn't said anything about it the day before.

"Some of the kids were talking about it last night. They had grandparents at the senior center when it happened." Ronnie shrugged. "I told them you were there, too, so you'd figure out who killed that girl."

Phyllis shook her head and said, "I'm afraid I don't really know much about it. Yes, I was there, but I don't have any idea what the police investigation has uncovered so far. And they certainly don't share the evidence with me."

"Well, they should. You've solved more murders than they have."

"I'm not sure that's fair. They have a lot of things to deal with."

"Well, so do you." Ronnie laughed. "You've had a crazy teenager in your house the past two years!"

"And I've enjoyed every minute of it, too."

"Yeah, so have I," Ronnie said. "Maybe not *every* minute …but pretty close." She grew solemn. "I'm going to miss all of you so bad. And Buck, too. He's the sweetest dog I've ever been around. Maybe…maybe I should rethink going to college back home. I mean, there's a college right here in Weatherford—"

"And if that's what you really wanted to do, that would be fine," Phyllis said. "But you've been over and over this in your head, haven't you? You want what's best for you, and for your parents. It's not my place to tell you what to do—"

"Sure it is. You're family, too."

"Well, I'm touched that you feel that way, but what I'm saying is that you shouldn't let the nostalgia of the moment overwhelm your common sense and the plans you've worked out. Of course you're feeling a little melancholy right now. You've reached a turning point in your life, and there are so many options ahead of you. It can be scary, and what you're used to may seem like the best and most appealing. But you never really know until you try new things."

"You don't do that," Ronnie said.

"What, try new things?" Phyllis had to laugh. "You think I've spent my whole life solving murders? I promise you, everything that's happened these past few years has been *extremely* new for me."

"Including getting together with my grandfather?"

The soft chime of the oven timer saved Phyllis from having to answer that question. She stood up and said, "That, young lady, is none of your business. Now, let's get those scones out of the oven and iced so you can have one or two of them before you get some sleep."

"Sounds good to me," Ronnie said.

Ronnie stayed awake long enough to eat a couple of the scones, but then she did as she said she was going to and went to bed. It was a quiet Saturday morning around the house, and Phyllis didn't wake the girl for lunch. She figured Ronnie needed the sleep more.

She and Carolyn had just finished cleaning up after the meal when the doorbell rang. Phyllis hurried from the kitchen up the hall, but Sam got to the door first and opened it. A stocky, dark-haired man in a suit stood there.

"Hello, Jimmy," Sam greeted him. "What brings you here?"

"The same thing that usually does," Jimmy D'Angelo replied. "Murder."

Phyllis came up beside Sam and said, "Come in, Jimmy. Can I get you some coffee or tea? And we have cookies."

D'Angelo shook his head and looked regretful. "I better not, no matter how tempting it is. The ol' blood pressure hasn't been as good as it could be lately."

Phyllis led them into the living room. Carolyn came up the hall from the kitchen and joined them. Eve was upstairs. As they all sat down, Phyllis asked, "Does this have something to do with Alfred Dorrington?"

"I'm not surprised you'd guess that," D'Angelo replied.

"I gave your name to his wife. And since you're here, I'm assuming that Mr. Dorrington decided he needed different representation, rather than his business attorney." Phyllis paused. "Has he been charged with murder?"

D'Angelo nodded. "Yeah, early this morning. He insists he's innocent." The lawyer shrugged. "Of course, most of my clients say the same thing. Sometimes they're telling the truth, and sometimes they're not."

Sam said, "What do you think about Dorrington?"

D'Angelo appeared to consider the question for a moment, then said, "I believe him. He seems pretty shook up to me. Not scared, really. He comes across as a cool customer. But I think he's genuinely upset about the girl's death and wants to know who poisoned her."

"There's no doubt she was poisoned?" Phyllis asked.

"No doubt. The autopsy confirmed it was a quick-acting toxin that paralyzes the nerves and shuts down the respiratory system. She couldn't breathe, but she didn't die of suffocation because it stopped her heart, too." D'Angelo shook his head. "Nasty stuff." He drew in a deep breath. "And the cops found a little vial of it in that tote bag Dorrington uses to haul around the stuff for his cooking classes."

"Wait a minute," Phyllis said sharply. "*That's* the evidence they used as a basis for arresting him and charging him with murder?"

"As far as I know, that's all they've got. Detective Largo isn't always as forthcoming as she might be."

"But Cliff Reynolds carried that tote bag in and out of the senior center," Phyllis said. "He could have planted the vial of poison in it. For that matter, all three of them had access to it."

Carolyn said, "That poor girl didn't kill herself. I didn't know her well enough to say whether or not she'd do such a thing, but I did see her face when that…that horrible poison took hold. She was completely shocked by what was happening to her."

Phyllis nodded. "I agree. Were Dorrington's fingerprints on the vial?"

D'Angelo spread his hands and shook his head. "I don't know yet. This is Saturday, so I can't file a motion to get copies of all the police and autopsy reports until Monday morning."

"So Dorrington *has* hired you?"

"Yeah. He called me about the middle of the morning. The guy he had representing him doesn't want anything to do with a murder case. He's a desk jockey, not a litigator."

Sam said, "Dorrington must've talked with his wife, since she's the one Phyllis gave your name to, Jimmy."

"Yeah, I met the lady. She was waiting for me at the station, in fact." D'Angelo gave a little shiver. "Talk about an iceberg! I got the impression she hates her husband, but she doesn't want him convicted of murder and sent to prison. That'd hurt her social standing."

Carolyn blew out a breath and said, "Yes, that sums her up very well, I'd say."

"So I'm on the case," D'Angelo said. He pointed at Phyllis and Sam, who had sat down together on the sofa. "And that means so are you two."

"We're gettin' a mite old for legwork," Sam said.

"Nah, that's crazy. I got other investigators I could use, but nobody better for a case like this than the two of you."

Several times in the past, D'Angelo had hired them as investigators, which Phyllis had gone along with because that status gave them some official standing to look into cases she wanted to investigate anyway. Sam liked it because he claimed it made them private eyes. And the arrangement had turned out well most of the time, Phyllis had to admit.

But in the back of her mind, she had figured the situation probably wouldn't come up again. This business of murder seeming to follow her around had to come to an end *sometime*.

"Do you really think we can help?" she asked.

"I know you can! People talk to you, Phyllis. They tell you things they might not say to anybody else." D'Angelo grinned. "I think it's because you remind everybody of their favorite grandma. And besides, you were right there when it happened. You saw what was going on. You know the people involved—"

"Not well," she broke in.

"Better than me," the lawyer insisted. "You know the best defense I can mount for Dorrington is to find out who really killed the girl, and nobody's more likely to do that than you two. So how about it? Can I count on your help?"

Phyllis looked at Sam and asked, "What do you think?"

"He never did strike me as the sort of fella who'd kill a young woman like that," Sam said. "And shoot, not only was the Reynolds boy there, but Mrs. Dorrington was, too. If you ask me, she's the most cold-blooded one of the whole bunch."

Carolyn said, "I feel the same way about her. *She's* the one I'd say was mostly likely to be a murderer." She stopped and frowned. "Of course, that means she probably isn't, doesn't it? Or does it actually work like that in real life?"

"There's only one way to find out," D'Angelo said.

Phyllis knew he was right. She nodded and said, "I suppose we can look into it. I liked Miss Thackery. Whatever she'd done, she didn't deserve what happened to her."

"Yeah," D'Angelo said, "with most of us, we're lucky if we *don't* get what's comin' to us!"

# Chapter 17

Nothing would happen in the case until Monday morning, when Alfred Dorrington would be arraigned and Jimmy D'Angelo would request bail for him.

That left Phyllis with the rest of the weekend before the investigation would begin in earnest. Vanessa and Phil took Ronnie out for dinner on Saturday evening, but Phyllis planned to have everyone there for a backyard cookout on Sunday afternoon. She and Carolyn made what preparations they could beforehand including making a cucumber and tomato salad, and a Texas Margarita trifle since none of them were able to taste the ones they made at the senior center. They then got busy getting the quick chuckwagon beans heating and making the vegetable tray with hamburger and hotdog makings and prepared the corn on the cob to have them ready to grill as soon as they returned from church.

It was a beautiful day, sunny and quite warm as days in late May usually were in Texas, but the old, towering post oak trees in the back yard provided plenty of shade and kept the temperature comfortable. There was a picnic table with benches that had been there for thirty years, and Sam brought out other chairs so people would have places to sit. It was a friendly gathering, complete with plenty of talk and laughter.

"I'm glad Dad found such a good place to live and such fine friends," Vanessa said to Phyllis as they sat together on the back porch and watched Sam and Phil grilling hamburgers. "With Mom gone, I was afraid that after he retired he'd just be at loose ends and wouldn't know what to do with himself."

"I think he would have been all right. He's a very strong man." Phyllis smiled. "But I'm glad he's been here with us, too. Of course, it was a bit of an adjustment at first, having a man living here. It was just us girls for quite a while."

Vanessa returned the smile and said, "He's so strait-laced, I'm a little surprised he agreed to it. I would have thought he'd consider living in a house with a bunch of women to be improper, somehow."

"No, he seems to be a man who's very comfortable with himself, wherever he is. That allowed him to fit in pretty quickly. He even won over Carolyn...and that's not easy!"

Vanessa hesitated a moment, then said, "I know he's very fond of you."

"And I'm fond of him. After my husband passed, I thought I'd never care about another man again, but Sam makes it easy."

"I, uh, don't really want to ask..."

"Then don't," Phyllis advised gently. "But if you're thinking about what the future might hold, well, then, all I can say is that Sam Fletcher isn't a man who can be rushed. He does things at his own pace, when and if he thinks the time is right."

"Yeah, I know that!" Vanessa laughed. "So what you're

saying is, wait and see what happens."

"Exactly. And in the meantime, enjoy what life brings us."

Vanessa smiled at Ronnie, who was trying to take a rope toy away from Buck. The Dalmatian growled playfully and tugged back on it.

"Right now, life is bringing my daughter back to me, and I couldn't be happier about that."

"I couldn't be, either," Phyllis said honestly. "Although we'll miss Ronnie when she's gone home."

"I think this will always be her second home now."

"That's fine with me," Phyllis said. "She'll always be welcome."

The two women sat in companionable silence for a few moments, then Vanessa said, "I will admit, it was a little worrisome when I kept hearing about all those murders…"

"It worried us, too."

"And my dad running around helping to catch criminals… Well, it seemed pretty dangerous."

"Mostly it wasn't. There were only a few times when things might have gotten out of hand, and those were my fault for not managing things better. Sam's never really seemed bothered by anything that happened, but maybe he just doesn't show it. He can be unflappable."

"I know! When I was a girl, all hell could be breaking loose around him, and you'd never know it because he stayed so cool and calm. I used to think he must have been, I don't know, a professional spy or something, to be so unruffled all the time."

"A professional spy," Phyllis mused, smiling. She shook her head. "No, I can't see that. He's too open and honest. But I know what you mean. There are depths to him that he doesn't let anyone see."

Sam turned from the grill and called, "Chow's on! Come an' get it, 'fore I throw it to the hogs!"

"Then there's that part of him," Vanessa said with a laugh.

"Yes," Phyllis said. "There certainly is."

Jimmy D'Angelo called Monday morning and asked that they meet him at his office in one of the buildings on the courthouse square at ten o'clock. Phyllis and Sam got there a little before that. D'Angelo hadn't arrived yet, so his secretary showed them into his private office to wait.

When the lawyer came in, he had Alfred Dorrington with him. Obviously, a judge had set bail for him. Dorrington stopped short when he saw Phyllis and Sam and frowned at them.

"I don't understand," he said. "I thought we were going to be meeting with your investigators, Mr. D'Angelo."

"And so we are." D'Angelo waved a pudgy hand toward Phyllis and Sam. "These are the people who are going to be helping me with this case."

"But that's… I understand that Mrs. Newsom is the one who gave your name to my wife, but… How is such a thing even possible?"

"You only ask that because you don't know how many murder cases these two have solved." D'Angelo opened a door. "Come on, let's go in the conference room. We have a lot to talk about."

Dorrington still looked befuddled, but he followed the lawyer into the conference room, as did Phyllis and Sam. They all took seats around a sturdy, polished wooden table.

Dorrington was wearing the same clothes he'd been wearing Friday. His hair was combed, but he hadn't shaved. He was far from the elegant chef he had been when he came into the senior center...but a weekend in jail would do that to a person, Phyllis reflected.

D'Angelo's secretary brought in coffee for everyone, and when they were settled around the table, the lawyer said, "I'll start by going over what I've been able to get out of Detective Largo and the district attorney."

Dorrington held up a hand to stop him. "Before we do that, I want to say one thing to Mrs. Newsom and Mister...?"

"Fletcher," Sam supplied. "Sam Fletcher."

"I don't believe we were ever actually introduced, although I do recall seeing you at the senior center." Dorrington cleared his throat. "What I'd like to say to both of you is that if you're going to be assisting Mr. D'Angelo in defending me, I want to know if you believe I'm innocent."

"Is that important?" Phyllis asked.

"It is to me. No matter what the task, a person is less likely to put forth their best effort if they're doing whatever it is simply for the money."

D'Angelo laughed and said, "I promise you, I don't pay 'em enough for that!" He grew serious as he went on, "These two just like to dig out the truth, no matter what it may be."

"That's right," Phyllis said. "But for the record, I don't mind saying that I don't believe you're responsible for what happened to Becky Thackery."

"Neither do I," Sam added. "Although Phyllis was a lot closer to everything that went on. I trust her opinion, though, and I saw for myself how upset you seemed to be when that poor girl died."

"There's no 'seemed to be' about it," Dorrington said. "I

was shocked. Horrified. I still am. And I'm furious that a fine young woman was struck down when her life had barely had a chance to begin. Her killer *must* be brought to justice."

"We're all on the same page, then," D'Angelo said. He opened a file he had taken from his briefcase and brought into the conference room with him. He took a photograph from it and slid it in front of Dorrington. "Ever see that vial before?"

Dorrington studied the picture for a few seconds and then shook his head. "It looks just like any other vial of that size. I don't recognize it or see anything special about it." His hands clenched on the table. "Is that the vial that contained the poison?"

"Yeah. The cops found it in a little zippered pocket on the inside of your tote bag." D'Angelo took out a photograph of the open tote bag and showed it to them. An area on the photo had been circled with a marker. "Right there."

Dorrington shook his head. "I don't normally use that pocket for anything. There are several such pockets inside the bag, I believe."

"Were there any fingerprints on the vial?" Phyllis asked.

"No," D'Angelo said, "but Largo thinks Mr. Dorrington could have used gloves when he handled it. There was a box of plastic gloves in the bag, too."

"Of course there was," Dorrington said. "I'll often don a pair of gloves when I'm cooking, especially when I'm giving a class. In the restaurant business, we have to think of such things all the time when handling food."

"Yeah, the cops think about things like that all the time, too."

"Is that the only physical evidence they have?" Phyllis asked.

"That's all I know about right now."

Sam said, "Doesn't hardly seem like enough to get the D.A. to sign off on a murder charge."

"They're basing it on something else, to go along with the poison. They claim that Mr. Dorrington was having an affair with the victim." D'Angelo looked at Dorrington and added, "Sorry to be so blunt about it."

"That's quite all right. If you're going to be successful in your effort to clear my name, bluntness may well be required on a regular basis." Dorrington shook his head. "But it makes no sense. I've denied every way I know how that there was ever anything improper between myself and Miss Thackery...but even if there had been, why in the world would I want to kill her? I should think that two other people who were on hand had a stronger motive. I'm speaking, of course, of my wife and young Mr. Reynolds."

"Yeahhh," D'Angelo said, and something about the way he dragged out the word and made a face told Phyllis he was about to add something important. "But the autopsy did more than confirm the presence of the toxin that killed Miss Thackery." He looked around the table. "It also told the cops that she was pregnant."

# Chapter 18

Once again, Dorrington looked thunderstruck. Phyllis, on the other hand, had been halfway expecting such a revelation, so she wasn't shocked or even surprised.

"So they're going to claim that you got her pregnant, she confronted you with the news, and you killed her to keep her from telling anyone else," she said to Dorrington.

"But it's not *true!*" he blurted out.

"It's the way a police detective would think, though." Phyllis remembered something Patrick Flanagan had said. "The simplest solution to a case is usually the correct one. Statistics bear that out."

Dorrington leaned back in his chair and slowly shook his head. He looked more haggard than ever. After a moment he said, "Surely it's possible to do a DNA test on the…the child…and prove I'm not the father. It has to be the Reynolds lad."

"DNA tests aren't as conclusive as all the TV shows would have you believe," D'Angelo said. "But if you're *not* the father, there's a very good chance the test will indicate that. I'll have to get a court order for the test, but that shouldn't be hard, under the circumstances. It could take several days before we get the results back, though. *And* I'll get an order to have Cliff Reynolds' DNA tested, too."

"Well, there you go, then. It seems we're well on our way to disproving the case against me."

Phyllis said, "There's not *any* chance the test will show it's possible you're the father?"

Dorrington glared. "None at all. The very idea is ludicrous. Why, I'm old enough to be that poor girl's grandfather!"

"Wouldn't be the first time a gal's fallen for an older fella," Sam drawled. "Especially when that older fella is rich and influential and the girl works for him and is ambitious."

"I'm going to pretend I didn't hear you say that," Dorrington told him in a chilly voice.

D'Angelo said, "You can pretend anything you want, Mr. Dorrington, but it won't change the way the cops and the district attorney are going to approach this. What we have to do is give 'em a Plan B. An alternative. Reasonable doubt, if it ever gets as far as a jury."

Dorrington paled. "You don't think there's any chance it will, do you? You'll get the charges dismissed before it comes to that, surely."

"If we can find out who really killed her," D'Angelo said with a shrug. "But if we can't, we may have to take our chances with a jury. I'm confident you wouldn't be convicted on what they have now, but I'd rather not risk it at all."

"You and me both, my friend." Dorrington sighed and rested his head in his hands for a moment, adding in a muffled voice, "You and me both."

They sat there in grim silence for at least a minute, sipping their coffee and looking at the table. Phyllis finally said, "Tell us about Cliff Reynolds."

Dorrington lifted his head. He still looked despondent, but he asked, "What do you want to know?"

"Everything you know about him. How long Becky had known him, how they met, how serious they were about each other. Things like that." A thought struck Phyllis. "Did he work at your restaurant, too?"

"As a matter of fact, he did, and I believe that was how the two of them met."

"Was he a cook?"

"Hardly," Dorrington said. "He was a busboy. He worked occasionally as a server, when we were short-staffed, but he was never very good at that job. Too surly."

"Yeah, I can see that, and I wasn't even around him that much," Sam said. "Why was he working there?"

"I'm sure I don't know. Perhaps because he couldn't find anything better? You understand, I don't supervise the day to day details of running the place, and I don't hire or fire the staff except on rare occasions. I keep my hand in enough to know what's going on, but if you want details, you'll probably have to ask my general manager."

"We will," D'Angelo said. "I'm going to see if Reynolds himself will talk to me, too."

"Good luck with that. As I said, he's surly." Dorrington shook his head. "Honestly, I never really understood what Becky saw in him. As for how serious they were about each other, I don't know that, either. I don't recall ever hearing any talk between them about marriage, but that doesn't mean the subject was off the table, I suppose."

"Did they live together?" Phyllis asked.

"I don't believe so." Dorrington shrugged. "But how often

they spent the night at one or the other of their places, I really couldn't say."

There was a lot that Dorrington couldn't say, Phyllis thought, but she supposed that made sense. After all, Becky had worked for him and Cliff Reynolds had come along just to help Becky. If Dorrington was telling the truth about there not being anything illicit or improper in his relationship with Becky, there was no reason for him to know very many personal details about their lives.

"Let's move on to your wife," D'Angelo suggested.

Dorrington made a face, then sighed. "I suppose we must. She was present when that horrible incident occurred, and at least in her own fevered brain, she had reason to wish ill on poor Becky."

"But no actual reason to be mad at her, right?"

"Absolutely right," Dorrington declared.

Phyllis said, "From the way she talked, this wasn't the first time she'd accused you of being unfaithful."

"Unfortunately, it wasn't. Sophia possesses a jealous streak in her personality that's a mile wide, as you phrase it so colorfully here in Texas."

"But you never gave her any reason to be jealous?"

Dorrington frowned, cleared his throat, gazed down at the polished surface of the table, and looked distinctly uncomfortable. After several long seconds had gone by, he lifted his head and said, "I won't lie to you."

"Under the circumstances, that'd be wise," D'Angelo told him.

"In the past, I have given in to temptation on several occasions. There have been times when attractive women...*very* attractive women...have become enamored of me, and I'm only human, shall we say?"

"So you've got a history of steppin' out on your wife," Sam said.

"Calling it a history makes it sound like a regular occurrence. It was no such thing. More like occasional moments of weakness on my part." Dorrington leaned forward in his chair. "And this is the important thing. Nothing of the sort has happened in recent years. I promised Sophia that such behavior on my part was a thing of the past, and I've kept my word." A pained expression crossed his face. "She may not believe it, but I truly love her. I don't want to cause her any pain."

"But she still believes you're cheating on her," D'Angelo said.

Dorrington sighed. "As I've mentioned, once darling Sophia gets an idea lodged in her head, *dislodging* it becomes well nigh impossible. It might require the proper application of high explosives to blast it loose."

D'Angelo frowned and said, "I'd be careful about making comments like that, especially anywhere but in the privacy of your lawyer's office."

"Yeah, it kinda sounded like you were talkin' about blowin' her brains out," Sam added.

"Perish the thought! No, I just meant that in addition to being extremely jealous, she's also extremely stubborn." Dorrington shook his head. "A potentially dangerous combination."

"Would she know anything about poisons?" Phyllis asked.

The question seemed to take Dorrington by surprise. He frowned again and shook his head. "I don't know. I wouldn't *think* so. But Sophia has always been able to find a way to get whatever she wants, whether it's a designer dress from Paris, shoes from Milan, or perfume that's incredibly expensive. Just because I don't see how she would have gotten her hands on such a thing doesn't mean it's impossible. Not by any means."

"But there's nothing in her background to indicate that she would have special knowledge? She didn't go to medical school or anything like that?"

"Absolutely not."

"Do the two of you still live together?"

"We live under the same roof." Dorrington inclined his head. "That's not exactly the same thing, is it? Sophia and I tend to go our separate ways, unless there's some function where it looks better if we attend together, of course."

"Does she have any boyfriends?" D'Angelo asked.

Dorrington arched an eyebrow. "I see we're being blunt again. To answer your question, I suppose it's possible. Sophia and I spend enough time apart that I can't account for every minute of her day. You've seen her. She's a very attractive woman for her age, and certainly many men have been drawn to her over the years. But if you're asking for my instinctive reaction to the suggestion, I'd say that it's unlikely." He smiled faintly. "I'm no longer sure the man exists who actually meets her standards."

D'Angelo spread his hands and said, "I was just curious. Sometimes when one half of a couple acts really jealous and is always accusing the other partner of cheating, it's because they're, what do you call it, projecting their own behavior. Don't worry, we'll find out."

"To be honest, I'm not sure I want to know." Dorrington shrugged. "But, if it becomes necessary to tell me, then do so, of course. My primary concern is clearing my name—"

"And stayin' out of prison," Sam said.

"And staying out of prison," Dorrington agreed, "along with seeing poor Becky's killer brought to justice. But if at all possible, I'd also like to come out of this with at least a chance of salvaging my marriage."

"But what if it turns out that your wife is responsible for what happened to Miss Thackery?" Phyllis wanted to know.

"Well, in that case," Dorrington said as he looked around the table at them, "I'm sure that you'll all do your very best to burn the witch."

# Chapter 19

They interviewed Alfred Dorrington for a while longer, going back over some of the ground they had covered already, but without turning up anything different from what he'd told them the first time through.

Finally Jimmy D'Angelo rested his hands flat on the table and said, "All right, I guess that's all for now. The terms of your bail require you not to leave Dallas, Tarrant, or Parker County, Mr. Dorrington, so you'd be better off just staying home unless you have to come back over here for a court appearance."

"I'm allowed to go to my place of business, surely," Dorrington said.

"You are. I'm just saying you should be careful about where you go and what you do. I doubt that the district attorney's office is going to keep you under surveillance in the hope that you'll do something else incriminating, but we can't rule out the possibility entirely. So be discreet."

"As you wish, counselor. Right now, after everything that's

happened, I want nothing more than to go home, take a nice hot bath, and wash off the jail smell. Then perhaps a drink and some decent food."

D'Angelo lightly slapped the table top and said, "Sounds like a plan."

"You'll stay in touch and let me know how things are going?"

"You can count on it."

The three men got to their feet. Dorrington shook hands with all of them, including Phyllis, and said, "Thank you for taking up arms, figuratively, in my defense. It's nice to know that there are people fighting for me who believe in me."

He left the office, and when he was gone, Sam and D'Angelo sat down again. Sam clasped his hands on the table and asked, "Do we?"

"Do we what?" D'Angelo asked.

"Believe in him." Sam looked at Phyllis.

After a moment, she nodded. "I don't believe he poisoned Becky Thackery, anyway," she said. "As for whether he was telling the truth about the extent of his cheating, or that he'd been faithful to his wife in recent years...well, that I'm not so sure of."

"You reckon he's a hound dog?" Sam asked.

"I just get the feeling that he doesn't have quite as much self-control as he claimed to, let's put it that way."

D'Angelo said, "I've learned to trust your instincts, Phyllis. As long as he's not a killer, though, that's all we're concerned with."

"He seems genuinely shaken by what's happened, and I think he was sincerely fond of Becky and feels sorrow at her death. I hope I'm not wrong about him."

"We'll find out, one way or another," D'Angelo said. "For

now, I'll start the ball rolling on DNA tests and trying to find out what else the cops and the DA might have up their sleeves."

"What do you want us to do?"

The lawyer frowned in thought. "Dig into this Reynolds kid. Talk to him if you want. I'll send you his contact info. Unfortunately, he lives in Dallas, so it's a pretty good drive over there."

"That's all right," Sam said. "I don't mind drivin', as long as it's not at night. These old eyes o' mine don't handle night driving as well as they used to."

They left the law office. Sam had brought his pickup today, and it was parked on one of the rows of parking places surrounding the majestic old courthouse. As they walked toward it, he nodded toward a café in one of the business blocks surrounding the square and asked, "You want to get some lunch? It's a little early, but not much."

"I told Carolyn and Eve we might not be back until sometime this afternoon, so they'd have to fend for themselves today," Phyllis said. "So I think that would be fine."

They were just finishing up their meal—a salad with strawberries, pecans, and grilled chicken for Phyllis and a thick bacon cheeseburger for Sam—when Sam's phone rang. He slipped it out of his pocket and checked to see who was calling.

"Patrick Flanagan," he said. "Wonder what he's up to?" He thumbed the phone's screen to answer the call and said, "Hey, Patrick... Yeah, it is Monday, sure enough...I don't know... Hold on." He cupped his hand around the phone where the microphone and speaker were and looked at Phyllis. "Were we gonna try to talk to the Reynolds boy this afternoon? Patrick, Ansel, and Carl want to know if I'm playin' dominoes today or if they should hunt up somebody else at the center?"

Earlier during the meal, Phyllis had gotten a text on her phone from Jimmy D'Angelo, giving her the phone number and address of Cliff Reynolds. He actually lived in Irving, not Dallas, but the location was still at least an hour's drive from Weatherford, depending on the traffic.

"We'll go tomorrow," she told Sam. "I don't see any reason you can't enjoy some dominoes this afternoon."

He nodded and said into the phone, "We're just finishin' up lunch, Patrick. I'll be there in fifteen or twenty minutes. So long."

Sam paid the bill and they went back to his pickup. He opened the door for Phyllis, as he nearly always did, and as she was getting in, he asked, "You want me to drop you off at the house? I can go that way to get to the senior center just as easily as any other way."

"No, I'll come along," she said. "There aren't any classes of any sort this afternoon, as far as I know, but there's usually something interesting going on."

They headed out what both of them still referred to as "Old Highway 80" to the west side of town and parked in the senior center lot. Quite a few cars and pickups were in the lot, but no TV news vans, for which Phyllis was grateful. Becky Thackery's murder had gotten some press coverage over the weekend, but with the 24-hour news cycle and the "outrage *du jour*" attitude of the media, Becky's death was already largely forgotten except by those directly affected by it.

Patrick Flanagan, Ansel Hovey, and Carl Benford were waiting at the domino table. The dominoes lay face down in the middle of the table, and Flanagan had his big hands resting on them, idly shuffling them.

He grinned as he spotted Sam and Phyllis coming in and then waved. Hovey and Benford smiled, too. Sam turned to Phyllis and said, "Any time you get ready to go, you just let me know."

"Go ahead and have a good time," she told him. "We'll forget about murder for the afternoon."

It wasn't likely she actually would forget about what had happened to Becky Thackery, though. She wasn't sure she would ever get the image of the young woman's agonized face out of her mind.

She spotted Sheila Trent and Ingrid Gustafson sitting at one of the tables and talking to Darla Kirby, who stood next to the table. Phyllis headed in that direction. Darla glanced at her and seemed a little relieved to see her coming. Phyllis wondered if Sheila and Ingrid had been complaining to her about something.

"Let's see what Phyllis thinks of the idea," Darla said. "She's one of the regulars here."

"You might have more regulars if you'd listen to good advice once in a while," Ingrid said, confirming Phyllis's hunch that the two of them weren't happy about something.

"I'm always happy to listen to advice," Darla said. "After all, this is *your* center, yours and the others who come here, and I just want all of you to be pleased with the services we offer."

"What are we talking about?" Phyllis asked.

Sheila said, "We think Darla should get a yoga instructor to come in here a couple of times a week. It wouldn't hurt any of us to get in better shape, especially me. I've really let myself go."

Ingrid rolled her eyes. "Oh, sure, you have. If you're not careful, you might get all the way up to a hundred and ten pounds, instead of a hundred and five."

"For your information," Sheila said, "I weighed a hundred and eight this morning. So you're not far wrong."

"Well, I'm not telling you or anybody else what *I* weighed this morning. Anyway, what do you think, Phyllis? Don't you think having yoga classes is a good idea?"

"Actually, I do," Phyllis said. "Yoga is supposed to be a good workout for, ah, people of a certain age because it's gentle."

"There you go," Ingrid said to Darla.

"You know, I was never against the idea," Darla responded. "I just said I wanted to talk to some of the others and make sure there's enough interest before I look into it any further."

"Well, now you know." Sheila smiled at Phyllis, but it was really more of a smirk. "Of course, if you *do* start a yoga class and Phyllis signs up for it, someone's bound to drop dead in the first class, and then it'll turn out that whoever it is was murdered."

Ingrid snickered and said, "Yeah, that's exactly what would happen. So I might not sign up for it after all!"

"That might be wise," Sheila agreed.

Phyllis tried to tamp down the anger that threatened to well up inside her. They were just having a little good-natured fun at her expense, she told herself. It really wasn't anything to get mad about.

"Well, if you decide to go ahead with it, I'd be happy to take part," she told Darla. "I believe I'll go see how the domino game is going."

"Should someone warn Sam and those other fellows?"

Sheila asked.

"Sam doesn't have anything to worry about," Phyllis said. As she turned and walked across the room, she told herself that her voice had been a little sharper than she'd intended...but she couldn't bring herself to care about that, either.

The men had just finished a hand when she walked up to the table. Ansel Hovey began to shuffle. Sam raised an eyebrow and said, "I figured you'd be over there talkin' to the ladies longer than that."

"Let's just say I didn't care for the way the discussion was going."

"In that case," Patrick Flanagan said, "you may not like it over here, either. We've been pumping poor Sam about that girl's murder." He reached behind him, snagged a chair at one of the other tables, and pulled it over so it was at the corner of this table between him and Sam. "Why don't you sit down and tell us what you've figured out so far?"

# Chapter 20

"Who says I've figured out anything?" Phyllis asked. She adjusted the chair and sat down anyway, figuring the company would be better here than with Sheila and Ingrid.

"You're investigating the case, though, aren't you?" Flanagan said. "Sam said you're working with the lawyer for that Dorrington fellow?"

"Patrick interrogated me," Sam said with a shrug and a grin. "Old cop habit, I guess. And I, uh, didn't hold up well under questionin'."

Phyllis laughed, shook her head, and reached over to pat his left hand. "That's fine. There's nothing secret about what we're doing." She looked at Flanagan and went on, "Yes, we're working with Jimmy D'Angelo. He's representing Mr. Dorrington. We've worked with Jimmy on several cases in the past."

"Have you now? I've run into a number of private investigators who worked for lawyers, and I must say…no offense, mind you…you two are nothing like them!"

"Maybe that's why we get good results," Sam suggested. "Folks look at us and just see kindly ol' Grandma and Grampa, not somebody who's tryin' to pin a murder rap on 'em."

Flanagan smiled and said, "I can see how such a deceptive appearance could be helpful." He leaned forward. "So, have you found out anything yet?"

"We've barely gotten started," Phyllis said. "We met with Mr. D'Angelo and Mr. Dorrington this morning, after Mr. Dorrington was released on bail."

"I suppose he's still claiming innocence?"

"That's right. He insists he didn't have anything to do with Miss Thackery being poisoned."

"Well…that *is* what killers nearly always say, isn't it?" Flanagan asked. "It's rare you'll find one who comes out and admits his guilt, unless he's one of those madmen who does his killing in public and there's no way to deny it. Or else he's trying to make some sort of point, and so he claims responsibility proudly."

"Like terrorists do," Ansel Hovey said.

"Terrorists…and freedom fighters. Sometimes there's not much difference between the two."

Sam frowned and said, "I'm a little surprised to hear an ex-cop say something like that. I figured you'd be against all terrorists."

"Oh, I am, I am. I'm just talking about how some of them convince themselves they're on the side of the angels, no matter what they do, so they don't mind admitting it when they blow up a building or slaughter a bunch of innocent people. They believe it's a *good* thing they've done. A justified thing." Flanagan shook his head. "But we're getting kind of far afield from the subject of poor Miss Thackery's murder. Does Dorrington still deny that he was having an affair with the lass?"

Phyllis wasn't sure that was any of Flanagan's business, but he had been here at the senior center every time those emotional fireworks broke out, so he already knew the basics of the case. Also, given his background as an investigator, naturally he was curious.

"He denied it adamantly," Phyllis said.

Flanagan studied her for a second, then said, "But you don't believe him, do you? Not completely, anyway."

"Would you?"

Flanagan chuckled. "Probably not. But remember, I'm in the habit of believing the worst of just about everybody."

"What about me?" Benford asked. "What deep, dark secret do I have?"

Flanagan narrowed his eyes in thought for a moment, then said, "Carl, the worst thing I can come up with about you is that sometimes you think your dominoes are better than they really are. There's no way you should have bid thirty-two on that last hand you had!"

Hovey laughed and said, "He's right about that! We didn't have any trouble settin' you, did we, Sam? It doesn't take any detective work to figure that out, though."

"Perhaps not," Flanagan said, "but taking note of a tendency toward overconfidence *could* come in handy in solving a case sometime. We were talking about terrorists taking responsibility for their actions. Even more rare is the criminal who'll actually boast about what he's done because he's confident that he's so much smarter than everyone else and has covered his tracks so well. That gives him as much pleasure as the actual killing itself."

Phyllis shivered. "Someone like that would have to be an

absolute monster."

"Oh, indeed, without a doubt. Thankfully, I never encountered any in my career, but I heard about a few."

"You know," Sam mused, "maybe *you* ought to be workin' for Jimmy D'Angelo, too. You've actually got the experience necessary in solvin' crimes."

Flanagan held up both hands, palms out, and shook his head. "I'm retired, remember. I've put in my time catching lawbreakers." He chuckled. "No, a hard-fought game of Forty-Two is about as exciting as I want to get these days. I shouldn't have even been picking your brains about the case. Just instinct, I guess."

"You wouldn't mind if we came to you now and then to ask your advice, would you?" Phyllis asked. "We'd be picking *your* brain, I guess you could say."

"Any time, dear lady, any time." Flanagan reached for the dominoes in the center of the table. "Now, let's get this next hand underway, shall we, gentlemen?"

Ronnie was on the front porch steps with Buck when Phyllis and Sam got home later that afternoon. Sam sat down on the step beside his granddaughter and asked, "You all right, kid? You look a mite down in the mouth."

"Just missing my folks a little, I guess," Ronnie said. Vanessa and Phil had headed to the airport the previous day to fly back home. They had said their goodbyes here in Weatherford, although Sam had offered to drive them to the airport so Ronnie could go along. Vanessa had thought it would be better to have their farewell here, rather than in the middle of a crowded terminal.

"Well, that's understandable," Sam said now as he sat beside Ronnie. "You weren't expectin' 'em, and then suddenly they were here, and then after just a couple of days they're gone again."

"Don't get me wrong, I'm glad they were here to see me graduate, but in some ways, it just made things harder."

Sam scratched Buck's ears and nodded. "I know. Seems like things are just in a total uproar right now with everything changin' at once, and you probably just wish it'd all settle down for a while."

"Exactly!"

"Life hardly ever does that, though. You get one thing squared away, and then something else comes along that you've got to deal with. You think you're headed straight ahead on one trail, and then it takes a sharp turn without any warnin'. That's what life is, gettin' thrown for one loop after another."

"But doesn't that wear you out eventually?"

Phyllis sat down on the other side of Sam, on the next step up, so she could rest her hand easily on his shoulder. "It certainly does," she said. "But as the old saying goes, it beats the alternative."

"Anyway," Sam said, "if things started goin' too smooth and stayed that way for a while, chances are we'd get bored."

Phyllis laughed. "Yes, but I wouldn't mind giving it a try. Just for a little while."

That evening after supper, Phyllis indulged her curiosity and sat down at the computer in the living room to see what she could find out about Alfred Dorrington. The others were elsewhere in the house, doing other things, so she had the room to herself for the moment.

A search for Dorrington's name and the name of his restaurant in Dallas turned up plenty of hits. Actually, the establishment was located in Highland Park, technically a suburb and a separate city, even though it was bordered on three sides by Dallas and on the fourth side by University Park, where Southern Methodist University was located. The wealthiest city in Texas and one of the richest in the entire country, it was the perfect place for an ultra-elegant, ultra-expensive restaurant.

Evidently, the upper echelon of society thought so, too, because there were a number of newspaper and magazine articles about the restaurant, complete with photographs of the rich and famous dining there. Politicians, sports stars, entertainment personalities...all of them patronized Alfred Dorrington's restaurant.

However, there were surprisingly few pictures of Dorrington himself, and in the ones that had caught him, he looked almost as if he were trying to avoid the camera. Usually, a man as vain as Dorrington seemed to be didn't mind being photographed. Just the opposite was true, in fact. From the looks of things, though, he didn't seek the spotlight.

The same couldn't be said of his wife. There were many more photographs of Sophia Dorrington, usually at some sort of fancy ball or charity fund-raising dinner. Her husband was in a few of the photos with her, but mostly she was alone or with some of the other so-called beautiful people.

On a whim, Phyllis tried looking into Sophia's background. She came from an old, wealthy British family, but she and Dorrington actually had met and married in Boston, nearly thirty years ago. The marriage had gotten some press coverage because of Sophia's position, but Dorrington, apparently, hadn't been nearly as well-known at that time.

That made sense, Phyllis thought. He might have run a successful restaurant in London, but that wouldn't necessarily translate into any real notoriety in the United States. Evidently, he hadn't been in the U.S. for very long when he met Sophia, and it was really her wealth and prominence that had enabled his success.

She couldn't find any explanation for why they had moved to Dallas. Dorrington's fame as a restauranteur had grown fairly quickly once they were in Texas. Or rather, the restaurant's fame had grown. Dorrington wasn't really a celebrity chef, and again, Phyllis was struck by his avoidance of the limelight.

There was no doubt that he loved what he did, though. If he hadn't, he wouldn't be spending his time traveling around giving cooking classes in senior centers. Those classes had to be a labor of love for him.

She scrolled through page after page of results, searching for any stories about controversy or trouble involving him and his restaurant. She came up empty. As far as she could tell, Alfred Dorrington had lived a scandal-free life since coming to America, at least in public.

But what about before that? Everything she had found so far came from the time following his arrival in this country. He had lived more than half his life in England and had been famous in culinary circles there. Phyllis tried to recall the name of his restaurant in London so she could search for any stories about that part of his life, but she wasn't able to pull it out of her memory.

That was odd. Usually she was able to remember things

like that without any trouble.

A sudden worry nibbled at her mind. At her age, she didn't like it if she couldn't remember something when she felt as if she should. She had seen too many friends, relatives, and acquaintances struggle with their memory slipping away, bit by bit. Some of that was normal and nothing to worry about; everybody forgot things from time to time. But it could be a sign of something else, something Phyllis didn't even like to think about.

The sound of a footstep was a welcome distraction. She looked over her shoulder and saw Sam come into the living room, carrying one of his old Western paperbacks. He headed for the recliner, obviously intent on reading for a while, but Phyllis said, "Sam, would you mind coming over here for a minute?"

"Sure. Computer actin' up? You know more about those things than I do—"

"No, it's not that. Do you remember those stories Mr. Dorrington told in class about all the funny things that happened in his London restaurant?"

"You're askin' the wrong person," Sam said as he moved up behind her. "I was busy playin' dominoes. I heard some of what he was sayin', but I didn't really pay much attention to it."

"Maybe Carolyn knows," Phyllis said as she stood up from the chair in front of the computer.

"Maybe Carolyn knows what?"

The question came from Carolyn herself as she walked into the room carrying her needlework bag.

"I'm trying to remember the name of Mr. Dorrington's restaurant in London. You know, the one he talked about all the celebrities going to, as well as some members of the royal family."

"Who are also celebrities," Carolyn pointed out. "More so than they have any real reason to be, as far as I'm concerned, but that's not important, I suppose. You want the name of the place? Let me think…"

A frown creased her forehead. She looked surprised as she said, "You know, I don't think he ever mentioned it. He just referred to it as 'the restaurant' or 'my restaurant'. That's odd, isn't it?"

"It seems so," Phyllis agreed. She sat down again. "Let me see what I can find anyway."

"What are you looking for?" Carolyn asked as she settled herself comfortably on the sofa and took out the needlework she was working on.

"Just more background information on Mr. Dorrington." Phyllis clicked the keys, then peered intently at the screen that came up. She typed more, hit ENTER again. The results still didn't satisfy her. She typed again, then shook her head and sighed in apparent frustration.

"Somethin' wrong?" Sam asked.

Phyllis looked over her shoulder at him and said, "I don't know. As far as I can determine from searching the Internet, Alfred Dorrington didn't exist until he got off a plane in America thirty years ago."

# Chapter 21

"That's not possible," Carolyn said with a shake of her head. "He told us all those funny stories about the queen's cousin. And that one about the bishop and the actress."

"Yes, I remember those," Phyllis said. "So I searched for anything about those incidents using their names, and I couldn't find anything. It's like those things never happened."

Sam said, "Maybe he made up the stories. I mean, the guy strikes me as pretty slick. It's not surprisin' he'd have a line of snappy patter to keep folks entertained in those classes he gives." He shrugged. "And if he was just spinnin' yarns about England, it's not very likely anybody in Weatherford, Texas, would ever know the difference."

"Oh, I don't know if I'd go that far," Carolyn objected. "There are British aristocracy buffs everywhere."

"Yeah, but I'm bettin' Dorrington's quick-witted enough that if anybody called him on it, he'd just change the story a little and claim he'd misremembered it for a minute. Think about it. You could change the characters in most of those stories and they'd still work, wouldn't they?"

"Sam has a point," Phyllis said. "Let's accept that he's an entertainer as well as a chef. A showman." She gestured toward the monitor. "There should still be *something* about him that I could find."

"You'd think so," Sam agreed.

"So what does that mean?" Carolyn asked. "You think he's not who he says he is?"

Phyllis said, "It's starting to look like it. But I'm not sure that actually means anything."

Sam held up the book he was still holding. "In these old Western novels, a fella might ride away from wherever he'd been, put his past behind him, and start over with a new name somewhere else. And it wasn't considered polite to ask him where he'd come from or what he'd done. You just took him for what he was, right then and there. Could be Dorrington's the same way, especially if he came from humble beginnin's."

Carolyn leaned forward and said, "Remember how he said he started working in a fish and chips shop? What if he never advanced beyond that? I can see how he would make up colorful stories about being a rich and famous London restauranteur if he was teaching classes about British cooking."

Phyllis nodded slowly. "That makes perfect sense, all right. I'm not sure it has any bearing on the case—"

"Other than the fact that perhaps he owes all of his success in this country to his wife. If that's true, then he really would be foolish to chase other women and jeopardize his meal ticket."

"Fellas do plenty of foolish things where women are concerned, though," Sam pointed out. "They might even know they're foulin' up, but they can't help themselves."

"Are you speaking from experience?" Carolyn asked.

Sam grinned. "I'll take the fifth on that, thank you."

Phyllis switched off the monitor and said, "Well, at some point I may ask him about that, but for right now, we need to concentrate on the other suspects in this case."

"Which means talkin' to Cliff Reynolds," Sam said.

She nodded. "Are you up for a trip to Irving tomorrow?"

"I'll be ready when you are," Sam said."

For years, Irving had been known as the home of Texas Stadium, where the Dallas Cowboys played their football games. But the Cowboys had moved to Arlington, another of the many suburban cities located between Dallas and Fort Worth, and eventually Texas Stadium had been demolished. Irving itself continued to grow, like all the municipalities in north central Texas, as more and more people moved in from elsewhere in the country.

Because of that, the traffic on the freeway that bisected the city was usually terrible, and today was no exception. From the passenger seat of Sam's pickup, Phyllis looked at all the cars and trucks around them moving along at seventy, eighty, even ninety miles an hour, shook her head and said, "I'm glad it's you driving and not me. I don't think my nerves could stand it."

"It's not a lot of fun for me," Sam admitted. "I'm not sure there's anywhere you can go to get away from the crowds anymore, though."

Phyllis had Cliff Reynolds' address pulled up on her phone's GPS. She hadn't called to let him know they were coming, so he might not be home. But she had a feeling—and

Sam agreed—that taking him by surprise was probably the only way to get him to talk to them. If they had called ahead, he would have refused to see them or made sure they couldn't find him.

Sam followed the directions Phyllis gave him, exited the freeway, and turned north under an overpass onto a smaller road. The side streets were crowded with traffic, too, but at least here the cars weren't going like greased lightning. A couple more turns brought them to an apartment complex that looked like it had been built in the Seventies or Eighties and only haphazardly maintained since then.

"This place strikes me as bein' a little sketchy," Sam said as he pulled into the parking lot. "I don't see any drug dealers hangin' around, but it sure looks like the kind of place where they might operate."

"We'll keep our eyes open," Phyllis said. "And our phones ready to call 9-1-1."

They got out of the pickup and made sure it was locked before walking over to a set of stairs that led to the complex's second floor. All the apartments opened directly outside, like the rooms in a motel, which was what the complex resembled.

Both of them could still climb a flight of stairs without getting too winded, which Phyllis regarded as a blessing at their age. They reached the second-floor balcony and went along it looking for the right apartment number. It was at one of the corners of the U-shaped building. There was no bell, so Sam rapped his knuckles on the door.

After a minute with no response, Sam knocked again, a little harder and louder this time. He had lifted his hand to give it a third try when a muffled voice called from inside, "Yeah, yeah, I'm coming."

A chain rattled on the other side of the door, which opened

a few inches to reveal a bleary-eyed, unshaven Cliff Reynolds. He wore a T-shirt, boxer shorts, and a ragged old bathrobe. His hair, which seemed to be on the verge of dishevelment at its best, went every which way. He glared out at Phyllis and Sam and looked confused, as if he didn't recognize them and couldn't figure out why two elderly people would be standing there at his figurative doorstep.

Then he blinked several times as the light dawned, and he said, "I know you. You were at the senior center in Weatherford when...when Becky...ohhhh!"

He turned and lurched away from the door, leaving it open behind him. Phyllis heard his bare feet slapping rapidly across the floor, then a door slammed somewhere in the apartment.

Sam waved a hand in front of his face and said, "Judgin' by the smell of booze, the young fella's been self-medicatin' his grief for the past few days."

"Or his guilt," Phyllis said.

"You think?"

"That's what we're here trying to find out, isn't it?"

Sam inclined his head in acknowledgment of that point and asked, "Do we invite ourselves inside?"

"I don't see why not."

They went into the apartment and left the door partially open. The ugly sound of Cliff Reynolds being sick came from behind a closed door on the other side of the living room. Phyllis glanced around and saw that the apartment was a furnished one, based on the seedy, worn look of everything in it. The stained, dusty sofa had probably been there since the Seventies, too.

The bathroom door opened and Reynolds stumbled out. He had closed the bathrobe and tied the belt around his waist. His pallor made him look sick. He plunged his fingers through his hair to get it out of his face and rasped, "What do you want?"

"We came to talk to you about what happened at the senior center last Friday," Phyllis said.

"You mean my cheating girlfriend getting murdered?" Reynolds' jaw clenched and his mouth worked a little. Phyllis couldn't tell if he was trying to hold in his rage or control the urge to throw up again...or both.

"Are you sure about that?" Sam asked. "The cheatin' part, I mean."

Reynolds glared at them and demanded, "What business is it of yours?"

"We're involved in the investigation into the case," Phyllis told him.

Reynolds looked confused again and muttered, "You're not cops. You can't be cops, not as old as... Wait a minute. You're working for Dorrington, aren't you?"

"We work with his lawyer," Phyllis said.

Reynolds stalked over to the door and jerked it open wider. He pointed and said, "Get out! I don't have anything to say to you. If you think I'd do anything to help that...that snake..." His face twisted. "Becky and I were in love. I was going to ask her to marry me! And then she... Dorrington went after her. She fell for his lies. He took her away from me, and then he killed her!"

"Listen, son," Sam said. "It's true that we're workin' with the fella he hired to defend him, but what we're really after is the truth, no matter where that trail leads. I give you my word, if we uncover proof that Dorrington killed that poor girl, we'll do everything in our power to see that he pays for it."

"You sound almost like you're telling the truth."

"I am. We just want to get to the bottom of this." Sam

pointed at Phyllis with his thumb. "You may not know it, but this lady right here has seen to it that quite a few murderers have paid for what they did."

"Yeah, I think I heard something about that," Reynolds muttered. He frowned at them for a moment longer, then gave the door a half-hearted push and stumbled over to the sofa. A little cloud of dust rose from the cushions as he plopped down limply on it. "What do you want to know?"

"How certain are you that Becky was having an affair with Alfred Dorrington?" Phyllis asked.

"You heard Dorrington's wife. She claims she has pictures of them."

"Yes, but that's *her* claim. What do *you* know?"

Reynolds sat there for several seconds, apparently gazing at nothing. Then he said, "I caught them a few times when they didn't know I was anywhere around. Dorrington...had his hands on her. He was holding her shoulders or stroking her arms or touching her hair. You could tell just by the way they were acting that they were...intimate."

"Well, not necessarily," Sam said. "Might as well admit it, some fellas in my generation and on back could get a little handsy whenever they were around a good-lookin' woman. Things like that might not fly in today's world, but that doesn't mean there was anything serious about it. That's just the way things were when we were growin' up, and Dorrington's right there in that same age group."

"How did Becky react when he touched her?" Phyllis asked.

Reynolds snorted. "Yeah, that's just it. It's easy to say that he's just an old perv, but Becky wasn't just putting up with it. She *liked* the attention. She never tried to get him to stop or even told him that he was being inappropriate."

"Well, she worked for him," Sam pointed out. "Could be she was afraid to."

Reynolds looked at him as if he were speaking a foreign language, then said, "Are you kidding? She could have sued him or just crucified him on social media. She didn't have to let him get away with anything, unless she wanted him to."

Phyllis nodded and said to Sam, "He's right, at least to a certain extent. I'm sure there's still a lot of harassment that goes on, but it's more difficult now for anyone to get away with it."

"What I saw wasn't harassment," Reynolds insisted. "They were acting like lovers. Talk to Mrs. Dorrington. If she's got proof…"

"If she does have proof," Phyllis said, "and if Becky and Dorrington actually were romantically involved…it seems to me that gives you a very strong motive to have slipped that poison into the trifle yourself, Mr. Reynolds."

He just gaped at her, as if the implications of what he'd been saying had never occurred to him until this very moment.

# Chapter 22

For a long moment, Cliff Reynolds didn't say anything. Then he muttered, "I think you'd better leave now."

Phyllis ignored that and said, "Do you mind telling us more about your background? How did you come to work at Mr. Dorrington's restaurant? That was where you and Becky met, isn't it?"

Reynolds shook his head. "I'm not telling you anything else. I don't even have to talk to you. You're not cops." His voice rose a little and shook. "I want you to get out. I'm going to call the police if you don't!"

"Take it easy, son," Sam said. "We're goin'." He put a hand on Phyllis's elbow as they both turned toward the door, which was still open a few inches. "You think about one thing, though. If Dorrington's innocent and we prove it, the next most likely suspect will be *you*. You might be better off helpin' us figure out who actually did kill that poor girl."

"I know who killed her," Reynolds muttered. "Dorrington did. You'll never convince me that he didn't. The old goat."

There was no point in talking to him anymore. Phyllis and Sam both knew it. They left the apartment and went down the stairs to the parking lot. On the other side of the lot from where Sam's pickup was parked, a couple of men were leaning on a car and talking. Phyllis kept an eye on them as discreetly as possible and tried not to seem nervous as she and Sam went to the pickup and got in. As he had said earlier, the apartment complex looked like the sort of place where drug deals might go down on a regular basis.

Nothing happened, though. Phyllis heaved a sigh of relief as they pulled away from the place.

"Yeah, I feel the same way," Sam told her with a smile. "What now?"

"We're all the way over here on this side of the metroplex. I wouldn't mind taking a look at Mr. Dorrington's restaurant."

Sam arched an eyebrow. "They probably won't let us in. We don't have a reservation."

"I still wouldn't mind seeing it. You know, just to get a feel for the place."

"Sure, we might as well. You have the address, don't you?"

"Yes, it was in the information Jimmy gave us."

Phyllis brought up the location on her phone and gave Sam directions. Back on the freeway, they drove past the former site of Texas Stadium, merged with another highway, and then cut across the northwest part of Dallas on Mockingbird Lane, going past Love Field.

Despite the city's affluence, most of the houses in Highland Park weren't ostentatious mansions. Rather, they were older residences that were very impressive in their solid, dignified appearance. Huge shade trees lined the road. There was nothing garish about the shopping centers. They were low-key and blended into the quiet elegance of the area. Alfred Dorrington's restaurant Great Expectations was in one of those centers, at the end of a red-brick building with ivy on the walls.

It was close to midday, well within the lunch hour, so the parking places in front of the restaurant were mostly full. Nearly all of the vehicles were either luxury sedans or luxury SUVs, but there were a couple of big, expensive pickups, too. This might be Highland Park, but it was still Texas.

"Look over there," Phyllis said as she leaned forward abruptly and pointed at a woman getting out of a car. "That's Mrs. Dorrington, isn't it?"

"Yeah, sure looks like it," Sam said.

"Let's talk to her. We were going to need to do that sometime, anyway."

"No time like the present," Sam agreed as he maneuvered the pickup into one of the few available parking spaces.

Sophia Dorrington closed the door of one of those luxury sedans and walked toward the restaurant entrance, which was set behind a covered courtyard with flower beds and shrubs and small, wrought iron tables and chairs that no one was actually using. Phyllis and Sam caught up to her as she was crossing that courtyard. Phyllis said, "Mrs. Dorrington, could we talk to you for a minute?"

Sophia stopped and turned to face them. She wore a gold-colored dress and short jacket that went well with her dark blond hair and was short enough to show off her still-good legs. Several rings glittered on her fingers, but she wore no other jewelry. Sunglasses covered her eyes.

"Yes, what is it?" she asked, giving them a blank look that said she didn't recognize them.

"My name is Phyllis Newsom," Phyllis said. "This is my

friend Sam Fletcher. We were at the senior center in Weatherford last week on Wednesday and Friday when you were there, too."

Sophia took her glasses off so she could glare at them better. "I don't see why you'd think I have anything to say to you. I've washed my hands of Alfred and of the whole sorry mess he's brought down on his own head." She added archly, "The law will take care of him now."

"But what if he's innocent?" Phyllis asked.

"Are you a reporter, dear? You seem a bit...mature for that profession."

Phyllis shook her head and said, "No, we're just trying to get to the truth, that's all."

"The truth is what you want? Well, I can tell you the truth. Alfred Dorrington is a philandering scoundrel who is finally going to get his comeuppance because he panicked and slew his latest doxy when she turned up with child and tried to blackmail him into dumping me and marrying her." Sophia's voice had a chilling note of satisfaction in it as she went on, "The little tramp should have known better. Alfred was never going to leave me for her. All he was interested in was some recreational canoodling on the side. If he ever tried to divorce me, my lawyers would leave him in shreds, not to mention poverty-stricken."

"You claimed to have photos to prove what you alleged—"

"Again, what business of yours is any of this?"

Phyllis wasn't going to lie. "We work for the attorney who's representing your husband."

Sophia laughed. "Oh, my. Then you have a formidable challenge facing you, dear. Because Alfred is guilty. He had every opportunity to slip poison into that trifle, and he knows about such things."

Sam said, "How's that? What does he know about poison?"

"Heavens, Alfred knows a great deal about a great many things. I may despite his character failings, but I'd never doubt that he has a keen, inquisitive mind. Why, there have been many occasions in the past when he's surprised me with his knowledge of esoteric matters. Ask *him* how he knows about it, why don't you?"

"We'll do that," Phyllis said. "What about those photographs?"

Sophia's eyes narrowed. "If such photographs exist, I should think they'd be in the hands of the prosecuting attorney by now, in order to help build his case against Alfred. Not that it needs much help. He's obviously guilty."

"Are you saying—"

"I'm saying that I'm done talking with you, Mrs.... Newsom, was it? I'm not sure what made you believe that I'd ever do anything to help that husband of mine."

"He says he still loves you."

"If he does, he's had an exceedingly strange way of showing it all these years. Honestly, you shouldn't believe a word he tells you. Lying is in his blood." Sophia paused, then said, "I seem to recall a colorful turn of phrase I once heard from one of the natives. I don't remember about whom he was speaking, but the gist of it was that there was a simple way to tell if this person was lying."

"His lips were movin'," Sam said.

That actually brought a smile to Sophia's face. "That's it exactly, darling." She shook her head admonishingly. "You stepped on my line, though."

"Sorry," Sam said.

"Think nothing of it. Just bear that advice in mind any time you're talking to Alfred."

Sophia turned away and started toward the restaurant entrance again. Phyllis said to her retreating back, "You hate your husband, but you're going to eat at his restaurant?"

"Just because he's a miserable excuse for a human being doesn't mean the food is bad," Sophia responded over her shoulder.

She walked on into the restaurant, her high heels clicking on the courtyard's flagstone paving. Phyllis and Sam watched her disappear into the building, then Sam said, "It's lunch time. You want to eat here?"

"We don't have a reservation, remember?" Phyllis smiled. "Besides, I saw what looked like a nice hamburger place a few blocks back. Wouldn't you rather have a good burger and fries?"

"Now you're talkin'," Sam said."

The burgers were good, although since the shop was in Highland Park, there was no such thing as a plain cheeseburger, only several different kinds of what the place billed as "gourmet hamburgers". Sam opted for one that had goat cheese, roasted red pepper, and horseradish on it, while Phyllis went a slightly lighter route with a burger that included honey mustard, brie, and thin slices of apple. Both were good, although Sam did point out that his would have been better with bacon on it.

They were finishing up the artisanal potato chips that came with the burgers when Phyllis said, "You know, I've been thinking about something Mrs. Dorrington said a little while ago."

"What's that?"

"She mentioned that Becky was pregnant. Jimmy told us about that because he was able to get the autopsy results, but how did *she* know?"

Sam frowned in thought. "That's a good question. She hinted pretty strongly that she was workin' with the DA over in Weatherford. Maybe he told her."

"That doesn't sound like something he'd do," Phyllis replied, shaking her head, "even if Mrs. Dorrington provided evidence he intends to use against her husband."

Sam pondered some more, then said, "I can think of one other way she might've known. Maybe she overheard the girl tellin' Dorrington about her condition. Maybe Becky Thackery actually did try to blackmail him into leavin' his wife and marryin' her."

"And if that's true, it just makes the case against Mr. Dorrington stronger."

Sam shrugged. "It might not have happened that way. It's just a possibility."

"But the theory explains why Mrs. Dorrington would know about the pregnancy. And that lends more credence to her claim that her husband was cheating on her."

"The cards are kind of stackin' up against Dorrington, all right." Sam smiled. "Or maybe I should say he's not drawin' very good dominoes."

"This doesn't eliminate Mrs. Dorrington from suspicion at all, though. Learning that Becky was pregnant might have been enough to push her over the edge to murder."

"Do the Dorringtons have any kids themselves?"

Phyllis shook her head. "None that I could find any record of."

Sam rubbed his chin and nodded slowly. "If they wanted kids…and she couldn't have 'em…and then she found out

that her husband got some other woman in the family way...
Yeah, that might be enough to do it, all right."

"We need to tell Jimmy about this," Phyllis said. "And then
I think we need to have another talk with Alfred Dorrington.
I want to see how he reacts when he finds out that his wife
knew Becky was pregnant."

# Chapter 23

Traffic was even worse on the way back to Weatherford, and by the time they got home, Phyllis and Sam were too tired to do anything else connected with the investigation. The next day, Wednesday, Jimmy D'Angelo was in court all day, so they weren't able to set up a meeting with the lawyer and Alfred Dorrington. D'Angelo's secretary penciled that in for Thursday morning, however, and promised to notify Dorrington and ask that he be there.

With things in the case on hold for the time being, Phyllis and Ronnie went shopping with Carolyn and Eve. The girl wanted to look at clothes for college that fall. Phyllis suspected that what Ronnie really wanted to do was spend some time with them before she left. She didn't believe that Ronnie actually was interested in their opinions on fashion. But no matter what the reason, she was happy for the opportunity. All too soon, Ronnie would be off on her new life.

After lunch, Sam was ready to head to the senior center to play dominoes with his friends. Phyllis said, "I'll come along, if that's all right. There's something I've been thinking about."

"I'm never gonna turn down the chance to spend more time with you," Sam said with a simple, honest affection that was touching. "Sure, come along."

When they got there, they found Patrick Flanagan sitting on one of the wooden benches along the building's front wall, near the door. He stood up and greeted them with a smile.

"I was hoping you'd be here, Patrick," Phyllis said. "There's something I want to ask you."

"About this investigation you and Sam are carrying out?"

"That's right."

The retired detective's smile widened into a grin. "Then it's true what they say about great minds thinking alike, because I've got something stirring around in my brain that I want to discuss with *you*."

Phyllis nodded toward the bench and said, "Why don't we sit down out here, if that's all right?"

"A good idea," Flanagan agreed.

They sat, Flanagan at one end of the bench, Sam at the other, and Phyllis between them. When Flanagan motioned for her to go first, she said, "The last police department you worked for was in Dallas, wasn't it?"

"That's right."

"Does the Dallas police department handle law enforcement in Highland Park, since it's so small? Or does it have its own police department?"

"Why would you want to know that, if you don't mind my asking?"

"I was just wondering if you might be able to find out whether or not the police were ever called to get involved in the Dorringtons' marriage."

"Ah, you mean like a domestic disturbance call," Flanagan

said, nodding.

"That's right. Mr. Dorrington has been adamant that he wasn't having an affair with Becky Thackery, but everything we turn up seems to indicate that isn't true."

Flanagan chuckled. "Remember what I said about great minds? I was about to suggest that I look into that very thing for you, since I have the contacts to do so. But I didn't want to stick my nose into your investigation without talking to you about it first."

"Please, go right ahead," Phyllis told him. "I'd appreciate it."

"Well, then, I'll make a call." He slipped his phone out of his shirt pocket. "Why don't you and Sam go on in while I reach out to an old friend of mine? I'll let you know what I find out."

"Thank you, Patrick," Phyllis told him as she and Sam got to their feet.

"My pleasure," he assured her.

They went into the building while Flanagan made his call. Sam headed for the domino table where Ansel Hovey and Carl Benford were waiting.

Phyllis looked around. The center was in sparse use today. No activities were going on, and she didn't see anyone she wanted to talk to.

The door of Darla Kirby's office was open, though, and the center's director was sitting at her desk. She looked up, caught sight of Phyllis, and motioned to her, indicating that she should come over. Phyllis did so, stopping in the office doorway to ask, "How are you today, Darla?"

"Frustrated, that's how I am," Darla replied. "Ever since that poor girl died, it's almost like people are afraid to come here. And it's getting worse every day. Did you see how empty it is out there today?"

"I noticed," Phyllis said.

"I'm not sure what they're afraid of. After all…and I don't mean for this to sound callous…the girl who died wasn't from here, and it's not like she was around the center all the time. She only spent a few hours here, all told."

Phyllis nodded and said, "I know, but once people get an idea in their heads, it's very difficult to change their minds. They make an assumption, and then it's stuck there."

"Well, I wish people would quit assuming that it's dangerous to come here. If they stop using the senior center, the city and county are liable to stop funding it. That would be a loss for everybody."

Including Darla, who was paid a salary—although certainly not a generous one—as the center's director. Phyllis knew Darla well enough to feel like that wasn't the woman's primary concern, though. She had worked tirelessly to make the center a good place for the seniors of Parker County to come together.

"What you need to do," Darla continued, smiling slightly to take any sting out of the words, "is hurry up and find out who the killer is, so folks will know that the murder had nothing to do with the center and will feel comfortable enough to come back."

"I'm working on it," Phyllis promised, "but I can't guarantee anything."

The front door opened, prompting her to glance over her shoulder. Patrick Flanagan came in, looked around, and spotted her standing in the doorway of Darla's office. He started toward her.

"In fact, I have to discuss the case right now," Phyllis went on.

"Good luck. I hope you solve it."

Phyllis nodded and turned away from the office. She moved to meet Flanagan in the middle of the room.

"Were you able to find out anything?" she asked.

"Maybe. Why don't we sit down?" He nodded toward an empty table.

From the domino table on the other side of the room, Ansel Hovey called, "Hey, Patrick, are you about ready to play? We've got the bones all shuffled."

Flanagan lifted a hand and said, "I'll be there in a minute, lad." He pulled out a chair and held it for Phyllis, then went around the table and settled down in the chair opposite her.

"So, I reached out to an old buddy of mine," he continued. "We used to work together before he took a job with the Highland Park Police Department. He did some checking for me...strictly unofficial, you know...and told me that they had answered several calls to the Dorrington residence over the past year, all of them for reported domestic disturbances. The last time, which was only two weeks ago, they found Mrs. Dorrington attacking Mr. Dorrington."

"Attacking him how?"

"The usual...throwing things, slapping, kicking," Flanagan answered with a shrug. "With a lot of screaming and cursing for punctuation."

"Did your friend have any idea what the fight was about?"

"He talked to the officers who answered the call. They said the lady was upset about her husband's girlfriend...and the results of a certain test."

"A pregnancy test?"

Flanagan shrugged. "I don't know, and my friend couldn't get all the specifics. But I can't think of any other test where the results would make a woman want to bounce a lamp off her husband's head, especially if there was another woman involved."

"You're right about that," Phyllis agreed.

Flanagan gave her an intent look and said, "This doesn't help Dorrington's case, though, does it? If anything, knowing that the girl was pregnant just gives him more of a reason for killing her."

"But it also strengthens the motive for his wife and for Cliff Reynolds," Phyllis pointed out. "We know that Sophia Dorrington was aware of Becky's condition. There's a good chance Cliff was, too. This raises the stakes for both of them…and doesn't put me any closer to finding the real killer."

"I was just trying to help. If I think of anything else…"

She patted his hand where it lay on the table and said, "I know that, Patrick. And now, instead of rumors, I have confirmation that Mrs. Dorrington was aware of the pregnancy situation. That may be important in the long run."

"Well, if I can do anything else to help, you let me know. In the meantime…I suppose I'd better go over there and play some dominoes before poor Ansel has a conniption fit."

Phyllis talked to some of the other ladies at the center for a while. Sheila Trent and Ingrid Gustafson weren't there, but Phyllis wouldn't have sought their company anyway. Eventually she wound up watching the domino game.

That's what she was doing when her phone buzzed. She slipped it out of her pocket and checked the screen, raising her eyebrows in surprise when she saw that the call was coming from the Weatherford Police Department.

Then she felt a sharp surge of worry. Calls from the police were almost always bad news. Something could have happened at the house...

That reaction lasted only a split second before she did the only logical thing and answered the call.

"Mrs. Newsom?" a familiar voice asked.

"That's right."

"Ralph Whitmire here."

It wasn't likely that Weatherford's long-time chief of police would be calling to deliver bad news, she thought—unless it was *really* bad news.

"What can I do for you, Chief?"

"Would it be possible for you to stop by my office this afternoon? I need to talk to you for a few minutes."

"Can I ask what this is about, Chief?" Phyllis said.

Whitmire hesitated, then answered, "The Thackery murder...and your investigation into it."

"Sam and I are assisting Jimmy D'Angelo, who's representing Mr. Dorrington. We have a right to question witnesses and anyone else who might be involved in the case."

"Yes, ma'am, you sure do. But I need to speak with you anyway."

Whitmire had never seemed to resent her getting mixed up in those previous cases. A little annoyed at times, maybe, since a civilian poking into murder investigations went against the procedural grain, but overall, she believed he appreciated the help she had given him and his department. She wasn't sure why this case would be any different.

However, there was one good way to find out.

She had stepped away from the domino table to take the call, but when she glanced back at the game, she saw Sam place a double-five at the end of one leg of a serpentine layout of dominoes.

"That makes twenty-five," he said, "and that puts us out."

All four men began turning their remaining dominoes face-down.

"You want me to come to your office now?" Phyllis asked into the phone.

"Yes, ma'am, if you can," Whitmire said.

"I'll be there in ten or fifteen minutes," Phyllis said.

# Chapter 24

Sam didn't mind leaving, although Ansel Hovey and Carl Benford groused a little about losing the fourth player for their games.

"We can play three-handed," Patrick Flanagan said. "Whatever errand you're about, Phyllis, go ahead and steal this big fellow to help you."

"Thanks," Phyllis said. She hadn't explained what the call was about or who it was from, instead saying that she needed to run an errand and asking Sam if he'd mind leaving.

"Will you be back?" Hovey asked.

Phyllis shook her head and said, "That's hard to say. I just don't know."

"Well, see you later, fellas," Sam told them as he heaved himself to his feet. The two of them started out of the senior center.

Flanagan caught up to them in the parking lot before they reached Sam's pickup. With a slight smile, he said, "I told the boys I'd remembered something I needed to tell you before you left, but actually, I want to ask a question. This is about the Dorrington case, isn't it?"

"To be honest, I'm not sure what it's about," Phyllis told him.

"I believe you," Flanagan said, "but remember, if there's anything I can do to help you, let me know."

"Thanks, Patrick," Sam said. "We sure will."

Flanagan nodded and went back into the senior center. Sam opened the pickup door for Phyllis, then climbed behind the wheel. As they drove again, he said, "Likable cuss, isn't he?"

"Patrick? Yes, he is. I think he's a little bit at loose ends, though. After a long career like he had, to go from being involved in the hustle and bustle of police work on a daily basis to having nothing to do but..."

"But play dominoes?" Sam finished for her. "Yeah, he probably is a mite bored. When it comes to detectin', though, you've already got a partner."

Phyllis smiled, reached over, and patted him on the shoulder. "The best one I could ever ask for," she said.

"So, where are we headed?"

"The police station."

Sam's bushy eyebrows lowered as a frown creased his forehead. "Who was that on the phone?" he asked. "Detective Largo?"

Phyllis shook her head. "No. Ralph Whitmire."

"The chief his own self. Did he say what it was about?"

"Not really, only that it has to do with Becky Thackery's murder."

"So you didn't quite tell the truth, the whole truth, and nothin' but the truth to Patrick when he asked you."

"Not exactly," Phyllis admitted. "But I know so little at this point, it didn't seem worthwhile to go into it."

"I can understand that," Sam said.

He knew all the back streets and shortcuts, so they got across town pretty efficiently and pulled into the police department parking lot fourteen minutes after Phyllis had spoken with Chief Whitmire. They would have made it easily in the time she had told the chief if Patrick Flanagan hadn't delayed them slightly.

When they went inside the sprawling brick building, Phyllis gave their names to the officer on duty at the reception counter. Chief Whitmire must have told the man to expect them. Within moments, they were being ushered into the chief's office.

Behind the big desk, Whitmire stood up and motioned them into leather chairs. "Please, have a seat. Thank you for coming, Mrs. Newsom." He leaned forward and shook hands with Sam. "Good to see you again, Mr. Fletcher."

"Likewise, Chief."

All three of them sat. Whitmire, who had already announced that he was going to be retiring as police chief in another few months, clasped his hands together in front of him and said, "I didn't mean to be so cryptic when I was talking to you earlier, Mrs. Newsom. It's just that... Well, I've never run into anything quite like this before."

"Well, that certainly sounds...foreboding," Phyllis said.

"Honestly, I don't know whether it is or not, because I don't know what to make of it."

"Why don't we stop talkin' around whatever it is and get to it?" Sam suggested.

Whitmire nodded. "Right. The two of you questioned Sophia Dorrington yesterday in Dallas, didn't you?"

Phyllis was surprised that the police chief knew about that, but she kept the reaction from showing on her face. At least, she tried to. Coolly, she said, "It was in Highland Park, actually. And we spoke briefly to her, but it wasn't what I'd call an interrogation."

Whitmire held up a hand and said, "Didn't mean to imply it was. But I got a call about it a little while ago."

"Mrs. Dorrington called you to complain? What did she think you could do about it? Technically speaking, we're on opposite sides of this case, Chief."

"It wasn't Mrs. Dorrington who called. It was the State Department."

"The State Department?" Sam repeated. "As in, Washington D.C.? That State Department?"

"The one and only," Whitmire confirmed.

"What in the world does the State Department have to do with a murder in Weatherford, Texas?" Phyllis asked. "Or with Sophia Dorrington?"

Whitmire looked frustrated as he said, "Again, I don't really know. But the lady I talked to, who works for the Secretary of State, told me they'd been in contact with the British Embassy, and the Brits would appreciate it if Sophia Dorrington wasn't the focus of any sort of investigation. They didn't come right out and say that they would claim diplomatic immunity for her, but again, according to the person I talked to, that option appears to be on the table."

Phyllis and Sam looked at each other. He appeared to be as flabbergasted as she felt. He spoke up first.

"Those folks can't come in here and tell us what to do. They don't have any business meddlin' in a criminal investigation." He paused and then chuckled. "Although we've been accused of doin' the very same thing in the past by your boss, haven't we?"

"The district attorney's not my boss," Whitmire said. "And I don't like the Brits sticking their noses into this case, either. But Sophia Dorrington is a British citizen, and I guess she has a right to complain to her embassy. And then they have an obligation to pass along the complaint to the State Department, which bumped it on to me."

"And now you've passed it along to us," Phyllis said. "I suppose you'll be talking to Jimmy, as well?"

"That's right. He's in court today, though, so I figured I'd touch base with the two of you first." Whitmire leaned back in his chair and laced his fingers together over his thickening belly. "Look, we've always gotten along all right"—he smiled—"even when you made us look bad. I just want the criminals caught, you know that. I resent a bunch of outsiders trying to dictate anything about how an investigation is run, on either side of a case. That's just not the way things work. So I'm telling you right now, if you want to ignore this, there's nothing I can do about it. But I can't guarantee that the Feds will see things the same way."

"So you're sayin' the State Department may come after us if we don't lay off Mrs. Dorrington," Sam said.

"I honestly don't know. I've given you the information. What you do with it is up to you."

"Wait a minute," Phyllis said. "You said Mrs. Dorrington is a British citizen. What about Mr. Dorrington?"

Whitmire nodded. "Yes, he is, too. They've both lived here in the United States for more than thirty years, but they never gave up their British citizenship. Dorrington informed us of that when he was arrested and asked that the British consul in Dallas be notified."

"But the British Embassy in Washington was worried specifically about *Mrs.* Dorrington?"

Sam said, "She hollered to somebody higher up the chain of command."

"That's what it sounds like to me," Whitmire nodded. "Also, she hasn't been arrested or charged with anything. Her husband has. The British ambassador would be less likely to try to influence an active criminal case."

"But he doesn't mind bullyin' civilians."

"Like I said, I don't care for being an errand boy. I've done what was asked of me, and now I'm finished with the matter. You folks carry on however you feel is best."

Phyllis said, "We appreciate that, Chief. We'll have to talk to Jimmy and see what he wants to do." She drew in a breath. "And I want to ask Alfred Dorrington why his wife would try to pull such high-level strings to keep us away from her."

"Sort of makes you wonder what she's afraid of, doesn't it?" Sam mused.

They didn't go back to the senior center but headed home instead. Phyllis went straight to the computer to see what else she could find out about Sophia Dorrington. She was vaguely aware of Carolyn and Eve asking Sam if something was wrong, but she didn't hear what he replied because all of them moved on down the hall toward the kitchen and their voices faded.

Earlier, when she had looked up Sophia's background, she had found that the woman was a member of a wealthy, influential, aristocratic family named Courtenay. The family's money seemed to come from vast real estate holdings in England and Ireland. Sophia Courtenay had attended the best finishing schools on the continent, and as a young woman, she had been a fixture at the casinos in Monaco and on the beaches of the Riviera, back in the days when Europe had been a glittering, glamorous place.

Phyllis opened a drawer in the desk and took out a notepad and pen. Computers were invaluable, of course, but at her age, sometimes writing things down helped her thought processes. She started working on a timeline of Sophia Courtenay Dorrington's life.

After fifteen minutes of clicking back and forth between links and writing on the paper, Phyllis leaned back in the chair in front of the computer desk and frowned. She picked up the pad and looked intently at it for several seconds, then got up to look for Sam and took it with her.

She found him in the kitchen, sitting at the table with Eve. Carolyn was standing at the counter and mixing something in a bowl.

"Find what you were looking for?" Sam asked.

"I don't know," Phyllis said. "I came across something odd, though." She moved to the table and sat down on the chair next to Sam. Placing the notepad in front of him, she went on, "Take a look at this."

Sam leaned forward to study what she had written and asked, "What am I lookin' at?"

"This is the chronology of Sophia Dorrington's life."

Carolyn said, "Sam told us she complained to the British embassy about you investigating her. Who does she think she is?"

"Somebody who's rich and has connections to the royal family," Eve said. "I'm sure she's used to having her every whim catered to. I don't know how they could threaten to invoke diplomatic immunity since she's not a member of their diplomatic corps."

Phyllis said, "I believe that was just a bluff calculated to strike fear into the hearts of us backwoods yokels. Chief Whitmire's not afraid of them, though, and we shouldn't be, either."

Sam rested the tip of his index finger on the paper and slowly ran it down the list of things Phyllis had written. He pursed his lips, frowned, and looked up at Phyllis. "I think I see what you're talkin' about."

"Well, let the rest of us in on it," Carolyn said.

"Sophia Dorrington's life is pretty well documented," Phyllis said, "from the time she was born until about thirty-five years ago. She was married once before she was married to Alfred Dorrington, to a man named Edward Alderdice. He was killed in a car wreck when she was in her mid-thirties. There are a few mentions of her in British newspapers for a couple of years after that, but then…she seems to drop off the face of the earth for almost a decade before resurfacing in Boston and marrying Dorrington. Where was she during that time?"

Sam said, "And when you can't find any record of Dorrington even existin' during that same time period and before, it gets sort of interestin', doesn't it?"

"There has to be a connection," Phyllis said. "Alfred Dorrington was living *somewhere*, likely under some other name, during that time. If his history has been scrubbed, and hers has, as well, it seems likely to me that the two of them were together."

Sam nodded and said, "That would explain it. Throw in the British government gettin' involved now, and it says that one or both of 'em were mixed up in something pretty hush-hush."

"You mean like they were *spies*?" Carolyn exclaimed. "Really, Sam."

"Maybe not spies, necessarily," Phyllis said, "but something to do with high levels of government. Something that everyone involved wants to keep quiet."

Eve said, "People have all kinds of dark secrets. Things that you'd never suspect them of. Not everyone's life is such an open book as, say, Sam's."

He grinned and said, "I don't know whether to consider that a compliment or an insult. But I might have secrets, too. Shoot, for all you know, *I* could've been a spy, way back when I was a young fella. When I was growin' up, there was an older man I knew, ran a hardware store and seemed about as mild a fella as you'd ever find, but come to find out, he'd been part of the OSS back in the war and fought Nazi agents down in Panama. So I reckon somebody who teaches British cookin' might have something like that in his background, too."

Carolyn said, "How in the world would you go about finding out something like that?"

"That," Phyllis said, "is the question."

# Chapter 25

After supper, Phyllis went back to searching on the Internet. She had determined that the London restaurant supposedly owned by Alfred Dorrington hadn't existed. But if he had been living under another name, the restaurant could have been called something else, too.

It didn't take Phyllis long to find articles about London's fine dining establishments during the late Eighties: Kensington Place, the River Café, Bibendum, Le Caprice, San Lorenzo, The Gavroche…

It was while she was scrolling through those stories that a headline caught her eye.

DEADLY EXPLOSION AT POSH LONDON EATERY

Frowning, she began reading the story. It was about a restaurant calling Babbingham's, after its owner and head chef, Warren Babbingham.

Sidetracked by wondering if Alfred Dorrington might really be Warren Babbingham, she did a quick image search and came up with several photos of the man from British newspapers. He appeared to have been in his fifties thirty-five years earlier, which would make him a little too old to be Dorrington. The mostly bald, jowly, pear-shaped head ruled out the possibility as well. Phyllis went back to the story about the explosion.

The blast had taken place on an evening when the restaurant was packed and had killed eleven people at the scene. Four more had died later from their injuries. Eighty-seven people were hurt but survived.

One of the fatalities was Warren Babbingham himself. If she had just kept reading, Phyllis thought, she wouldn't have had to search for a photo to know that Dorrington and Babbingham weren't the same man.

The cause of the explosion hadn't been a mystery for long. Almost right away, the Irish Republican Army had taken credit, or at least, a splinter faction of the group led by someone calling himself Eamon McMullen. According to spokesmen from Scotland Yard and MI5, McMullen was well-known to them as a violent extremist whose fanaticism had drawn his entire family into his crusade against the British government. McMullen, if indeed that was his real name, was something of a mystery man, as well. The authorities had never managed to get a good photograph of him.

It was an interesting, if tragic, story, but it wasn't getting Phyllis anywhere in her research on Alfred Dorrington. She was about to click the back arrow when she paused and leaned toward the screen, squinting at a grainy photograph in the newspaper story.

It was a picture of the restaurant after the explosion, with a gaping, ragged hole in its front wall. Several men stood there, looking into the building and facing partially away from the photographer, who had been standing down the block and shooting at an angle. The caption underneath the photo read: *MI5 AGENTS PROBE IRA TERROR BLAST.*

And one of those agents, Phyllis realized as her heart suddenly thudded harder in her chest, bore a distinct resemblance to Alfred Dorrington.

She was imagining things, she told herself. Seeing what she wanted to see. Caught up in the effort to discover the truth about Dorrington's past, she had fabricated the resemblance. The angle was so bad, she couldn't possibly put any stock in what she thought she saw.

And yet, she was looking right at the photograph, and she still thought the man in the picture looked like Dorrington. Not exactly, maybe, but close enough, given the circumstances and the passage of time...

She needed another set of eyes. Sam had sat at the same table as Dorrington in Jimmy D'Angelo's conference room and seen the man close up, for a good amount of time. She could get Sam to take a look at this. She just wouldn't tell him what he was looking at or what she expected him to see, so she would get an unbiased opinion.

He had gone upstairs to his room after supper. She went up there now, knocked on the door, and opened it without waiting for him to respond.

Sam was sitting at his desk with his laptop open when she came in, but he closed it before she could get a good look at whatever was in the screen. It was some sort of image, that was all she knew. But the look he gave her as he turned in his chair had a hint of guilt in it, as if she'd disturbed him at something...unseemly.

"What were you looking at?" she asked, knowing it wasn't really any of her business but curious anyway. They had been through enough together that she didn't think there was any reason he ought to keep secrets from her. Other than the fact that he had every right to, of course.

"That?" He gave a negligent wave toward the closed laptop. "Oh, nothin'. Just something I was lookin' at. Nothing important." He stood up. "You need me for something?"

"As a matter of fact, I do. Can you come downstairs and look at something for me?"

"Sure. Be happy to. Are we talkin' about some kind of odd bug, or...?"

"Something on the computer."

They went downstairs, and Phyllis told him to sit at the desk so he could get a better look at the screen. Then she reached past his shoulder and wiggled the mouse to wake up the display, which had gone dark.

She had left the computer zoomed in on the image as much as she could without blurring it beyond recognition. Sam couldn't see the caption beneath it. She said, "Take a good look at that and tell me if you see anything familiar."

"All right." Sam leaned toward the monitor, just as she had a few minutes earlier. He tipped his head to the side, then leaned over, giving in to the universal impulse to peer *around* something on the screen to get a better look, even though the brain knew perfectly well that wasn't going to work in two dimensions.

Then he straightened, reached out a hand, and pointed without his fingertip quite touching the screen.

"That fella right there looks a powerful lot like Alfred Dorrington."

"Then you think it could be him?"

"I think there's a mighty good chance of it." Sam shrugged. "Can't guarantee it. I can't see him *that* good. Where was this taken, and what in the Sam Hill is goin' on there? It looks like somethin' blowed up real good."

"A terrorist attack in London," Phyllis said as she reached past him again, took the mouse, and zoomed back out so he could read the newspaper story. "It happened a little more than thirty years ago."

"Middle Eastern terrorists?"

Phyllis shook her head. "Irish Republican Army."

"Ah. The Troubles. Don't really know much about all that, but I've heard of it, of course. They set off a bomb in this place?"

"That's right, or at least they claimed responsibility for it. A man named Eamon McMullen, specifically. Evidently the patriarch of an entire terrorist family."

Sam pointed again. "Where is this? In London?"

"Yes. A restaurant called Babbingham's."

"Babbingham..." Sam looked around quickly at her. "Holy cow! You think Babbingham and Dorrington—"

"Babbingham was killed in the explosion," Phyllis said. "And I saw a picture of him. They look nothing alike. But whoever *that* is..." She nodded toward the screen. "Certainly looks like Alfred Dorrington."

"Yep, he does. An MI5 agent, huh?" Sam smiled. "A spy! Just like we talked about."

"I don't know if someone who works for MI5 would be considered a spy. I think they just investigate cases in Great Britain, not in foreign countries."

"Oh, yeah," Sam said. "That's right. It's MI6 agents who are spies. I know that from books and movies. I should've remembered." He rubbed his chin. "So if Dorrington was an MI5 agent and investigated this bombing...you think that could have anything to do with what happened here?"

"You mean Becky Thackery's murder? I don't see how. She

wasn't even *born* when Eamon McMullen blew up Babbing-ham's. There has to be more to the story if it means anything."

Sam stood up. "Then why don't you keep lookin'? You un-covered this much. See what else you can dig up."

Phyllis resumed her seat in front of the computer. "This had to be a pretty big story in London. There must have been quite a few follow-up stories."

With as much to go on as she had, it wasn't difficult to find more newspaper coverage of the deadly explosion at Babbing-ham's. An MI5 agent identified as Patterson Flint, the lead in-vestigator in the case, vowed that Eamon McMullen would be brought to justice and pay for the murders he'd committed. An intensive investigation was undertaken, and a couple of months later, a task force composed of members from MI5, Scotland Yard, and Special Air Services commandos had closed in on McMullen and his family/gang at their headquar-ters in Dublin. A fierce battle had resulted, with fatalities on both sides. But the McMullens had been wiped out, except for Eamon McMullen himself. His wife, two teenage sons, two brothers, three nephews, and a couple of cousins had died. Somehow, he had escaped.

Sam had been reading over Phyllis's shoulder as she went through the stories. He said, "Sounds like it should've been a movie based on one of those thriller novels that are four or five hundred pages long. Shoot, Patterson Flint would be a great name for the hero of a book like that. Not that I have the pa-tience to read 'em much anymore. These days, if a book's more than three hundred pages, I take a good hard look at it before I decide to give it a try."

"I haven't seen a picture of anyone else in any of these sto-ries who looks like Alfred Dorrington, though," she said.

"Maybe we were wrong. Maybe the man we saw in that picture just resembled Dorrington, and that's all."

"Maybe," Sam said, "but remember, we're supposed to meet with Dorrington again at Jimmy's office tomorrow, and maybe it's time we see if we can throw him for a loop and shake his story."

"You mean we should march right in there and accuse him of being..." Phyllis glanced at the screen again. "Patterson Flint?"

"Even if he's not, if he's connected with what happened back there, just hearin' the name's liable to shake him up pretty good."

Phyllis smiled. "I like the idea."

"Just look him right smack dab in the eye and tell him we know his name is Flint...Patterson Flint."

# Chapter 26

Their meeting with Alfred Dorrington at Jimmy D'Angelo's office was set for ten o'clock the next morning. Phyllis and Sam were both fairly early risers, so they had plenty of time for a leisurely breakfast before they left. They were at the kitchen table, enjoying pancakes, bacon, and eggs with Carolyn and Eve, when the doorbell rang.

"I'll get it," Sam said as he rose to his feet. He went up the hall and returned a moment later with Patrick Flanagan.

"Good morning, ladies," Flanagan greeted them.

"Hello, Patrick," Carolyn said. "Would you like some coffee? We have plenty of food, too."

"I've already had breakfast, but I certainly wouldn't mind a cup of coffee. I'm beholden to you."

"Not at all," Carolyn said as she got up to take a cup from the cabinet and fill it. She set it on the table in front of the empty chair next to hers. "There you go."

He pulled out the chair and sat down. "Many thanks." He

took a sip of the coffee and nodded. "Excellent, just as I expected."

"What brings you here this morning, Patrick?" Phyllis asked. She wondered briefly how he knew where they lived, but she supposed Sam must have told him. Also, it was no secret. He might have found the address on the Internet.

"I just wanted to see how the case was going." Flanagan smiled. "I might as well admit it. I was going to try to stay out of this, because it's really none of my business. But I suppose I'm like an old fire horse hearing a bell. With a murder investigation going on, it's almost impossible for me not to be interested."

"That's understandable, and perfectly all right," Phyllis told him.

"And there's a new angle on the case that you haven't heard about yet," Carolyn added. During breakfast, Phyllis and Sam had told her and Eve about their discoveries of the previous night.

"Is that so?" Flanagan asked as he wrapped his hands around his coffee cup and leaned forward. "Anything you'd care to share?"

"I don't see why not," Phyllis said. "With your law enforcement experience, there might be something you can add to our thinking. Were you ever involved in any terrorism investigations?"

Flanagan's eyebrows rose in surprise. "Terrorism?" he repeated. "I thought this was a simple case involving cheating, jealousy, and pregnancy."

"And that's probably what's behind everything that's happened," Phyllis admitted. "More than likely, we've let ourselves be sidetracked into something completely unconnected."

"But it's a pretty wild story, if there *is* a connection," Sam put in.

Flanagan chuckled and said, "All right, now you've got to tell me about it."

For the next few minutes, they did so. Flanagan's eyes widened even more. When Phyllis and Sam were finished, he said, "You're right, that's quite a bizarre tale." He slipped his phone out of his shirt pocket. "I have to look up some of those things."

"I'll save you the trouble," Sam said as he took out his own phone. "I've got the pages still open." He woke up the phone, tapped the screen a couple of times, and then handed it to Flanagan.

A couple of times as he scrolled through the stories, Flanagan let out low whistles of amazement. He passed the phone back across the table to Sam and said, "All right, let me get this straight. You believe that Alfred Dorrington is really Patterson Flint, one-time MI5 anti-terrorism agent, who came to this country, changed his name to Dorrington, wiped out his past, and became a chef and cooking teacher?"

"Well, when you boil it down like that, I suppose it does sound a little silly," Phyllis admitted.

"But stranger things have happened," Sam said. "Like all those fellas who've been assassinated in James Bond-like ways, and it turns out the Russians were behind it."

Flanagan nodded slowly. "Yes, things go on behind the scenes in international espionage and crime that the general public would believe was the stuff of Hollywood fantasy if they knew about them. But say that you're right and Dorrington is really Flint—"

"He wouldn't have to be Flint," Phyllis interrupted. "He

could be one of the other MI5 operatives or even an SAS commando."

"Yeah," Sam said excitedly. "Remember how easy he handled Cliff Reynolds the first time the young fella jumped him? That was like something a commando would do."

"All right," Flanagan said, "we'll go with the idea that Dorrington was involved in this…this affair at Babbingham's. Why would he go into hiding?"

"Because of Eamon McMullen," Phyllis responded without hesitation. "He masterminded the attack on Babbingham's, but then he escaped and the rest of his family died when the task force caught up to them." She shook her head. "If that's not enough to make someone swear vengeance on you, I don't know what would be. Especially someone who's already a violent extremist like McMullen. Actually, the fact that Flint was in charge of the task force is what makes me lean toward the theory that Flint and Dorrington are the same man." She smiled. "But of course, we could be way off in our guesswork. This could be nothing more than a bizarre fantasy."

Flanagan rubbed his chin and frowned in thought. "I don't know," he said. "I always tend to trust the instincts of an experienced investigator, and I'd say that you qualify after all the murders you've solved. But I still don't see how that poor girl could have gotten mixed up in all that."

After coming across those new possibilities the night before, talking them over with Sam, sleeping on it, and then discussing the case again this morning, the wheels of Phyllis's brain were really turning over. She said, "The only thing that makes sense is that Becky was never the target. Dorrington was. The poison was slipped into the trifle because the killer thought *he* would eat it, not Becky."

"The killer," Flanagan repeated. "You mean Eamon

McMullen?"

"You don't think that's possible?"

Flanagan held up a finger. "Two things, the first being that there was no one at the senior center who could have been this McMullen fellow." Another finger went up. "And the second is that I've dealt with a lot of criminals in my career, and they're very much creatures of habit. McMullen was a terrorist, a bomber! If he was going after Dorrington, he'd have blown the place up."

"Here's another possibility," Sam said. "Maybe somebody besides McMullen was after Dorrington because of what happened all those years ago in London. Maybe he had some other relative who's been holdin' a grudge all this time."

"Such as Cliff Reynolds?" Phyllis suggested. "We don't really know much about him." She shook her head. "But how would he have found out who Dorrington really is, assuming we're right about that?"

"It sounds to me as if you still have a lot of questions that need to be answered," Flanagan said. "And I'll tell you who can answer them."

"Alfred Dorrington?"

"Right the first time," Flanagan said.

Patrick Flanagan was still drinking coffee and talking with Carolyn and Eve when Phyllis and Sam left the house to head for Jimmy D'Angelo's office.

"Patrick brought up some good points," Sam commented as he piloted the pickup through Weatherford's streets.

"He did," Phyllis agreed. "I'm glad he stopped by this morning. Talking to him helped me pull some things together in my mind."

Sam glanced over at her. "You know who the killer is?"

"Not yet," she said honestly. "But I feel like there are only one or two more pieces I need to find before the picture makes sense."

"Maybe Dorrington'll give us those pieces. Or should I say Flint?"

"Not yet," Phyllis replied, shaking her head. "That's still pure speculation."

"Like Patrick said, though, you've got to trust the instincts of an experienced investigator."

Phyllis smiled. "My instincts have been wrong plenty of times. Remember that time when I came up with three different solutions to the case?"

"Yeah, but you didn't give up until you had the right answer. I don't reckon you will this time, either."

When they arrived at D'Angelo's office, Alfred Dorrington was already there, seated at the table in the conference room. D'Angelo ushered them in and offered them coffee, which both of them refused graciously. When they were all seated, D'Angelo said, "All right, what have the two of you turned up that we need to talk about?"

There were quite a few things, actually, Phyllis thought: the interview with Cliff Reynolds, the encounter with Sophia Dorrington at the restaurant in Highland Park and the revelation that she had known about Becky's pregnancy before the murder, the knowledge that Highland Park police had been called to the Dorrington residence more than once because of domestic disturbances...

But all of that paled in comparison to the information Phyllis had uncovered the previous evening. She placed her hands flat on the gleaming hardwood, looked intently across the table at the urbane Englishman sipping from a cup of coffee, and said, "Mr. Dorrington, is it true that your real name is Flint?" Then, unable to resist, she added, "Patterson Flint?"

# Chapter 27

Dorrington choked on the coffee. For a second, Phyllis thought he was going to drop the cup. Then he recovered and set it on the saucer in front of him. It rattled slightly, just enough to tell Phyllis that his hand had trembled.

"Coffee go down the wrong way?" Sam asked dryly.

Dorrington cleared his throat. "Yes. Yes, I suppose so," he said. He frowned at Phyllis. "What in the world would make you ask me such a bizarre question?"

"I think I'd like to know the answer to that myself," D'Angelo said.

"Which one?" Phyllis said. "Why I asked the question…or if your client's real name is Patterson Flint?"

"How about both?" D'Angelo gave Dorrington a look that was just short of a scowl. "It's not a good idea to withhold information from your attorney that might help your case."

"I assure you, I haven't done that."

"So your name's not really… What was it? Patterson Flint? I should remind you, if Phyllis and Sam have found out about it, there's a chance the prosecution will, too. Although I don't think anybody who works in that office is as good at digging things out as these two."

"My name is Alfred Dorrington. I can provide ample documentation of that."

Phyllis said, "Did MI5 provide you with that documentation when they gave you a new identity so Eamon McMullen couldn't track you down and kill you as revenge for what happened to his family in Dublin?"

D'Angelo waved his hands in the air and said, "Okay, hold it. This is getting *way* out there. Tell me what's going on, Phyllis."

"She must be hallucinating," Dorrington said.

Sam narrowed his eyes at the man. "You won't find anybody more level-headed than Phyllis Newsom, mister. Whenever she talks, there's something to it, no matter how strange it might seem at first."

"Then you admit that this whole idea is strange?" Dorrington said.

"Weird things happen in life," D'Angelo responded. "How about it, Phyllis? Fill me in before I get too confused here."

The websites that Sam had up on his phone would help with that. Phyllis took it from him and passed it along to D'Angelo, telling him, "Read through those, and then the theory we've come up with will make more sense."

D'Angelo's frown deepened as he went through the stories. While he was doing that, Alfred Dorrington sat on the other side of the table wearing an outright scowl on his face.

Finally, D'Angelo looked up and said, "All right, I've heard of things like this bombing happening before, but I'm not sure how it ties in with Mr. Dorrington's case...unless he really is that guy Flint, like you claim."

"I only thought it was a possibility," Phyllis said. "He might be one of the other MI5 agents involved with that task force and the battle with the McMullen family. But his reaction when confronted with the name makes me believe we came upon the truth."

Coldly, Dorrington said, "I'm right here, you know. Surely you realize how ludicrous this whole thing is."

Sam said, "Yeah, it's pretty far out...but it sure does explain why there's no record of you existin' before you married your wife in Boston thirty years ago."

"And it would explain why almost a decade of *her* life is missing before that, if she was married to you during that time," Phyllis added. "Wiping out any signs of Patterson Flint's life would have taken care of that, too."

Dorrington shook his head. "I'm not going to dignify this lunacy with a denial.

D'Angelo said, "Whenever I hear somebody say that, I always figure that whatever they've just been accused of is true. Juries think the same way, you know."

"If you put any stock in the ravings of these two, perhaps I should start thinking about different representation."

"Maybe you should," D'Angelo said with a shrug. "But if you get another lawyer and lie to them, too, you'll be cutting your own throat. Tell us the truth...lay out the whole story...and you'll stand a lot better chance of coming out of this without a murder conviction."

A tense silence hung in the air of the conference room for several heartbeats before Dorrington sighed. He picked up his coffee, took a swallow, and this time when he set the cup down, it didn't rattle. He had regained control of himself after being startled by Phyllis using the name Patterson Flint.

"I trust that everything said in this room is covered by attorney-client privilege?" he said.

"Of course. And as employees of mine, Phyllis and Sam are covered by that, too."

D'Angelo paid them a token salary just for instances such as this. Phyllis said, "We just want to find out who's responsible for Becky Thackery's death, Mr. Dorrington. We're not out to cause trouble for you."

Dorrington sighed. "I want the same thing, Mrs. Newsom. But do you actually believe that what happened so long ago could have anything to do with this terrible business?"

"That was a terrible business, too," Phyllis pointed out. "A lot of people died. And the past has a really bad habit of not letting go of the present."

Dorrington nodded slowly. "That's all too true. Very well." He took a deep breath. "I am… I used to be… Patterson Flint. How in the world did you find that out?"

"There's a picture of you in a newspaper story available on-line."

Dorrington winced and said, "Really? All of those were supposed to be expunged. But with newspapers putting more and more of their archives on-line all the time, I suppose it's all but impossible to keep up with everything. And it *has* been thirty years or more." His mouth tightened. "Honestly, I doubt if anyone at MI5 today actually knows or cares much about what happens to me. I'm a dinosaur to them. Ancient history. So they probably don't have anyone monitoring the Internet for things like that."

"I assume your government helped set you up with a new identity?"

"Yes, after three attempts on my life by Eamon McMullen, all bombings. My wife was almost killed in one of them, and while they might not have gone to that much trouble for a civil servant such as myself, they didn't want even a distant relative of the royal family to come to any harm. That happened often enough during The Troubles as it was." His mouth quirked. "That was what prompted the attack on Babbingham's, you know. A member of the royal family was supposed to dine there that night. For once, an attack of gastritis was well-timed and prevented that party from being on hand when the bomb went off."

D'Angelo shook his head and said, "You're talking about a whole different world from Weatherford, Texas."

"Yes. Unfortunately, the ugliness is spreading. There are few places that are truly safe anymore…and fewer of them all the time."

Phyllis hated to think it, but she knew Dorrington was right. However, that was a bigger problem than she could deal with, so she stuck to the business at hand.

"You dropped out of sight and resurfaced in this country with a new identity," she said. "But your wife didn't. She was still Sophia Courtenay Alderdice, until she married you."

"Well, not exactly. Her marriage to Patterson Flint was a matter of public record, after all. But Patterson Flint was dead, so she was a widow for the second time when she married Alfred Dorrington."

Sam said, "MI5 made it look like that last attempt on your life was successful, is that it?"

"That's right. By then it was obvious McMullen wasn't going to stop until I was dead…so we gave him what he wanted. I was smuggled out of the country, and my grieving widow went to America to put her tragic past behind her, and in due time she met and married a charming restauranteur named Alfred Dorrington. There seemed to be no need for her to hide who she was."

Phyllis said, "But if McMullen believed he'd succeeded in assassinating you, why keep up the deception? He wouldn't be looking for Patterson Flint anymore."

"It was a precaution, plain and simple, against the truth coming out someday." Dorrington smiled. "Besides, I came to love the life I was leading. I actually am a wonderful cook, you know. It was a much more pleasant life than hunting down terrorists and criminals and spies."

"I can see how it would be," Phyllis admitted.

"In time, I forgot all about Patterson Flint. I was Alfred Dorrington. I was rich and successful and married to a beautiful woman—"

"Who you cheated on," D'Angelo said with painful bluntness.

Dorrington winced. "I freely admit that I have more than my share of human failings. I try to conquer and control them, which is more than some people can say."

D'Angelo stood up and started to pace back and forth at the head of the table. "All right, this is a wild story," he said. "But does it tell us who killed Becky Thackery? As far as I can see, it doesn't."

"Eamon McMullen," Phyllis said. "Somehow, he discovered that Patterson Flint was still alive, figured out his new identity, and tracked him here to Weatherford."

"McMullen wanted *me* dead," Dorrington said. "He wouldn't have even known who Becky was, other than someone who worked for me."

"You said your wife was almost killed in one of the attempts on your life. Something like that could have happened here. That poison could have been intended for you."

D'Angelo stopped his pacing and pointed a finger at Phyllis. "That's right! Becky's murder could have been an accident." He turned to look at Dorrington. "Is McMullen even still alive?"

"I have no idea," Dorrington replied with a shake of his head. "He dropped out of sight after the last bombing. Friends of mine from MI5 contacted me occasionally, strictly back-channel, and let me know that he hadn't resurfaced. Over time, those friends retired or passed away, and I simply haven't heard a word about the man in more than ten years. I suppose I stopped thinking about him. The threat seemed to be over."

"Unless he was just bidin' his time," Sam said. "Waitin' for just the right moment to get his revenge. Does that seem like something he'd do?"

Dorrington said, "I wouldn't put *anything* past the man. He was a lunatic, a fanatic. And it wasn't just devotion to his cause. I think he enjoyed wreaking havoc and spreading death and destruction wherever he went. If it hadn't been political strife, he would have found some other reason to do the things he did."

"His family was killed," Sam pointed out. "Regardless of anything else, that's enough to make a fella want revenge."

"He's the one who put them in harm's way," Dorrington said sharply. "And they helped him carry out his campaign of terror. I felt bad about the youngsters, I really did…but they were killers, too. Not only that, but McMullen ran out on them, the night we raided the flat where they had holed up. We found out later that he'd stepped out just before we struck, and he must have seen what was going on. But he turned and ran, while the rest of them died." He shook his head. "I'm not going to waste much sympathy on any of that lot."

"Would you recognize him if you saw him?" Phyllis asked.

"After all this time? I very much doubt it. I probably wouldn't have known him then, either. That was what made McMullen so devilishly hard to catch. He was incredibly camera-shy. We had only vague descriptions of him to go by, and it was rumored that he made an effort to change his appearance fairly often. He was a bit of a phantom, I suppose you could say."

"So he could walk right up to you," Sam said. "Why didn't he? If he found out who Alfred Dorrington really was, why didn't he just shoot you?"

"Because that would have meant he'd have to face justice for his actions," Dorrington said, adding with a note of contempt in his voice, "As I told you, Eamon McMullen is a coward. He would want to have his revenge on me while protecting his own skin."

"Let's say the poison was meant for you," Phyllis said, "but the attempt backfired and Becky wound up dying instead."

Dorrington's expression was bleak as he nodded and said, "If we accept the other parts of your theory, it could have happened that way."

"But even though McMullen failed in his primary goal, then you were arrested and charged with Becky's murder," Phyllis went on. "Is it feasible that he might have decided *that* would be his revenge on you? To see you go to prison for a murder you didn't commit?"

"That seems awfully subtle for him," Dorrington said, "but I suppose it's possible. He might even think it was appropriate. After all, I tried my best to capture him and put him in prison. If he succeeded, even by accident, at putting me behind bars... Yes, I can see that."

"There's one big problem with all of this," D'Angelo said.

"We don't have a single bit of evidence. If we try to tell this story in court, the jury may be entertained, but they won't believe it. Not without proof to back it up. While the prosecution, on the other hand, will have your affair with Miss Thackery, her pregnancy, your wife's jealousy, her boyfriend's attacks on you—"

Dorrington held up a hand to stop him. "Wait a moment. I'm still not admitting that Miss Thackery and I ever had an affair."

"Your wife certainly believes you did," Phyllis said. "What other motivation would she have had for that argument Cliff Reynolds overheard, or the domestic disturbance calls to the Highland Park Police Department?"

Dorrington frowned at her. "How many times do I have to tell you, my wife gets ideas in her head and they're impossible to budge. And there were never any domestic disturbance calls. For that matter, there is no Highland Park Police Department."

"What are you talking about?" Phyllis asked. "Highland Park does have its own police force, doesn't it?"

"It has a Department of Public Safety," Dorrington explained. "All the officers serve as police, firefighters, and emergency medical technicians, on a rotating basis. It's a unique arrangement. But there is no 'Police Department', as such."

Phyllis drew in a deep breath, sat back in her chair, and looked out the window, which didn't have much of a view, just the northern part of downtown Weatherford. But she wasn't really seeing what she was looking at, so it didn't matter.

Dorrington and D'Angelo both started to say something, but Sam held up a hand to stop them.

"She's thinkin'," he said. "And I know that look on her face."

D'Angelo breathed, "Does that mean—"

Sam motioned again for him to be quiet. After a few more seconds went by, Phyllis smiled.

"Can I talk again?" D'Angelo blurted. "What is it, Phyllis?"

"Eamon McMullen," she said. "He's alive. And there's only one person he can be."

# Chapter 28

Sam stopped the pickup in the driveway at the house. Phyllis didn't wait for him to come around and open her door, as she normally would have. She was out of the vehicle quickly, heading for the front door.

It opened before she got there, and Ronnie stepped out, stopping short and looking surprised at the intense expression on Phyllis's face.

"Gosh," she said, "what's wrong?"

Phyllis didn't answer the question but asked one of her own, instead. "Where are you going?"

"I'm meeting some friends out at the lake." Ronnie lifted the big tote bag she carried. "It's a beautiful day for a swim and a picnic."

Sam had come up behind Phyllis in time to hear Ronnie's answer. He nodded and said, "Sounds like fun. You go and have a good time."

"All right, thanks." The girl frowned as she hesitated. "*Is* something wrong?"

"Not really," Phyllis said. "Have fun, like your grandfather says."

"Okay." Still wearing a slightly confused expression, Ronnie headed for her car, which was parked at the curb.

Quietly, so Ronnie wouldn't overhear, Sam said, "She'll be safer away from here for a while, I reckon."

Phyllis nodded. "Yes. Unless—"

She caught her breath and turned swiftly toward the street, intending to call out and tell Ronnie to wait. But it was too late for that. Ronnie was in her car, the engine cranking as she turned the key...

The engine caught, running smoothly as Ronnie put the car in gear, pulled out, and drove off.

Phyllis closed her eyes and blew out a soft, relieved breath.

Sam swallowed hard and looked shaken. He said, "You thought of the same thing I did, didn't you? A fella who's got a history of plantin' bombs..."

"It seemed like a pretty remote possibility, but I was worried anyway."

"Like they say in the memes, the odds may be against it, but they're never zero."

Phyllis nodded and went into the house through the front door that Ronnie had left partially open. Sam was right behind her.

They found Carolyn and Eve in the living room. Phyllis said, "Patrick Flanagan's not here anymore?"

"No, he left a little while after you did," Carolyn said. She hesitated for a second, then added, "He does seem like a nice man."

Phyllis and Sam just glanced at each other, then Phyllis asked, "Did he say where he was going?"

"To the senior center, I believe. He thought he might be

able to rustle up enough players for a domino game, even though you weren't going to be there, Sam."

"Maybe we'll head that way, too," Sam said.

Eve started to set aside the book she was reading. "We'll come with you."

"No!" Phyllis exclaimed. Then, when her friends stared at her in surprise, she went on, "I mean, I probably won't stay. I'll just drop Sam off and then come back here. There's a, uh, recipe I've been meaning to try."

"But if you don't want to go, why doesn't Sam just go by himself, dear?" Eve asked.

"And if you drop him off, you'll have to go back and get him," Carolyn added.

Both comments fell on deaf ears, because Phyllis and Sam had already turned around and were heading for the door."

"You don't think he'll come back to the house, do you?" Sam asked as he drove across town toward the senior center.

"He doesn't have any reason to. You and I are the ones who figured out the truth about him."

"Yeah, but Carolyn and Eve know about it, too."

Phyllis shook her head. "Not as much as we know. They had no idea that Patrick Flanagan is really Eamon McMullen."

"We don't have any proof of that," Sam said.

"We will, once Jimmy gets through digging into Flanagan's background and discovers that everything he told us about his life and career were lies." Phyllis shook her head. "He must have been tracking down Dorrington and setting this up for a long time, in order to move to Weatherford a couple of months before Dorrington was supposed to teach those cooking classes here."

"He figured he could fool a bunch of rubes like us," Sam said. "So he puts together this whole elaborate masquerade and laughs at us the whole time, more than likely." Sam shook his head, as well. "It's a blasted shame, that's what it is. I actually liked the fella."

"So did I," Phyllis said. "And I think Carolyn was starting to. That's what makes me as mad as anything. The way he played up to her, when there was no strategic reason for doing so. That was just pure meanness on his part."

"Yeah, and he stayed friendly after the murder so he could keep tabs on what we were doin'." Sam groaned. "And we fell for it and kept him up to date on the whole thing. He knows now we're on his trail, even if he can't be sure we've figured out who he really is. Why doesn't he just disappear like he did before? Drop out of sight and stay gone?"

"You heard what Dorrington said. He likes to wreak havoc on people's lives..."

"He's done a good job of it here," Sam muttered.

They had reached the senior center. Sam pulled into the parking lot. As Phyllis looked at the other cars, she realized she didn't know what sort of vehicle Patrick Flanagan drove. He had been at her house earlier when she and Sam left, but several cars had been parked along the street and she didn't know which was his.

Maybe he *had* "taken it on the lam", as Sam would say. Phyllis almost hoped that was the case, so that he wouldn't threaten anyone else around here. But without Flanagan, they might not be able to prove their theory about the murder, which would make it more difficult to clear Alfred Dorrington's name.

Before they got out of the pickup, Phyllis took her phone from her pocket and thumbed it to redial the last call she'd made. After a moment, she grimaced and said, obviously talking to voicemail, "This is Phyllis Newsom again. Please meet us at the senior center as soon as you can."

"Detective Largo's still not answerin' her phone?" Sam asked as Phyllis put her phone away.

"No. She must be busy on another case, or perhaps she's in court and has it turned off."

"Why don't you call Chief Whitmire? I'm sure he'd be willin' to come over here."

"That's a good idea."

A few minutes later, though, Phyllis shook her head and slipped her phone back into the pocket of her jeans once again.

"He's not available, either, but I left a message."

"Never a cop around when you need one, as the old sayin' goes." Sam nodded toward the building. "You want to wait and keep an eye on the place until one of 'em calls you back?"

"I suppose we could do that…"

"But you don't want to, do you? You want to go in there and tell Patrick that we've figured out he's really Eamon McMullen."

"He's lied to us, manipulated us, and like you said, laughed at us. That doesn't sit well with me."

"Me, neither."

Phyllis opened the pickup door. "We won't come right out and accuse him. He knows we were going to see Jimmy and Dorrington. We can pretend we're just bringing him up to date on the case. For one thing, that will keep him from leaving before either Detective Largo or Chief Whitmire get here."

"Sounds good to me," Sam said. He got out of the pickup, too.

When they stepped into the senior center and looked around, both of them spotted Flanagan right away. He was sitting at the domino table with Ansel Hovey and Carl Benford. They weren't playing, just talking. Flanagan saw Phyllis and Sam and smiled as he raised a hand to signal for them to come over.

Phyllis managed to return the smile as they stepped up to the table. "Hello, Patrick," she said.

"Thank goodness you're here, Sam," Hovey said. "Even though it's not our usual day for a game, now we can get one going."

"Sure, I reckon that'd be all right," Sam said as he pulled out one of the empty chairs at the table. He glanced at Phyllis. "You don't mind?"

"No, go right ahead," she told him. "I'll just sit and watch."

As Flanagan started shuffling the dominoes, he said, "I believe they have a yoga class going on in the community room, Phyllis. You don't do yoga?"

"I've tried it," she said. "It's enjoyable, but I don't really have time for a regular class."

"No, I imagine not. Solving crimes keeps you busy and on your toes, doesn't it?"

Before, she wouldn't have thought anything of the comment. She would have considered it playful joshing on his part. Now, she didn't feel that generous.

"I just don't like to see people get away with murder," she said. "Something about it really rubs me the wrong way."

"Aye, the feeling is a familiar one. I suppose that's what made me become a detective."

"Where was it you said you worked before coming to Dallas?"

Flanagan stopped shuffling, and the four men began drawing dominoes. "Boston and then St. Louis," he replied.

"That's funny. I would have sworn you said you were a police detective in New York, not Boston."

"Yeah, that's what you told us, Patrick," Ansel Hovey chimed in, unaware of the implications.

Flanagan waved a hand. "Boston, New York, it's easy to get confused. They're both big cities in the Northeast, aren't they?"

"Well, yeah, but they're pretty different," Carl Benford said. "I don't think I've ever heard anybody mix them up before. Most guys I've run into from either place wouldn't be caught dead claiming to be from the other one."

Flanagan shot a glance toward Phyllis, then let out a rueful chuckle. "Clearly, the years are catching up to me. My memory's not what it used to be."

The door to the center's community room opened, and eight women wearing workout clothes came into the main room, trailed by the young, leotard-wearing yoga instructor. Sheila Trent and Ingrid Gustafson were among the students. Sheila looked like she had handled the exercise fairly well, but Ingrid was red-faced and puffing.

Darla Kirby emerged from her office and started talking to the instructor. The other women sat down and began drinking from bottles of water.

Ansel Hovey, sitting to Flanagan's left, played six-four to start the game. Carl Benford shook his head a little and played double-four. Sam said, "That must be the only thing you've got that'll play, Carl, if you're settin' me up like that. But I'll take it."

He played double six and moved the peg in his and Hovey's scoreboard four holes.

Flanagan played six-two and said, "Well, I'll get half of it back, anyway," as he moved the peg in his and Benford's board two spaces.

The center's front door opened. Phyllis looked that direction and saw Detective Isabel Largo step into the building. She had a curious frown on her face as she looked around.

"Mixing up Boston and New York is one thing," Phyllis said. "Not knowing that Highland Park has a Department of Public Safety instead of a police department is another."

Flanagan scowled. "Are we back to that again? Can't a man have a senior moment now and then?"

"When you've told so many lies, I suppose it *is* difficult to keep up with them."

Flanagan's expression darkened even more. Hovey and Benford looked surprised at what seemed like a tactless comment on Phyllis's part.

Then Flanagan glanced over his shoulder, saw Detective Largo coming toward them, and said quietly, "Feeling brave now that the cavalry has arrived, are you?"

"Feeling like it's time for the lies to stop," Phyllis said.

"Speaking of stopping…" Flanagan unbuttoned the middle button on his shirtfront and pulled the garment open enough for Phyllis to see the thin bricks of a waxy-looking substance held in a belt of some sort strapped around his torso. "You'd better tell your detective friend to stop right where she is, or I'll blow this whole place to smithereens."

# Chapter 29

Phyllis was shocked but didn't lose her head. Sam retained his composure, too, and reacted quickly, raising a hand and saying, "Stay right where you are, Detective."

From where Largo was, she couldn't see the bomb under Patrick Flanagan's shirt. She glared at Phyllis and demanded, "What's this all about? Your call sounded urgent, Mrs. Newsom."

"It is urgent," Phyllis said, working hard to keep her voice level and steady. She nodded toward Flanagan and went on, "This man killed Becky Thackery, and he just threatened to blow up the senior center."

Largo's eyes widened, and her hand started to move toward the gun on her hip. Flanagan said, "Ah, ah, lass, I wouldn't do that if I were you."

He turned on the chair so Largo could see. She swallowed hard and said, "Please, sir, I don't know what's going on here, but take it easy. You don't want to hurt anybody."

"Ah, but I do." Flanagan looked at Phyllis and went on,

"Call that lawyer friend of yours right now and tell him to have Flint come here. There's no time to waste. I thought I was going to have some nice delicious revenge, seeing that murderer sent to prison for something he hadn't done, but you've ruined that, haven't you, Phyllis?"

"I found out the truth," Phyllis said.

"Just like you always do."

"Like I try to."

"Who's Flint?" Largo asked.

Flanagan answered her. "Patterson Flint. The man who massacred my family and ruined my life. You know him as Alfred Dorrington."

"Patterson Flint," Phyllis repeated. "Patrick Flanagan. You took his initials."

"A little tribute," Flanagan said with a smile. "Tribute to a monster."

Sam said, "He was just tryin' to do his job. You're the monster, mister."

Ansel Hovey had been staring at Flanagan. Now, with his voice rising, he blurted out, "Is that a *bomb?*"

"Bomb!" Sheila Trent screeched.

"Gangway!" Ingrid Gustafson bellowed as she burst out of her chair and headed for the door. "We're all gonna die!"

Flanagan lurched to his feet and twisted around, yelling, "Stop!"

His hand came out from under his shirt as he turned. Sam lunged out of his chair, dived across the table, and grabbed both of Flanagan's arms from behind.

"Give me a hand, boys!" he called to Hovey and Bradford. "Hang on to his arms!"

They did as Sam said, clearly confused but knowing that fast, desperate action was called for. They pinned Flanagan's arms behind his back. He staggered back and forth, but he couldn't shake them loose, nor could he reach whatever trigger or detonator he had concealed under his shirt with the plastic explosive.

"Everybody out!" Largo shouted as she drew her gun. She waved the others toward the door. "Go! Call 9-1-1!"

Darla and the other people left in the center stampeded out of the place. Largo covered Flanagan, and Sam, Hovey, and Bradford hung on to him for dear life.

"You'd better stop fighting," Largo said, "because if you break loose from those men, I'm going to shoot you in the head, just to make sure you don't do whatever it is you're trying to do."

With his lips drawn back from his teeth in a hate-filled grimace, Flanagan said, "I'm only trying to do what I've dreamed of for thirty years now! I just want to avenge my family!"

"And all you really accomplished was killing an innocent girl," Phyllis said.

"She wasn't innocent! She was a harlot consorting with that devil Flint! She wasn't my target, but she got what was coming to her!"

Phyllis looked at Largo, who still held the 9mm pistol in a rock-steady grip. "I'd say that was a confession."

"Maybe not an admissible one," the detective said, "but I have a feeling this man, whoever he really is, wants to talk."

And so Patrick Flanagan—Eamon McMullen—talked. Talked up a storm, in fact. According to what Isabel Largo told Phyllis later, it was hard to get him to shut up. He had so much hate and bile built up in him, once it started spilling out it didn't want to stop.

It had taken quite a while to get him locked up. First, several uniformed officers had carefully replaced Sam and the other two older men and kept Flanagan's arms pinned. Then explosives technicians from the sheriff's department had had to defuse the bomb strapped to his body. It was a viable, working device, according to them, and would have caused considerable death and destruction if Flanagan had been able to set it off.

Phyllis's son Mike, who was a deputy, had heard about what was going on and showed up at the senior center, on the edge of being frantic. He relaxed when he saw that Phyllis and Sam were all right and Flanagan was in custody, but he said, "Mom, you've got to stop confronting murderers like this. You're making me old before my time!"

"Me, too," Sam said. "And I don't have that much more time to spare."

Phyllis was more shaken than she let on, but she just nodded and said truthfully, "It would be just fine with me if this is the last murderer I ever set eyes on."

When they finally got back to the house, Carolyn and Eve had no idea what had happened. Ronnie was back, too, having returned from the excursion to Lake Weatherford with her friends. They all gathered in the living room, where Phyllis laid out the facts of the case, culminating in Patrick Flanagan's capture.

Carolyn sat back in her chair, eyes wide. "I...I never would have dreamed that he was like that," she said. "He seemed so...friendly and helpful."

"I'm sorry," Phyllis said. "I know you liked him—"

"You don't think I'm upset about that, do you?" Carolyn interrupted her. "Goodness, no. Patrick Flanagan, or whatever his name really is, didn't mean anything to me."

But he might have, in time, Phyllis thought, if things had worked out differently.

That was true of everything. That was why *What might have been* were such poignant words…

That evening, after supper, Sam was waiting for Phyllis at her bedroom door. He followed her into the room and sat down on the end of the bed while she sat at the small desk.

"You look like you have something on your mind," she said.

"I do. I figure I owe you an apology."

"You do? What in the world for?"

"I probably shouldn't have tackled Patrick like that this afternoon. He might've set off that bomb and blown us all to kingdom come."

"That's exactly what he was already threatening to do," Phyllis pointed out. "You saw an opportunity to grab him while he couldn't reach the detonator, and you seized it. Honestly, there's a good chance you saved all of our lives." She smiled. "You're a hero, Sam."

"Heroism is ten per cent seein' a chance and ninety per cent luck," he said.

"And you always say you'll take all the luck you can get," she reminded him.

"Yeah, those are words to live by, all right. And I was never luckier than the day I moved in here."

"I'm not so sure about that. Being friends with me has been a lot of work…not to mention being dangerous now and then."

"I wouldn't trade a minute of it," Sam said. "But what happened today reminded me, I don't have nearly as many minutes ahead of me as I do behind me."

"That's true of both of us," Phyllis said softly.

Sam drew in a deep breath and got to his feet. "And I don't want to waste a single minute of the ones I *do* have left."

Phyllis stood up as well and told him, "Neither do I."

*One week later*

"Just get down here to the courthouse as fast as you can," Phyllis said, then broke the connection and slipped the phone back in her purse.

Sam had been making calls, too. He put away his phone and grinned. "That's all of 'em, I think," he said. "They ought to be here pretty soon. I made it sound pretty urgent."

"It *is* pretty urgent," she said. They sat down on a bench in the courthouse hallway to wait.

Over the next half-hour, people began to arrive: Carolyn, Eve, and Ronnie; Mike, his wife Sarah, and their son Bobby; Chief Ralph Whitmire, Detective Isabel Largo, and Detective Warren Latimer; Sheriff Ross Haney; and Jimmy D'Angelo. They gathered around Phyllis and Sam wanting to know what was so important that they had all been called down here.

Finally, Sam raised his hands to get their attention and said solemnly, "It looks like everybody's here, so I might as well go ahead and tell you...Phyllis has been arrested for murder."

Startled cries and denials filled the hallway. Phyllis slapped him lightly on the arm and said, "Sam!"

"Sorry, I couldn't resist," he said as a happy grin broke out across his face. "Here's the real news, folks." He slipped his arm around Phyllis's shoulders. "We're gettin' married, and all of you are invited."

"More than invited," Phyllis said. "You're going to be attending, because the ceremony is about to begin."

"Married!" Eve said. "And you didn't even let us help you plan the wedding!"

"We can have a reception, though," Carolyn said as the group practically mobbed Phyllis and Sam, hugging her and shaking his hand. "It's short notice, but I think we can put on an affair that no one will ever forget."

"Let's just hope no one is murdered at it," Eve said. "That seems like *exactly* the sort of thing that would happen in this town!"

The hubbub continued around them, but Sam leaned close to Phyllis and said quietly, "Somethin' wrong? You look a little wild-eyed all of a sudden."

"It's what Eve just said about someone being murdered at the reception," Phyllis said. "You don't think…?"

"Not this time," Sam said, and he kissed her to seal the promise.

## *Bonus Story*

# *The Coconut Bunny Butt Caper*

### A Fresh Baked Mystery Short Story

## Livia J. Washburn

I'm holding the cat, and that's one of my cousins about to
pull the cat's tail. I bet this didn't end well.

## Author's Note

This story was written before the COVID-19 virus made a
gathering like this impossible.

Both of my parents had six siblings. Easter was a big family
gathering in our Sunday best with Easter egg hunts at the
farm, with lots of food and love. Some of my best memories
are of those times.

# The Coconut Bunny Butt Caper

On a beautiful spring day under an almost cloudless blue sky, Phyllis Newsom smiled as she watched the crowd of children running and screaming across the vast green lawn. They descended on the shrubbery and flowerbeds like a swarm of locusts.

"Dang," Sam Fletcher said as he stood beside Phyllis. "Don't get between a kid and an Easter egg, that's all I've got to say."

"They're certainly enthusiastic," Phyllis agreed. "This reminds me of the big Easter egg hunts that went on when we were young, and even when Mike was a child. I remember taking him to several of them, sometimes put on by family, sometimes by the community or one of the local service clubs. People don't do things like that anymore. Not much, anyway." She shook her head. "Just another way that things have changed, I suppose."

"They've got a way of doin' that," Sam said. "But bringin' back the old days was sort of the whole idea of this fandango, wasn't it? That's what the fella told you?"

"That's right." Phyllis nodded toward a man who was walking across the lawn toward them. "Here he comes now."

The man approaching them was tall, although not as tall as Sam. He was broad-shouldered and had an air of vitality about him. His weathered, deeply tanned face, white hair, and white mustache, along with the liver spots on the back of his big, knobby-knuckled hands, showed his age, but nothing else about him did. He wore boots, jeans, a white dress shirt buttoned up to the throat, and a crisp straw Stetson.

Walking beside but just behind him was a younger, smaller man dressed in similar fashion, although his shirt was dark red instead of white. He had a closely cropped salt-and-pepper beard on his lean cheeks.

"Mrs. Newsom," the older man said as he extended a hand to Phyllis. "Phyllis. It's mighty good to see you again." After shaking with Phyllis, he turned to Sam. "I'm Buck Williams."

Sam clasped his hand firmly. The two of them were roughly the same age.

"Sam Fletcher," he said. "Pleased to meet you. No offense, but my dog's name is Buck."

"Is he a good dog?" Williams asked.

"A mighty fine one."

"Then it's an honor to share the name with him! There's not much better in this world than a good dog."

Sam grinned and said, "I reckon we're on the same page about that."

Phyllis was glad to see the two men hitting it off. She had known Zachary "Buck" Williams for many years. He and his late wife Lizabeth had been friends with Phyllis and her late husband Kenny, all of them attending the same church and belonging to the same Sunday School class.

She hadn't seen Buck in almost a decade, though. He had stopped attending church after his wife passed away. Phyllis had been surprised when he called her out of the blue to ask a favor of her.

They had chatted for a bit, with Williams and Phyllis catching up on old times, and then Williams got down to business.

"I've been keeping up with all those adventures of yours," he'd said.

"I wouldn't call them adventures," Phyllis had said. "More like…messes that I never wanted to be dragged into."

Several years earlier, after she had retired from her career as an American History teacher and she'd lost Kenny, she had decided to take in boarders—to use an old-fashioned expression—in her big, two-story house on a side street in Weatherford, Texas, a few blocks from the courthouse square. Not just any boarders, though. Phyllis had persuaded several other retired teachers to join her. Carolyn Wilbarger and Eve Turner were friends more than they were renters. In fact, they were like family.

And so was Sam. At first, Phyllis had balked at having a male boarder, but her old superintendent, who knew him, had convinced her to take a chance.

In the years since, Sam had become her best friend and confidant and partner in the other thing that had livened up her retirement far more than she had ever expected.

For some reason, she kept stumbling across murders and other mysteries, and somewhat to her own amazement, up until now she had always solved them. It was like something out of a TV show, as Carolyn pointed out from time to time with a touch of wry humor.

Phyllis had been thinking about that as she talked to Williams and continued, "Goodness gracious, Buck, you're not mixed up in some mystery, are you?"

"Nope, not at all. But if I ever was, you're sure the lady I'd call, I can tell you that! What I really wanted, though, was to see if I could recruit you for a little project I'm working on. Easter's coming up, you know."

"Yes, of course it is," Phyllis had said cautiously.

"You remember how folks used to get together and have big family parties for Easter, including Easter egg hunts for all the kids?"

"Of course I remember. It was always one of the best days of the year."

Those memories made Phyllis feel a warm, nostalgic glow. When she was a little girl, every year her parents had hosted an Easter party at their house out in the country, where there was plenty of room for all the cousins—and there were a lot of them!—to romp and play and hunt eggs. And all the good food! People brought a wide variety of delicious things to eat. Phyllis would never forget those wonderful times, as long as she lived.

"Well, I want to do the same thing," Williams had said. "I've got this big ranch house out here, with a front yard practically the size of a football field, and I want to throw a big Easter shindig with games and food and an egg hunt. I'll invite everybody from the whole county to join in the fun."

"Why, that sounds wonderful! But...you want my help with it?"

"I remember from the days we all went to church together that there's nobody better than you at putting together Dinner on the Grounds and ice cream socials and fish fries, not to mention all those holiday parties you've thrown. Seems to me that you're the perfect person to be in charge of this Easter blow-out."

"Well, I...I'm flattered, Buck, but that sounds like an awfully big job..."

"I'm sure you can get your friends to help you, and if it's a matter of money, well, don't worry about that, I'll pay for everything and we'll do it up nice. What do you say, Phyllis? For old time's sake?"

She'd been about to say that it sounded like too much work, but then she'd thought about how Sam and Carolyn and Eve always pitched in, and if Buck Williams was offering to pay for everything...then she couldn't really find a good excuse...and those Easter parties had been *so* much fun...

"All right," she had said, "I suppose I can give it a try."

Later, when she told Sam about it, he'd just grinned and said, "Any time I've seen you 'give something a try', you've succeeded. You're just like Yoda. Do or do not. There is no try."

"Thanks... I think," Phyllis had responded to that.

Now, as she stood in front of the large, white-painted ranch house and looked around the vast lawn, she was proud of what she and her friends had been able to accomplish.

The party had a definite fair-like atmosphere. Down one side of the lawn were booths for games like ring toss, as well as face painting and even a dunking booth. On the other side of the lawn was the food area. At Carolyn's urging—because Carolyn's competitive nature was always lurking just under the surface—there were two cooking contests going on. One was for goodies—cakes, pies, cookies, fudge, homemade ice cream, etc.—while the other included all sorts of potluck foods such as chili, beans, black-eyed peas, and casseroles. Phyllis hadn't entered either contest, but that didn't mean she hadn't come up with a special recipe for the Easter party. She made a flavorful Muffaletta pasta salad in the tradition of her favorite sandwich and chocolate chip cookies for the goodies table that weren't entered in the contest.

After introducing himself to Sam, Williams gestured toward the man with him and said, "This is Fred McKenzie, my foreman. He helps me keep this place going."

McKenzie shook hands with both Phyllis and Sam, then said, "It's a real honor to meet you, Mrs. Newsom. I'm a big fan of your recipes."

"You bake, Mr. McKenzie?"

"He does more than that," Williams said. "He represents this ranch in the chuckwagon cookoff they have every year. Nobody does up a better batch of chuckwagon beans than ol' Fred."

"That sounds mighty good," Sam said.

"You can try them if you want to. Fred's entered a pot of 'em in that potluck contest we're having."

"Now, that's not necessary, Mr. Williams," McKenzie said. "I don't like to brag. My beans aren't *that* good."

"Well, we'll just wait and see, I reckon."

"Speaking of that, I'd better go tend to them." McKenzie nodded to Phyllis and Sam. "Sure nice to meet you folks."

He headed off down the line of tables and booths where the contest entries were.

Williams motioned for Phyllis to come along with him and said, "While those kids are rooting around out there for the eggs, let me show you something, Phyllis." He added, "You, too, Sam."

They walked with him. The potluck dishes were first, with the wide assortment of desserts farther along. Between the two areas stood a large, blue-and-white striped canvas tent with an open front and sides, forming a shaded area in which a table was set up. A large wicker basket rested on that table.

Inside the basket rested two large golden eggs with a silver tray between them. The eggs were plastic, but their filigreed surfaces were quite impressive. A small, almost unnoticeable latch in the middle of each egg indicated that they opened into two halves.

Phyllis smiled at the silver tray with its round cover and said, "Is that…"

"It is," Williams confirmed. "The special treat you made for the prize basket. After you dropped it off earlier, I made sure it went in a place of honor."

Sam said, "You mean under there is the famous Coconut Bunny Butt?"

Phyllis looked sharply at him. "How did you know about that?"

He smiled and said, "I heard you mutterin' to yourself about it a few days ago. When you overhear somebody talkin' about a coconut bunny butt, believe you me, it gets your attention."

Williams reached out, took hold of the cover, and lifted it from the tray. "There you go," he said.

In the center of the tray rested a round cake with white icing covered in white coconut. It was small, about half the size of a regular cake, and bore a distinct resemblance to the rear end of a cottontail bunny. Large marshmallows also covered in icing and coconut were arranged to look like the tail and feet, and small pink rolled fruit were cut to make the pads on the hind feet. The cake sat on a round bed of green coconut that looked like grass, with jelly beans to represent eggs placed carefully around it. Pink and white ears were cut out of paper and stuck to the plate on the opposite side from the feet.

"I was trying to make it look like the bunny is going into his burrow, so that's why you can only see his, ah, rear end," Phyllis explained.

Sam chuckled, then said, "That's downright whimsical, especially for you, Phyllis."

She shrugged and said, "I just thought it would be funny."

"It is," Sam assured her.

"And it's a fine companion piece for those golden eggs," Williams said. He leaned closer to Phyllis. "One of those eggs is pretty special, you know. It's really a prize egg."

He picked it up, turned the catch in the middle, and opened the top half to reveal a roll of greenbacks with a string tied around them.

Sam let out a surprised whistle and said, "That's quite a wad of cash."

"Five thousand dollars," Williams said. "It goes to whichever kid is lucky enough to find the matching egg. There'll be a special hunt later, after I've announced the prize. The eggs out there now just have the usual candy and dollar bills, with a few fives and tens scattered among 'em."

Sam said, "When you throw an Easter egg hunt, you put on a good one."

"That was the idea," Williams said, smiling and nodding. He closed the golden egg and replaced it next to the coconut bunny butt cake.

At that moment, Eve Turner walked up and said, "Phyllis, Carolyn wants to talk to—" She stopped short, looked up at Buck Williams, smiled and said, "Why, I don't believe we've been introduced." She put out her hand. "I'm Eve Turner."

"Oh, I know who you are, Miz Turner," Williams responded with a smile of his own as he clasped Eve's hand and then patted it with his other hand at the same time. "I've read your book. It was mighty fine."

"Oh, aren't you kind? There's talk of making a television series out of it, you know."

"I heard that. Hope it comes about. It'd sure make a good one."

Phyllis had witnessed Eve flirting with men so many times that she'd come to expect it. She let the opening salvos in this exchange run their course, then asked, "Did you say Carolyn wants to talk to me?"

Eve said, "Yes, that's right."

"Do you know what about?"

Eve had already turned back to Williams. She said over her shoulder, "No, dear, you'll just have to ask her."

Phyllis nodded. As she looked around for Carolyn, Sam pointed with a thumb toward the line of food booths and said, "I'm gonna sample some of those, I think."

"Of course," Phyllis told him. "I'll see you later."

She spotted Carolyn down at the end of the line of tables where the desserts were set out and started in that direction. Before she got there, however, a man standing behind one of the tables stopped her by saying, "Hello, Mrs. Newsom."

She looked over at him and said, "Hello," then paused and added, "I don't mean to be rude, but do we know each other?"

He smiled. "I was in your class."

Phyllis hadn't been teaching for very many years before she realized just how quickly the children who went through her classes grew up. As eighth-graders, they were only a handful of years away from being adults, legally, at least, and

Phyllis had long since come to accept that many of the children she'd taught were not only grown-ups, they were parents themselves and, in many cases, grandparents. She figured that some of them might even be great-grandparents by now.

So she was used to encountering former students. She said, "I'm sorry, you'll have to refresh my memory…"

"I'm Darrell Culverhouse."

"Oh," Phyllis said, and she couldn't keep the surprise out of her voice.

For a second, she worried that she might have offended the man, but he grinned and said, "I see that you remember me."

"Well…"

He held up his hands and said, "No, I get it, believe me. I was such a monster the whole year, how could you ever forget me? I'm sure all the other eighth grade teachers have terrible memories of me."

"I wouldn't call them terrible—"

"I would." Culverhouse sobered. "And all those kids I went to school with, the ones I beat up and terrorized, I imagine most of them hate me."

You wouldn't think, looking at this handsome, clean-cut young man now, that he had been one of the biggest bullies Phyllis had ever dealt with in her teaching career. He was right: he really *had* terrorized many of his classmates.

"I'm sure people have forgotten all about that," Phyllis said, although she knew most of them probably hadn't. Such memories tended to stay with a person. "Anyway, when people grow up, they change. At least, sometimes."

"I hope I did," Culverhouse said. "I've tried, I can promise you that."

"What are you doing these days?"

"I was in the service for a while," he said. "Marines."

"You're to be congratulated for that. And thanked."

"Since I've been back, I never have really settled on any-thing, so I've been doing a little of everything. Some roofing, worked in a car wash…" He shrugged. "Just odd jobs. You know."

To change the subject, Phyllis said, "Have you entered the dessert contest?"

Culverhouse gestured with pride at the plates of cookies in front of him. "You wouldn't think a guy like me would be much of one for baking cookies, would you? I picked it up somewhere along the way. My mother passed away when I was pretty young, you know, so it was just me and my dad. He worked all the time, so I guess I figured if I was ever going to have anything like this, I'd have to learn how to do it my-self."

"Most boys would have just bought cookies, I think."

"I didn't have enough money for that. And after I'd gotten in trouble enough times for stealing them…well, I guess I shouldn't have said anything about that, should I?"

"Clearly you *have* changed since you were young, Darrell, and I'm glad. Now, if you'll excuse me…"

She'd been on her way to talk to Carolyn, and she hadn't forgotten about that. It was always good to talk to her former students, though—even the ones who had been a problem, like Darrell Culverhouse.

"Sure, I just wanted to say hi." He lifted a hand in farewell.

Phyllis walked along the line of tables until she reached the one where Carolyn was standing next to a couple of pies. She gestured toward them and said, "Phyllis, would you look at this?"

"Why, that's adorable," Phyllis said. She looked at the young woman standing behind the table. "Easter bunny pies?"

"That's right," the woman said.

The crust of each pie had a rabbit drawn on it with what appeared to be cake icing. An interesting technique, Phyllis thought. And definitely cute.

"Whoever heard of putting cake icing on pies?" Carolyn said.

"Well, it's unusual," Phyllis admitted, "but also very clever." She smiled at the young woman. "What's your name, dear?"

"Jessie Scribner."

Phyllis smiled at the little girl who was peeking out from behind Jessie Scribner's leg. "And who is this?"

Jessie put her hand on the girl's blond curls and said, "This is my daughter Ashley."

"Hello, Ashley," Phyllis said, then smiled again as the little girl turned her head and pressed her face against her mother's leg. "She's shy."

"Yeah, she really is."

Phyllis said to Carolyn, "I'm glad you showed me this. I really like it."

Carolyn frowned, and Phyllis could tell that her friend hadn't called her down here because she was impressed with what Jessie Scribner had done. Carolyn was upset about something, although Phyllis had no idea what it might be.

In order to find out, she said, "Why don't we take a look at some of the other entries?" and put a hand on Carolyn's arm to steer her further along the line of tables and booths. She smiled back at Jessie and added, "Good luck in the contest, dear."

"Thank you, Mrs. Newsom. That means a lot coming from you. I've read all your magazine columns and love your recipes."

When they were out of easy earshot, Phyllis lowered her voice and asked, "What's wrong, Carolyn? I know you've got something on your mind."

"It just seems *wrong* to me to use cake icing on a pie."

"I've seen recipes that call for that before. It's not that common, but I wouldn't call it *wrong*." Phyllis looked shrewdly at her friend. "You're not worried that Jessie's pies will beat yours in the contest, are you? I've never known you to get upset about honest competition."

"No, it's not that." Carolyn sighed. "You don't know who she is, do you?"

Phyllis shook her head. "No, I'm afraid not. A former student of yours? I just ran into one of mine. But Jessie didn't act like she knew you."

"She doesn't. But I've heard about her. Or rather, the little girl."

"That adorable little girl? Ashley, wasn't that her name?"

"Yes. She's very ill."

"Really?" Phyllis said. "She looked fine."

"It's some sort of heart defect, I believe. Anyway, she needs surgery, and her mother is, well, a single mother and has no insurance and can't afford it. She's been trying to raise money on-line. One of those crowd-funding things, you know. So I thought it might lift her spirits if she were to...well, win the contest..."

Phyllis's eyebrows rose. She said, "You know I'm one of the judges, Carolyn. Are you asking me to *fix* the contest?"

"No, of course not! But I didn't think it would do any harm to, well, keep all the circumstances in mind while you're coming to a decision."

"And here I thought you were upset about the silly cake icing and wanted that girl to be disqualified because of it."

"Good grief, no! Although to be honest, using icing that way still doesn't seem right to me. And I'm sure she used the store-bought kind, too, that you squeeze out of a tube."

Phyllis smiled but managed not to laugh. She had been accused many times of being old-fashioned, and there was some truth to that, but Carolyn was even more traditional.

She was also soft-hearted underneath the gruff exterior that had developed over decades of teaching elementary school.

"I don't know how the contest is going to come out, but maybe we can help somehow with Ms. Scribner's other problem. I'm sure we could come up with some donations for her crowd-funding campaign."

"All right," Carolyn said, nodding.

Most of the hidden eggs had been found by now, so the frenzied running around by the children was slowing down. Quite a few of them were trooping back to the area where dozens of picnic tables had been set up. They compared the eggs they had found, and kids being kids, some of them were throwing the brightly colored plastic eggs at each other, too.

Phyllis left Carolyn at the table where her Easter peanut thumbprint cookies were displayed and walked back toward the house, passing the blue-and-white-striped tent where Eve was still talking to Buck Williams as they stood in front of the prize basket display. She looked at the potluck dishes entered in the contest, many of them in crockpots plugged into power strips that were in turn plugged into long extension cords that ran toward the ranch house. Most of the food looked quite appetizing. Some of the contestants were already serving up samples, although the official tasting and judging would be later.

She spotted Sam standing closer to the ranch house in a group with several other men. Phyllis recognized them as retired teachers and knew some of them had worked with Sam when he taught and coached at Poolville. As she approached, he said, "See you later, fellas," and turned to meet her.

"You seem to be having a good time," she said.

"Who wouldn't be? Beautiful weather, friendly folks, fine food. Nobody could ask for much more than that."

"I'm glad," Phyllis said. "You sampled some of the potluck dishes?"

His grin was enough to answer that, but he said, "They were all good except one. That one was cold. I guess the fella was having trouble with his crockpot."

Buck Williams, accompanied by Eve, strode back to the ranch house's big front porch where a portable public address system was set up. He turned on the microphone and leaned closer to it. Phyllis and Sam turned toward him to listen.

"I want to thank all you folks for coming out today," he said. "It's really warmed this old codger's heart to see such a good old-fashioned Easter celebration. Looks like the kids have finished hunting eggs…for now. I say that because we're gonna have another hunt later this afternoon, with a very special prize egg for one lucky youngster. Now I'll invite you to play some games, get your little ones' faces painted, and listen to some good music. We've got a number of acts fixing to perform up here on the front porch. So have fun!"

He moved down from the porch and waved to a trio carrying guitars to take his place. They did, and in a few minutes began playing country music. Some of the people paired off and began to dance in front of the ranch house.

"Dancin' on Easter," Sam said to Phyllis with mock solemnity, shaking his head. "I thought ol' Buck was a good Southern Baptist. He must be backslid."

Phyllis watched as Buck talked to Eve for a minute, then went into the tent and closed the front and sides of it. Eve joined Phyllis and Sam.

Phyllis nodded toward the tent and asked, "What's Buck being so mysterious about? Is he getting that special prize egg so he can hide it?"

"That's right," Eve said. "He offered to let me hide it, but I told him since it was his idea…and his money…he should do the honors." She smiled. "He's a very nice man, Phyllis. You should have introduced me to him a long time ago."

"Well, I haven't really seen that much of him in recent years," Phyllis explained.

"I certainly hope to see more—"

Sam interrupted Eve by saying, "Hold on. Something's wrong."

Phyllis saw that he was looking past her and turned to see what had provoked that reaction. She caught her breath as she spotted Buck Williams pushing out of the tent, obviously unsteady on his feet. He lifted a trembling hand toward his head. He wasn't wearing his cowboy hat anymore, and Phyllis saw a splotch of red in his thick white hair.

She knew that had to be blood.

Eve saw it, too, gasped in alarm, and started toward Williams. So did Phyllis, but Sam, with his long legs, reached the rancher before either of them.

Other people were starting to notice Williams' behavior and realize that he was hurt. Several cried out in surprise and fear. Williams took another couple of reeling steps before Sam clasped his arm with a strong hand and steadied him.

"Take it easy, Buck," Sam said. "I've got you. What happened?"

"I...I dunno," Williams said. "I went in there...to get that prize egg...and when I picked it up and turned around...somebody walloped me from behind..."

"Oh, you poor man," Eve said as she clutched Williams' other arm. "You're bleeding."

"You need to go sit down," Phyllis said. "Sam, can you help Buck up to the porch?"

"Sure." Sam waved his free hand at the people who had begun to crowd around. "Step back if you would, folks. Give us some room."

With Sam on one side and Eve on the other, they began helping Williams toward the house as the crowd parted. The musicians on the porch had noticed some sort of commotion going on and had stopped playing, but the air still buzzed with talk as everyone wondered what had happened.

Phyllis started to follow Sam, Eve, and Williams, but she stopped short after only one step and pushed the canvas aside to look into the tent.

The whole prize basket was gone, including the coconut bunny butt cake.

Phyllis stepped closer to the table where the basket had been sitting but didn't touch anything. She leaned over to look at the ground behind the table. Like everywhere else on the big lawn in front of the ranch house, it had been mowed recently and cut fairly short. It had been long enough since any rain had fallen that the ground was completely dry. She didn't see any footprints or anything else that might be important.

Except that the canvas rear wall of the tent was bunched up in the middle, with a gap at the bottom, as if someone had pulled it up enough to crawl under it, taking the prize basket with them.

That was the only way it could have happened. Phyllis had seen Buck Williams enter the tent, and no one had gone in after him. No one had left the tent until Williams himself pushed the canvas aside and staggered out.

Phyllis's mind went back to the moment earlier in the afternoon when Williams had opened the prize egg and showed her and Sam the roll of money. He hadn't exactly waved it around and drawn attention to it, but anyone who happened to be looking into the tent and watching closely enough could have caught a glimpse of the greenbacks.

It seemed unlikely that anybody could have crawled into the tent and back out like that with no one noticing, but with music playing and people dancing and excited children running around and playing games, a lot had been going on. Such a brazen theft and assault would have taken both luck and daring—but someone could have pulled it off.

Obviously, someone had.

Phyllis stepped out of the tent and looked toward the ranch house. Most of the people at the party had gathered in front of the house to see what was going on. Some of those who had brought potluck dishes or goodies for the contest were still standing in their booths, but others had abandoned them to join the crowd.

Quickly, Phyllis moved to the side of the tent and went along it to the back. She looked at the ground there, too, and spotted a slight depression that could have come from someone's knee as they put weight on it while getting up. She looked both directions but didn't see anything out of the ordinary.

Then something caught her eye in a line of shrubbery about ten feet away, directly behind the tent. That growth might have helped conceal whoever the culprit was, too.

She didn't want to mess up any potential evidence—eventually the sheriff's department would have be called, since Buck Williams had been attacked—but she wanted to take a closer look at whatever she had spotted. Circling around the area where someone had crawled out the back of the tent, she walked carefully toward the thick shrubs.

When she got closer, she leaned down and put her hands on her bluejean-clad knees to brace herself as she peered through a gap in the branches. She caught her breath as she recognized the prize basket she had last seen inside the tent. She edged closer.

It looked like someone had shoved the basket back there to hide it, no doubt after taking the prize egg and the money it contained. The other egg was lying on the ground, open and empty. The silver tray was still there, too, with the cake on it, looking considerably the worse for wear. Phyllis's lips tightened.

Someone had scooped up a handful of coconut bunny butt and eaten it!

That paled in comparison to assaulting Buck Williams and stealing five thousand dollars, of course, but it still bothered Phyllis. She straightened from her crouch, pulled her cell phone from her pocket, and called her son Mike, who was a deputy in the Parker County Sheriff's Department. Mike would have come to the Easter party with his wife Sarah and Phyllis's grandson Bobby, but Bobby had a cold, and Mike had to work.

And since he was on duty, he was getting the call on this crime.

A fire department ambulance showed up a short time later, along with the Sheriff's Department cruiser, and a couple of EMTs checked out Buck Williams' head injury.

"That cut on your head isn't too bad, Mr. Williams," one of them told him. "But we need to take you to the hospital anyway. Any time you've been hit in the head like that, you need to be checked out more thoroughly than we can do here."

"Fine, but not yet," Williams responded firmly. He had gotten his senses back after the wallop and now seemed to be more angry than injured, as far as Phyllis could tell. "Not until we figure out the polecat who's responsible for what happened."

As he regained his composure while sitting on the ranch house's front porch and waiting for help to arrive, it hadn't taken long for him to ask about the golden egg with the money in it. He'd been furious when Phyllis told him it was gone.

That was when the ambulance and the sheriff's cruiser pulled up with their lights flashing, and while the EMTs were tending to Williams, Phyllis's son Mike took her aside and said, "All right, Mom, tell me what happened here."

"First of all, you need to make sure no one leaves. I can't be certain no one slipped off between the time I called you and when you got here. I might have missed it if they did. I didn't see anyone leaving, though. And the thief *could* have taken off before we realized that had happened, but I doubt that. It was all pretty quick."

"You're saying that whoever attacked Mr. Williams is probably still here."

"I think so, yes."

Mike spoke into the radio attached to his collar and got back a quick response that a unit would block the driveway leading from the ranch headquarters to the farm-to-market road half a mile away.

Once that was done, Phyllis filled him in on the afternoon's events and then led him to the tent where the attack had taken place.

Sam was standing at the tent's rear corner with his arms folded. "I've been guardin' the scene," he told Mike. "Nobody's messed with anything. The ground's just like it was, and that prize basket's over there in the bushes where Phyllis found it."

Mike took gloves from his pocket and started to pull them on so he could gather the evidence.

"You're not callin' out the crime scene fellas?" Sam asked.

"Assault and theft are serious crimes," Mike said, "but they wouldn't be considered major cases and the department has limited resources. We've all been trained to collect evidence and photograph and document a crime scene."

"What happened is a major crime to Buck Williams," Phyllis pointed out.

"And we'll get to the bottom of it," Mike promised.

He took pictures of the inside of the tent, the area behind it, and the prize basket that had been shoved up among the bushes.

"That's the famous coconut bunny butt your mom made," Sam pointed out.

"It's not famous," Phyllis said.

"With a name like that, it will be as soon as this story hits the news."

She was afraid he was right about that. That would teach her to give in to a fit of whimsy, she told herself with a sigh.

Mike gathered and bagged everything for evidence purposes, then he, Phyllis, and Sam walked back up to the house in time to hear Buck Williams declare that he wasn't going to the hospital until this crime was solved.

Mike introduced himself to the rancher and asked, "Mr. Williams, do you have any enemies who would do a thing like this?"

"A fella doesn't have to have any enemies to get robbed," Williams replied. "He just has to have something that some lowlife scoundrel wants bad enough to steal!"

His foreman, Fred McKenzie, was standing beside him while Williams sat on a bench. McKenzie put a hand on his shoulder and said, "Take it easy, Buck. You don't want to work yourself into a state when you've been hit in the head like that. We don't know yet how much damage that varmint did."

Williams sighed and nodded. "I reckon you're right." He looked up at Mike. "To answer your question, Deputy, no, I don't know of any enemies who'd want to do this. I get along pretty well with most folks, I think. All the people here this afternoon are either my friends or folks who wanted to come out on Easter Sunday afternoon for a good time."

"Well...if there's no likely place to start... I guess we'll have to search everybody."

Mike didn't sound happy about that, and Phyllis didn't blame him. There were so many people here that searching them would take a long time, and some of them were already starting to grumble about not being allowed to leave.

"Mike," she said, "could we talk for a minute?"

He had a look of gratitude on his face as he turned to her. "Sure, Mom. Excuse me, Mr. Williams."

The rancher pointed at Phyllis and said, "You listen to your mama, Deputy. I'll bet she's solved this thing already!"

Mike nodded politely, led Phyllis off to the side, and said quietly, "You *haven't* solved it…have you?"

He had a definite note of hope in his voice.

She hated to disappoint him, but she shook her head and said, "No, I'm afraid not." She wasn't very happy about what she had to tell him next, either, but she went on, "I have an idea, though. As you said, a place for you to start."

"You mean a suspect?"

Phyllis drew in a breath. "There's a young man here named Darrell Culverhouse," she said. "He was in my class, oh, ten or twelve years ago."

"All right," Mike said, nodding for her to go on.

"He was a terrible bully at the time, and he admitted that he used to steal things."

"A lot of kids do," Mike pointed out. "Petty stealing, I mean, not the bullying part. Although too many do that, too."

"Yes, but I was talking to Darrell earlier, and he told me that he's had a hard time of it since he got out of the service. Can't hold a job, doesn't have any real family life… He entered one of the cooking contests, and he was standing close enough to that tent where the prize basket was that he could have seen Mr. Williams showing Sam and me the money that was in that golden egg."

Mike's eyes widened. "He took out five grand and flashed it around?"

"Not blatantly, you understand. But he showed Sam and me, as I said, and other people could have seen, too."

Mike thought about it for a moment and then nodded. "From what you're telling me, it sounds like I need to talk to this Darrell Culverhouse."

"He's not the only one," Phyllis said.

"There's somebody else?"

Now Phyllis really hated to continue, but she did so anyway. "There's a young woman here named Jessie Scribner. I just met her today. She's a single mother with a small child, and Carolyn tells me that the little girl has a medical condition that needs surgery."

"Surgery that the mother can't afford, I'm guessing."

"That's right. She's trying to raise money for it with one of those crowd-funding things on the Internet."

"If you're talking about major surgery, then five thousand bucks would be just a drop in the bucket when it comes to the medical bills."

"That's true," Phyllis said. "But to someone who's desperate, the sight of that much money...especially a roll of cash...might be too much temptation to resist."

"Would this girl Jessie be able to wallop a big guy like Mr. Williams?"

"If she used something to hit him...maybe. I don't know what it would have been, but I don't think we can rule it out."

"Neither do I," Mike said. "At least we've got a couple of possible motives. Point them out to me, and I'll take it from there."

Eve didn't want to leave Buck Williams' side, and Carolyn wasn't going to leave Eve, so Phyllis and Sam waited on the porch with them while Mike talked to the two people Phyllis had told him about.

Everyone else had spread out around the lawn again. Some of the kids had started playing again, and the adults had congregated into small groups to gossip and complain about being forced to stay here while the investigation went on. Phyllis knew that Mike wouldn't be able to keep them here very long for a crime that didn't involve murder.

She had pointed out Darrell Culverhouse and Jessie Scribner to him, as he'd requested, and she watched as he approached Culverhouse and motioned for the young man to follow him. They moved off away from the others and spoke for a minute or so, and then Phyllis could tell the moment when Culverhouse realized he was a suspect. He stiffened and took a step backward. Mike raised a hand and moved a step forward, obviously telling Culverhouse to take it easy.

Instead, Culverhouse turned suddenly and broke into a run.

Mike reacted as he'd been trained to do. He pursued a possible suspect fleeing the scene. Within just a few steps, he started to catch up to Culverhouse. Reaching out, he clamped his hands on the young man's shoulders and took him down. Both of them sprawled on the ground and rolled on the recently mown grass.

The brief chase excited the crowd. A few people yelled questions about what was going on.

With Sam beside her, Phyllis hurried to the spot where Mike now had Darrell Culverhouse lying face down on the ground with his arms pulled behind his back. Mike fastened restraints around his wrists.

After climbing to his feet, Mike reached down and hauled Culverhouse upright. "What was that all about?" he demanded. "Why'd you take off like that?"

"You were about to arrest me for attacking Mr. Williams and stealing that money!"

"How did you know money had been stolen?"

"Everybody out here knows it," Culverhouse said. "That old bull was bellowing about it enough."

Mike looked over at Phyllis, who shrugged and nodded. Buck Williams had been so upset when he found out about the golden egg being gone that numerous people could have overheard him, and that would be all it took to spread the story throughout the crowd.

"All I did was ask you where you were when Mr. Williams was attacked," Mike said.

"Yeah, but I know where that goes," Culverhouse responded scornfully. "I've been questioned by the cops before. You were just getting ready to accuse me of walloping that old guy and taking his money."

"Do you have a record? You know it won't do any good to lie."

"I've been arrested before, but I've never been convicted of anything. I never did any jail time other than overnight in the city lockup."

"What were you arrested for?"

"Disorderly conduct, public intoxication, misdemeanor theft." Culverhouse's shoulders rose and fell. "Nothing that bad."

He turned his head and looked at Phyllis. She saw pain and humiliation and disappointment in his eyes. She knew he believed she had pigeonholed him based on his past and pointed him out to Mike for that reason.

*Once a bad guy, always a bad guy.*

And honestly, he wasn't wrong.

"So instead of answering my questions, you decided to run."

"I didn't figure you'd believe me," Culverhouse said. Again he glanced at Phyllis. "Seems like nobody does."

Again she felt a pang of guilt, but it was followed rapidly by the realization that Culverhouse had made his own decision to flee and couldn't lay that at her feet, even though he might like to.

Anyway, he hadn't established that he was innocent.

"Why don't you give it a try and answer my question?" Mike said. "Where were you when Mr. Williams was attacked?"

Sullenly, Culverhouse said, "I was at my table with the cookies I entered in the contest. I saw him when he came out of the tent with his head bloody."

"Is there anybody who can back up that story?"

"I don't know." Culverhouse looked frustrated now. "There was a couple with a kid...a little boy...I told him he could have one of the cookies, and he was eating it when Williams came out of the tent about fifty feet away. The dad saw him and made some comment about something being wrong. If you'll let me look around, I might be able to find them."

Phyllis felt a surprising moment of relief when she heard Darrell Culverhouse explain that there were witnesses who could clear his name—assuming, of course, that he was telling the truth.

"Which is your booth?" Mike asked the young man. Culverhouse nodded toward it. Mike took hold of his arm and went on, "Come with me. There are folding chairs behind those tables. You're going to sit down and not make any more trouble for a few minutes."

"Are you going to let me look for those people?"

"In a few minutes," Mike said again.

"They might have left already!"

"We'll both hope that they haven't." Mike took him behind the table in the booth. "Now park it."

"Are you going to take these cuffs off me?"

"No, and you're lucky I didn't put you in the back seat of my car. Those seats are really uncomfortable."

Culverhouse sighed and said, "Yeah, I know."

Phyllis and Sam had trailed Mike, hanging back a little so as not to get in his way. He rejoined them and said, "All right, now I'll talk to that lady with the sick little girl."

"I really don't think she would have done it," Phyllis said. "I don't think she *could* have done it."

Mike frowned at her. "Earlier you said she might have."

"I know, but I just don't believe she would—"

"That's your good nature and kind heart kicking in," Mike told her. "I have to question all the likely suspects, and I need to find that golden egg." His forehead creased again. "You said it was a match for the other one in the prize basket?"

"That's right."

"Same size and everything?"

"Yes, I think they were identical."

Mike took out his phone and looked at the photos of the evidence he had made before locking it in his cruiser. He pointed to the other golden egg as Phyllis and Sam leaned in to peer at the screen.

"That's too big for somebody to just stick it in a pocket," he said. "A lady could put it in a big purse, I suppose."

"But it would have to be done quickly," Phyllis said. "The thief couldn't walk around with it. He must have hidden it as soon as he got rid of the prize basket."

Mike looked from side to side along the row of tables where the contest entries were set up. "Then it's got to be around here somewhere," he muttered. "The woman you mentioned, Jessie Scribner, she was close by. In fact, she's standing behind her table with her little girl right now." He squared his shoulders. "I'd better go question her." He paused, as if he expected Phyllis to object again. "Mom? I said I was going to question Jessie Scribner—"

"Yes, dear, go ahead," Phyllis told him. She patted him on the arm. "You do what you need to do."

Mike looked a little confused, but he headed down the line of booths toward Jessie's.

Sam's eyes narrowed as he gazed at Phyllis. "I've seen that look before," he said. "You got all distracted for a minute, and then the light dawned. I could see it. You've solved the case, haven't you?"

"It was the talk about where the egg could be hidden. There was something you said earlier, Sam, that made sense the way you said it...but it could make sense another way, too. But there's only one way to find out." She started back toward the house, Sam keeping up easily with his long legs. "When you sampled some of the potluck dishes, you mentioned that one of them was cold and said that the person's crockpot must not be working. But what if that crockpot was turned off?"

"Son of a gun!" Sam said. "Because you couldn't put a plastic egg in a pot of hot beans without riskin' it meltin' a little. And you wouldn't want it to melt if it had five grand in greenbacks inside it."

"That's right. Do you remember which—"

Sam didn't let her finish the question. Instead, two swift strides brought him in front of a table with a large crockpot full of pinto beans sitting on it. He plunged his hand into the beans and came up clutching a large, golden, plastic egg with beans and sauce dripping off of it.

Phyllis turned and called, "Mike!"

The urgency in her voice made his head snap around. He had been talking to Jessie Scribner, and she looked both upset and angry. Her expression turned baffled, though, as Mike abandoned his questioning and hurried toward his mother.

Mike looked past her at Sam standing there holding the egg aloft. "Is that—"

"It is," Phyllis said. "Sam just found it in that pot of beans."

"Phyllis told me to check there," Sam added. "She was right, just like always."

"Whose crockpot is that?" Mike asked.

Phyllis picked up the entry card on the table next to the pot and showed it to him. Mike nodded, took the card, and started toward the house.

"Hang on to that, Sam, and bring it with you," Mike said over his shoulder. "I don't want to break the evidence chain just yet."

People saw what was going on. Excited muttering followed them to the ranch house, where the crowd parted to let Mike, Phyllis, and Sam through. As they went up the steps onto the porch, Buck Williams caught sight of the egg in Sam's hand and exclaimed, "That's it! That's the prize egg! Where'd you find it?"

"Where Mr. McKenzie put it," Mike said, nodding toward Fred McKenzie, Williams' foreman. "In the pot of beans he entered in the potluck contest but left cold so that no one would be too interested in them."

McKenzie, who had been standing near Williams, tried to look flabbergasted and stammered, "But…but I never… Anybody could've put that egg in my beans!"

"But I have a witness who saw *you* do it," Mike said, half-turning and pointing toward Jessie Scribner, who was still frowning angrily in his direction. "And the fact that you brought a pot of beans and left them cold indicates premeditation. That's proof you planned this whole thing."

Phyllis knew that Mike was bluffing about the witness. Jessie Scribner hadn't told him any such thing. But Fred McKenzie didn't know that.

McKenzie looked around wildly as if he were going to continue denying his guilt, but then a snarl suddenly twisted his face.

"Of course I planned it," he said. "You reckon a measly five grand is enough to pay me for all the hard work I put into making this place a success. But Buck never appreciated that, not ever! So I figured I'd ruin his little Easter party. That'd hurt him worse than losing the money!"

With his face as dark as a thundercloud, Buck Williams rose from the chair where he'd been sitting. McKenzie's head darted back and forth as he looked like he was going to bolt, but then he snarled again and lunged at Williams.

Mike was ready and grabbed him from behind, pinning his arms. He wrestled McKenzie to the porch and fastened restraints on him.

Sam held out the egg toward Williams. "It's a mite sticky," he said, "but I think this is yours."

Half an hour later, the Easter party was back in full swing. There were still potluck and goodie contests to be judged and ribbons to be awarded.

There wouldn't be a second egg hunt, though, because the prize egg—and the five thousand dollars—had already been given out. All it had taken was for Phyllis to tell Buck Williams about Jessie Scribner and her daughter Ashley's plight as Williams was being loaded in the ambulance.

He had still been holding the golden egg, but he tossed it back to Sam and said to Phyllis, "You make sure that gal gets this money, and I'll work with the hospital and the docs to see that her little girl gets the surgery she needs."

"I think we can raise a lot of donations," Phyllis had told him. "My friend Carolyn is very good at things like that."

A grin had plucked at Williams' mouth. "You tell your friend Eve to come visit me."

"I don't think I'll have to tell her," Phyllis said. "I have a feeling you'll be seeing a lot of her."

Williams was still grinning as the ambulance doors closed.

Now that the celebration was continuing, even with Buck Williams gone for the moment, Phyllis went looking for Darrell Culverhouse with Sam at her side. They found the young man at his booth.

"Mind if I try one of those chocolate chip cookies?" Sam asked.

"I don't know," Culverhouse said. "You're with *her*."

"I understand why you're angry with me, Darrell," she told him, "but at the same time, if you're honest with yourself, *you'll* understand why I suspected you. I haven't been around you in years, and although you told me you'd changed, I had no proof of that."

"You still don't."

"No, I don't suppose I do," she said. "So what you need is a chance to prove yourself. How do you feel about ranch work? Mr. Williams is going to be short a hand now. Of course, you couldn't come right in and take over the foreman's job. You'd be at the bottom of the ladder."

Culverhouse grunted. "Not the first time." He cocked his head a little to the side. "You think he might consider hiring me?"

"I think I can convince him to give you a chance. If I can't, I have a friend who can, no doubt about that."

"Well…it actually sounds like a pretty good deal. I've always liked working outside, and I get along pretty good with animals. I never really thought about it but… I think I'd like to give it a try."

"We'll see if we can make it happen, then."

He summoned up a smile and said, "Thank you, Mrs. Newsom. I guess I was kind of a jerk back when I was in school—"

"You were."

"And I still can be now, but I'll try to do better."

"I'm sure you will," Phyllis told him.

As they walked back toward the ranch house, Sam said, "That was a nice thing you just did, tryin' to help out that young fella. I hope he doesn't let you down."

"I don't think he will. But just because there's a chance of that happening, it doesn't mean we can give up trying, does it?"

"Nope, it sure doesn't." Sam was quiet for a moment, then went on, "With the case bein' solved and all, I reckon Mike won't have to lock up that coconut bunny butt as evidence after all."

"It's a cake. You don't have to keep calling it by that other name."

"Yeah, but I *like* the other name."

"Anyway, what does it matter whether or not it's evidence?"

"I never got to try it," Sam said. "Now that I know there's such a thing as a coconut bunny butt, I figure I've got to eat some of it."

"After it was shoved in the bushes like that? Heavens, no." She linked her arm with his as they walked on. "I'll make you a fresh one."

# Recipes

# Lemon Blueberry Scones

## Ingredients

2 cups  all-purpose flour
1/3 cup  granulated sugar
1 tablespoon baking powder
1/2 teaspoon salt
6 tablespoons cold unsalted butter grated
1/4 cup heavy whipping cream plus more for brushing the tops
1/4 cup lemon juice
2 tablespoons lemon zest
1 large egg
1 cup fresh blueberries

## For the lemon glaze:

1 cup powdered sugar
1-2 tablespoons lemon juice

## Directions

Preheat oven to 400 degrees F (204 degrees C). Line a large baking sheet with parchment paper or a silicone baking mat and set aside.

In a large mixing bowl, whisk together the flour, granulated sugar, baking powder, and salt. Add the cold grated butter and mix into the dry ingredients.

In a separate mixing bowl, whisk together the heavy whipping cream, lemon juice, lemon zest, and egg. Add blueberries to the dry ingredients and lightly stir and then add the wet ingredients stirring until just combined. If the mixture is a little crumbly, that is fine.

Scoop the mixture out onto a lightly floured surface and work it together in a ball, then flatten into a 7-inch circle. Cut the dough into 8 equal-sized pieces and place them on the prepared baking sheet, making sure to leave a little room between each one.

Place the baking sheet in the freezer for 5-10 minutes or until the scones are chilled.

Brush the tops of each scone with a little heavy whipping cream.

Bake at 400 degrees F (204 degrees C) for 18-22 minutes or until the tops of the scones are lightly browned and cooked through.

Remove from the oven and allow to cool completely.

**To make the lemon glaze:**

In a medium-sized mixing bowl, whisk together the powdered sugar, and lemon juice until well combined. If the glaze is too thick add some milk to thin it out and if the glaze is too thin add more powdered sugar to thicken it.

Top the scones with the glaze and allow to harden for 10-15 minutes, then serve and enjoy.

**Notes**
Store scones in an airtight container at room temperature or in the refrigerator for 3 days.

Makes 8 scones

# Bubble and Squeak

### Ingredients

4 slices of bacon
1 tablespoon unsalted butter
1/2 medium yellow onion, finely diced
1/2 cup shredded Brussels sprouts or 1/2 cup shredded cabbage
1/2 cup raw or cooked grated carrots
2 cups leftover mashed potatoes
Salt and pepper to taste
Fried eggs, to serve (optional)

### Directions

Cook the bacon in a skillet, then remove from the skillet, drain, and crumble.

Add butter to the bacon fat in the skillet. Set on medium heat, and add the onion. Cook until the onion is softened.

Turn up the heat to medium-high and add the shredded Brussels sprouts or cabbage, and carrots. Season with a little salt and pepper. Cook for five minutes, until the vegetables start to color.

Add the mashed potatoes, and the crumbled bacon to the skillet and stir briskly, until the vegetables and potatoes are well combined. Season again, to taste.

Press down on the skillet and fry for five to seven minutes, until the bottom is lightly browned and crisp. Drizzle a little oil around the edges if the mixture looks like it's drying out. The potato mixture should start making squeaking sounds at this point.

Using the lid of the skillet, invert the bubble and squeak into the lid, then slide back into the skillet to cook the other side. Cook for an additional five to seven minutes. Serve cut into wedges and topped with fried eggs, if desired.

Serves 4

# Yorkshire Pudding

**Ingredients**

3/4 cup all-purpose flour
1/2 teaspoon salt
1 cup milk, divided
2 eggs
1/4 cup bacon drippings or 1/4 cup melted butter.

**Directions**

Mix flour and salt together until blended. Make a well in the flour, add the milk, and whisk until consistent. Beat the eggs into the batter until the mixture is light and frothy. Refrigerate batter 1 to 2 hours before cooking.

Preheat oven to 450 degrees F (230 degrees C). Pour 1 teaspoon of drippings into each of 12 muffin cups. Place muffin pan into oven and heat until drippings are very hot.

Remove muffin pan from oven and pour batter into each of the prepared muffin cups.

Bake in the preheated oven until puddings puff up and are slightly browned, 20 to 30 minutes.

Makes 12

# Chili Shepherd's Pie

## Ingredients

4 large baking potatoes, peeled and cubed
1 cup grated sharp cheddar cheese
1 tablespoon butter
1/4 cup milk
2 pounds ground beef
1 large onion chopped
2 tablespoons chili powder
1 tablespoon Worcestershire sauce
1 cube beef bouillon
1 (16 ounce) can pinto beans
1 (12 ounce) can canned Ro-Tel mild diced tomatoes
1 (15 ounce) can corn, drained
Salt and pepper to taste

## Directions

Preheat the oven to 400 degrees F (200 degrees C).

Place the potatoes into a saucepan and fill with enough water to cover. Bring to a boil, then cook over medium heat until tender enough to pierce with a fork, about 10 minutes. Drain and mash to your desired texture, add cheese, butter and milk

Meanwhile, crumble the ground beef into a large skillet. Cook and stir until meat is no longer pink. Season with chili powder,

Worcestershire sauce, and beef bouillon. Add the onion; continue to cook and stir until tender. Transfer the contents of the skillet to a large casserole dish.

Mix the beans, diced tomatoes, and corn in with the beef. Salt and pepper to taste. Dollop big blobs of mashed potatoes over the top and carefully spread evenly to cover the entire top. Rake over it with a fork to create a crispy texture on top when it browns.

Bake for 10 minutes in the preheated oven, until the top is browned and crisp.

Serves 4 -6

# Sticky Toffee Pudding Cake

## Ingredients

1 3/4 cups pitted, chopped dates
1 teaspoon baking soda
3/4 cup boiling water
1/3 cup butter
3/4 cup white sugar
2 eggs, beaten
1 1/8 cups self-rising flour

*Caramel Sauce*
3/4 cup packed brown sugar
1/3 cup butter
2/3 cup evaporated milk
1 teaspoon vanilla extract

## Directions

Preheat oven to 350 degrees F (175 degrees C). Grease an 8-inch square baking dish.

In a small bowl combine the dates and baking soda. Pour enough boiling water over the dates to just cover them.

Cream 1/3 cup of butter with the white sugar until light. Beat in the eggs and mix well to combine.

Add the flour and date mixture (including water) to the egg mixture and fold to combine. Pour the batter into the prepared baking dish.

Bake in the preheated oven until a tester comes out clean, 30 to 40 minutes. Let cool slightly and prepare the sauce.

To Make Caramel Sauce: In a small saucepan combine the brown sugar and 1/3 cup butter, and cook over medium heat and bring to boil. Turn heat down and simmer for 5 minutes, stirring occasionally until it reaches a "soft" ball stage. Remove from heat and stir in the milk and vanilla. Pour the sauce over individual servings of warm cake.

Perfect with a scoop of Bluebell Homemade Vanilla Ice Cream

Servings: 8

# Texas Margarita Trifle

## Ingredients

1 (3 ounce) package strawberry Jell-O
1 cup hot water
1/2 cup tequila
1/4 cup triple sec
1/4 cup fresh squeezed lime juice
2 pints fresh strawberries (reserve 8 for the top)
1/4 cup white sugar
1 (8 or 9 inch) yellow cake layer, baked and cooled
1 pint fresh blueberries (reserve a few for the top)
2 (3.5 ounce) packages instant cheesecake pudding mix
4 cups milk
1 cup heavy whipping cream
1 teaspoon vanilla
2 tablespoons white sugar

## Directions

Combine a small package of strawberry gelatin and 1 cup of hot water, and stir until the gelatin has dissolved. Stir in tequila, triple sec, and the lime juice. Set aside.

Hollow out 8 strawberries. Place them in a dish small enough to hold them upright. Carefully fill the strawberries with the gelatin, and then refrigerate.

Pour the remaining gelatin in the bottom of a large glass serving bowl. Slice 1/3 of the remaining strawberries and add them to the gelatin. Refrigerate until set.

Slice the remaining strawberries and sprinkle with sugar. Combine pudding mix with milk and mix until smooth. Cut the cake into 1 inch cubes.

Use half of the cake cubes place on top of the set gelatin in the bottom of a large glass bowl. Layer half of the sliced strawberries followed by half of the blueberries. Spread half of the cheesecake pudding over the fruit. Repeat layers in the same order without a second gelatin layer.

In a medium bowl, add vanilla and 2 tablespoons of white sugar to the cream, whip to stiff peaks and spread over top of trifle. Garnish with the whole strawberries filled with margarita gelatin and add a few blueberries.

Serves 8

# Cucumber and Tomato Salad

## Ingredients

2 cups cold water
1 cup distilled white vinegar
1/2 cup olive oil
1/2 cup sugar
1 tablespoon salt
1 tablespoon fresh, coarsely ground black pepper
6 medium cucumbers, peeled and sliced 1/4-inch thick (If using large cucumbers and it's too seedy, scoop out the seeds before slicing.
6 tomatoes, cut into wedges
1 purple onion, halved, sliced and separated into half rings

## Directions

Whisk water, vinegar, oil, sugar, salt, and pepper together in a large bowl until smooth; add cucumbers, tomatoes, and onion and stir to coat.

Cover bowl with plastic wrap; refrigerate at least 2 hours.

Serves 12

# Quick Chuckwagon Beans

## Ingredients

8 ounces bacon, diced
1 onion, diced
2 jalapeno peppers, diced
2 (15 ounce) cans pinto beans
1/2 cup ketchup
1/2 teaspoon dry mustard
2 tablespoons brown sugar
1 tablespoon Worcestershire sauce
1 pinch salt
1 pinch ground black pepper

## Directions

Heat a large pot over medium-high heat. Cook and stir bacon, onion, and peppers in pot until the onion is tender, add ketchup, dry mustard, brown sugar, Worcestershire sauce, salt, and black pepper.

Reduce heat to low and cook bean mixture at a simmer until hot, about 10 minutes.

Serves 6

# Coconut Bunny Butt Cake

## Ingredients (Cake)

1/2 cup white sugar
2 tablespoons plus 2 teaspoons butter, softened
1 egg
3/4 cups all-purpose flour
1 teaspoon baking powder
1 pinch salt
1/2 cup milk
1/2 teaspoon vanilla extract

## Directions (Cake)

Preheat the oven to 350 degrees F (175 degrees C). Grease and flour an oven safe round bowl. (This is for a smaller cake, so you're going to want to use a bowl that will make a 4-6" cake.)

In a medium bowl, cream together the butter and sugar until light and fluffy. Beat in the egg, mixing well. Combine the flour, baking powder, and salt; stir into the batter alternately with the milk. Stir in vanilla. Pour in the prepared bowl.

Bake for 25 to 30 minutes in the preheated oven, until the cake springs back when pressed gently in the center. Cool over a wire rack.

## Ingredients (Frosting)

1 cup butter, softened
1 1/4 cups confectioners' sugar
1/2 teaspoon vanilla extract
1/2 (13 ounce) jar marshmallow creme
1 cup flaked coconut, or more as needed, divided
2 drops green food coloring, or as needed
3 large marshmallows
1 pink fruit roll
pink paper bunny ears

## Directions (Frosting)

Cream butter in a bowl with the mixer on medium until soft and fluffy. Slowly beat in confectioners' sugar, about 1/2 cup at a time; beat in vanilla extract. Gently fold the marshmallow creme into the frosting until thoroughly combined.

Place 1/3 of the coconut into a resealable plastic bag; add green food coloring, seal the bag, and shake until coconut is shaded green. Repeat process until coconut is your desired shade of green.

Secure 2 large marshmallows, sides against the cake using frosting as "glue", to form bunny "feet." Secure remaining marshmallow, top-side against the cake, with a bit of frosting to the top of the cake to create the "tail."

Spread frosting over cake, "feet", and the "tail." Cover frosting with coconut.

Cut fruit roll to form 2 small ovals and 6 smaller circles. Using frosting as "glue", secure 1 oval and 3 circles to each "foot" to resemble foot pads. Secure paper bunny ears to the serving plate at the front of the bunny cake using frosting. Sprinkle green coconut around the cake to resemble grass and add jelly beans or peanut M&M's for eggs.

# Grandma's Chocolate Chip Cookies

Crispy edges and chewy middles.

## Ingredients

1/2 cup butter, softened
1/2 cup white sugar
1/2 cup packed brown sugar
1 eggs
1 teaspoons vanilla extract
1/2 cup all-purpose flour
3/4 cup oat flour (process or blend oats until it makes flour)
1 teaspoon corn starch
1/2 teaspoon baking soda
1/4 teaspoon salt
1 1/2 cups semisweet chocolate chips
1 cup chopped toasted pecans

## Directions

Cream together the butter, white sugar, and brown sugar until smooth. Beat in the egg, then stir in the vanilla. Add corn starch, baking soda, and salt to the batter. Stir in flour, chocolate chips, and nuts.

Preheat oven to 350 degrees F (175 degrees C).

Chill batter in refrigerator for 15-20 minutes.

Drop by large spoonfuls onto pans covered with parchment paper. Allow 2 inches between cookies.

Bake for about 10 minutes, or until browned lightly on the edges.

Makes: 2 dozen cookies

# Easter Thumbprint Peanut Cookies

## Ingredients

1/2 cup butter, softened
1/2 cup packed brown sugar
1 egg
1/2 teaspoon vanilla extract
1/2 cup all-purpose flour
1/2 cup oat flour (process or blend oats until it makes flour)
1/4 teaspoon salt
1/4 cup finely chopped peanuts
48 peanut M&M's

## Directions

Preheat oven to 300 degrees F. Grease cookie sheets.

Separate egg, reserving egg white. Cream butter or margarine, sugar, and egg yolk.

Add vanilla, flour and salt, mixing well.

Shape dough into balls. Roll in egg white, then peanuts. Place on cookie sheets about 2 inches apart. Bake for 5 minutes.

Remove cookies from oven. With thumb, dent each cookie. Put 2 M&M's in each thumbprint. Bake for another 8 minutes.

Makes: 2 dozen

# Muffaletta Pasta Salad

## Ingredients

1/4 cup red wine vinegar
1/4 cup finely diced shallots
1 tablespoon dried oregano
1 teaspoon celery seed
1 teaspoon Worcestershire sauce
1 teaspoon sugar
1/2 cup olive oil
1 16 ounce box tri-color penne
3 ounces sliced dry salami, cut into small pieces
4 ounces sliced provolone cheese, diced
3 stalks celery, finely chopped
1/2 cup chopped roasted red bell pepper
1/3 cup pitted sliced black olives
1/3 cup pitted sliced green olives
1/4 cup finely chopped pepperoncini
1/4 cup capers
1/4 cup chopped fresh flat-leaf parsley
Salt and freshly ground black pepper

## Directions

In a small bowl, mix the vinegar, shallots, oregano, celery seed, Worcestershire sauce, and sugar. Let sit for 15 minutes, then slowly whisk in the oil until emulsified into the dressing. Set aside.

Bring a large pot of salted water to a boil over high heat. Add the pasta and cook until al dente, or according to package directions. Drain and rinse well under cold water; drain again and transfer to a large serving bowl.

Add the salami, provolone, celery, pepperoncini, roasted red bell peppers, olives, capers, and parsley, and toss until evenly combined.

Add the dressing and toss again.

Season with salt and pepper. Serve at room temperature, or refrigerate up to one day.

Serves 6

# About the Author

Livia J. Washburn has been a professional writer for more than thirty years. She received the Private Eye Writers of America Award and the American Mystery Award for her first mystery, *Wild Night*, written under the name L. J. Washburn, and she was nominated for a Spur Award by the Western Writers of America for a novel written with her husband, New York Times bestselling author James Reasoner. Her short stories "Panhandle Freight" and "Widelooping a Christmas Cowboy" were nominated for a Peacemaker Award by the Western Fictioneers, and her story "Charlie's Pie" won. She lives with her husband in a small Texas town, where she is constantly experimenting with new recipes. Her two grown daughters are both teachers in her hometown, and she is very proud of them.

Ingram Content Group UK Ltd.
Milton Keynes UK
UKHW011309180723
425353UK00004B/289

9 798518 604551